HANGOVER HOUSE
BY SAX ROHMER

Assigned by her father to search out the reason for Lady Hilary's mysterious actions, private investigator Storm Kennedy promptly follows her from London to a party in Surrey. There on the steps of the terrace Peter Faraway, the host, discovers the body of a man—a man no one knows. He has been stabbed in the chest with a jeweled dagger. Before the police arrive, Kennedy examines the body and finds a small handkerchief and a woman's footprints on the scene of the crime. He pockets the handkerchief and eradicates the footprints. Later Lady Hilary admits to him the handkerchief is her property. Kennedy and Lady Hilary are suspected when a gold case belonging to the dead man is found on Kennedy.

In the midst of the police questioning there suddenly appears on the stairway the ghostly apparition of the man who was stabbed. He points to Lady Hilary and collapses.

Sax Rohmer, who created the insidious Doctor Fu Manchu, repeats his earlier successes in this suspense-packed tale of murder that grew out of a secret too dangerous to share!

Other Books BY SAX ROHMER

Bambushi Baruk of Egypt · Bat Wing ·
Daughter of Fu Manchu · Dope · Fire-Tongue ·
Fu Manchu's Bride · Grey Face · Moon of Madness ·
President Fu Manchu · Seven Sins · Shadow of
Fu Manchu · She Who Sleeps · Tales of Chinatown ·
Tales of Secret Egypt · The Bat Flies Low ·
The Day the World Ended · The Dream Detective ·
The Drums of Fu Manchu · The Emperor of America ·
The Golden Scorpion · The Green Eyes of Bast ·
The Hand of Fu Manchu · The Island of Fu Manchu ·
The Insidious Dr. Fu Manchu · The Mask of Fu
Manchu · The Quest of the Silver Slipper ·
The Return of Dr. Fu Manchu · The Trail of Fu
Manchu · The Yellow Claw · Yellow Shadows ·
Yu'an Hee See Laughs ·

BY SAX ROHMER

RANDOM HOUSE · NEW YORK

FIRST PRINTING

All the characters and incidents in this novel
are entirely imaginary

*Copyright, 1949, by Random House, Inc.
All Rights Reserved under International
and Pan-American Copyright Conventions
Published in New York by Random House, Inc.,
and simultaneously in Toronto, Canada,
by Random House of Canada, Ltd.
Manufactured in the United States of America
by The Colonial Press Inc., Clinton, Massachusetts*

To ROSE ELIZABETH
Who Helped to Write It

HANGOVER HOUSE

1

No! For the last time—*no!*"

She sat stiffly upright on the side of the bed, the receiver to her ear, but her glance always flashing to the closed door. Gray eyes blazed angrily, and her softly rounded chin hardened. She shook her head as if to expel that final *no* from between clenched teeth, so that pale gold hair brushed a bare shoulder.

A trunk and several suitcases, all partly packed, indicated preparations for a journey. All sorts of intimate personal belongings were littered about the room. The trunk was labeled, "Golden Arrow. Dover to Calais."

She listened awhile to the impassioned voice of a man on the other end of the line, but there came no tenderness, no hint of relenting, into the gray eyes. With the fingers of her free hand she began to beat an impatient tattoo on the edge of the bedside table and, presently:

"You are only wasting your time," she said coldly, "and mine. I didn't even know you were in England, until . . . Possibly—but I don't open your letters. They are destroyed, unread. Don't send me any more."

She was about to hang up, when something the man said checked her in the act. Her expression changed, subtly. The pupils of her eyes darkened. She was pale now.

"You would never dare!" The words were no more than whispered. "Even you cannot have sunk to that."

Another appeal, spoken in tones vibrant with emotion, answered her. But she interrupted:

"Now you are trying to excuse yourself. The threat, no doubt, was a slip of the tongue. But you said it, and you have thought of doing it. . . . Don't deny your own words. You can deceive me no longer. Never again."

She had stopped tapping the table. Her fingers were tensed nervously. . . .

"You have nothing to gain. I don't want to see you. I know you, at last, through and through. Nothing you could say could make the slightest difference. . . . Who told me is my affair. Any one of a hundred people could have told me. Listen!" A note of desperation sounded. "Whatever you do, or threaten to do, you can't come *here!* I shall refuse to see you."

Once more, she was on the point of hanging up, and once more she hesitated in response to the pleading voice, and listened, biting her lip. . . .

"Don't talk to me like that! You are making me more angry, more wretched. If you could only understand how I despise myself—not you, *myself*—perhaps you would realize how completely it is finished. . . . I tell you it's useless—useless—useless! Oh, God! What a fool I was! Go away! I want to forget it all!"

She was losing control, knew it, and hated her own weakness. She clenched her teeth, so that presently the rounded chin grew firm again. When she spoke, breaking in on a torrent of ardent words, her voice was calm.

"Stop. Listen to me for a moment. I refuse to see you here. That is final. I don't want to see you at all. Please understand that, too, if you can. . . ."

She clapped her free hand sharply over the mouthpiece.

Someone had knocked on the door.

"Don't come in!" she called. "I will ring when I'm ready."

The knock was not repeated. She spoke hurriedly, in a low voice, into the phone:

"You are driving me to desperation. I hope you know what that means? I will meet you, somewhere, later tonight. It will be our last meeting. Quick! Tell me where I can call you."

She was scribbling something on a pad when the door opened and a woman came in.

The girl on the phone hung up, and turned.

"Elfie!" she exclaimed—her expression was wild—"we can't go! It's too late!"

Elfie, a woman of fifty, at a glance, who wore workmanlike slacks and had a spotted handkerchief tied over her hair, pirate fashion, closed the door and stood with her back to it.

"Quiet, dear!" she whispered gruffly. "Your father's here!"

"Father! *Here?*"

Elfie nodded. "And I have a feeling he suspects."

"But I can't possibly see him! Elfie, Elfie! Don't ask me to see him, tonight! Tell him something—tell him anything. But, I beg of you, get him to go away! Oh, my God! What am I going to do . . . ?"

Less than an hour after this remarkable telephone conversation was interrupted, someone else's plans also were disturbed by an unexpected visitor. . . .

Storm Kennedy had had a tiring day. Every day was a tiring day. His service record had stood him in good stead on his return to private life, and although established only two years in his new profession, already he had been entrusted with several delicate official inquiries.

It was close on ten o'clock, he had dined alone and had no intention of going out again. Wearing a comfortably old dressing gown, his pipe well alight, and a drink at his elbow, he lay in a deep chair, reading. Around him, on the shelves of his cozy study, were many technical volumes, ranging from *Forensic Medicine* to works on the latest method of tabulating fingerprints. But the working day had closed. He was reading *Huckleberry Finn*.

The flat was very quiet. No sound of the ceaseless ebb and flow of London's tide penetrated. Then, faintly, he heard the doorbell.

He paid no attention. He was seeing nobody.

Footsteps. Silence again. More footsteps, a rap on the door, and Sergeant Whittaker, his granite-faced manservant, came in. He carried a visiting card.

Kennedy laid his book down.

"Whittaker," he said sharply, "did I, or didn't I, tell you to admit no one?"

"You did tell me, sir." Whittaker was unmoved. "I thought this caller might be an exception."

He offered the card. Kennedy frowned but picked it up.

It read, simply:

Lord Glengale
Guards Club London

But it meant, Major General The Marquess of Glengale and Dumferry, V.C., D.S.O., and a long list of civil distinctions and decorations—one of the few wealthy peers still spared by socialism to the House of Lords.

Storm Kennedy glanced at Whittaker.

"What on earth can *he* want? Where is he?"

"I showed him into the office, sir. . . ."

Little more than three minutes had elapsed when Storm Kennedy opened the door of the small room he used as an office. It was equipped with Spartan severity. Neat files, a typewriter on a side table, a severe oak desk and some leather armchairs. Sole wall decorations were two signed portraits: one, of Lord Wavell, the other of the Commissioner of Metropolitan Police and present chief of Scotland Yard.

A short, wiry man, his close-cut silvery hair retiring in good order from an exposed position on top of his head, stood with his back to the door, staring up at the Commissioner's picture. He wore a dinner suit.

"Lord Glengale?"

The visitor turned, spinning about on his heel. And Storm Kennedy found himself being dissected by a pair of lancet-gray eyes set in a lined, sun-browned face.

Lord Glengale noted the neatly-combed wavy dark hair, approved the heavy brows and the shape of the skull, liked the frank expression and wondered what that thin mouth looked like when it smiled. Build good, too; spare but muscular. Useful hands: long fingers, wiry. Not regularly handsome, by far. Bit on the rugged side.

"Why no pipe?" he inquired brusquely. "Sherlock Holmes always smoked a pipe, didn't he?"

Kennedy smiled, and Lord Glengale was satisfied. Strong, healthy teeth. He judged men as he judged horses and women: on points.

It happened that Kennedy had considered changing his dressing gown and had then discarded the idea. After all, the working day was over. This visit was not by appointment; and his rare hours of leisure were valuable.

"Left my pipe in the other room. Won't you sit down?"

Lord Glengale sat down, and Kennedy took a seat behind the desk. The disconcerting gaze remained fixed on him there.

"Got knocked out early, didn't you? With Archie Wavell in Africa?"

"Yes." Kennedy nodded, pushing a box of cigarettes across the desk. "Sniper trying to shoot a crow, and hit me."

"So they classified you Crock A, and shoved you into Intelligence. But Jerringham tells me you did well."

"Very kind of him."

Storm Kennedy was mildly interested to learn that the marquess had delved into his record, and wondered what he had come about. But he was getting annoyed. A further inquiry decided him.

"They parachuted you into Normandy, didn't they?"

"I believe they did."

"Good work. Can't stand office men."

Lord Glengale took a cigarette from the box, and Kennedy, leaning across the desk, lighted it. As he snapped out the lighter:

"Since I hadn't anticipated the pleasure of your call tonight, sir, perhaps you might tell me, now, why you came?"

Lord Glengale looked pleased. He liked men who stood for no nonsense.

"Certainly entitled to know. Colonel Mallory put me onto you. Remember Mallory?"

Kennedy lighted a cigarette and nodded.

"Rat of a nephew of his pinched some jewels, or something. Mary Mallory went to the police. You stepped in, got 'em back and saved a family scandal. Neat job."

"I did my best for Colonel Mallory. And now, Lord Glengale, what is it you want me to do for *you*?"

The marquess stood up, stared at Kennedy almost fiercely, and then sat down again.

"What I'm going to tell you is—painfully intimate. Understand?"

"Entirely."

Storm Kennedy was tapping the rubber end of a pencil on the empty page of a notebook.

"Concerns my daughter, Hilary. Know her?"

Kennedy gave no sign. But the statement—wholly unforeseen—had shaken him from his mood of bored toleration. Lady Hilary Bruton! Most exquisite debutante of postwar society. Gay, lovely, wealthy; a cast-back, he always thought of her, to those gracious pages of social history which Adolf Hitler seems to have blotted out forever.

"I have had the pleasure of meeting her. I cannot claim to know her well."

Lord Glengale's wrinkles deepened.

"Easy looker. But poor judgment. Gets her looks from my family. Most of the Brutons stand up well. Her mother's dead, you know." Lord Glengale was suffering the tortures of the damned in exposing his domestic life to a stranger. "Mettlesome stuff. Never jibbed her fences. Hilary's her mother's daughter. Bit of a handful. Briefly —she's in deep, somewhere."

He paused, pathetically.

"What about a drink?" Kennedy suggested. "I could do with one, myself."

"Thanks. Should appreciate it."

Kennedy pressed a bell on the desk.

Sergeant Whittaker entered, as if he had been standing outside the door, carrying a tray on which were bottles, a crystal jug, a soda-water siphon and a bowl of ice. Setting the tray down:

"Whisky, milord?" he inquired.

Glengale glanced up at him.

"With water. No ice."

He was served. A Scotch and soda was placed before Kennedy. Whittaker set the tray on a convenient side table and withdrew, silently.

"Good man, that," said the marquess. He raised his glass. "All the best."

He resumed: "Know I've outlived my generation. Don't understand 'em, today. Hilary's of age; lives her own life. Can't keep her locked up in Dumferry. Hate London, myself. Used to love it. Never be the same. Well, she got in a bit of a mess a while back—more particulars later—and now she stays in town a lot with her aunt, my late wife's sister. Damned old fool, but sound stock. Well, she's in some sort of bad trouble. Want someone to keep an eye on her."

Storm Kennedy frowned at his lifted glass. Did Lord Glengale suppose that he went in for the sort of private inquiry that meant collecting evidence from hotel chambermaids and bribing servants to snoop on phone conversations?

"If you mean, someone to spy on her movements, I'm afraid Colonel Mallory has sent you to the wrong address."

Glengale glared. "Spy on her movements be damned, sir! What d'you take me for? Don't want her followed about. Want her protected. I tell you she's in deep—involved with some blackguard, in a big way. You don't know Hilary as I do. If anybody got her cornered, by God, I think she's capable of killing him—or trying to."

And, Kennedy reflected, he was talking about his own daughter, Lady Hilary Bruton, who, in the days of the Regency, would have been "The Toast of the Town!"

But he didn't interrupt, and Lord Glengale suddenly stood up again.

Resting brown, muscular hands on the desk, he stared down at Kennedy. The cold gray eyes of this grim old soldier met the glance of equally steady blue eyes.

"Believe I know the man. If these were my grandfather's times, I'd shoot him out of hand not later than tomorrow morning. Other days, other ways. Came up to make a few inquiries. Found the man I'm talking about was in London. Called on Hilary tonight about an hour ago, and she wouldn't see me! Wouldn't see her own father! Lot of baggage in the lobby. Believe she was ready to bolt!"

Kennedy preserved a completely expressionless face. He was sincerely sorry for Lord Glengale; but what part he was expected to play in this comedy of a wayward girl and an outraged parent became more and more obscure.

"You are possibly afraid," he suggested patiently, "that she may rush into some undesirable marriage?"

The piercing stare remained focused on him.

"Do you understand, sir, that apart from the estate which will be hers one day, Hilary, under her mother's will, controls a very large fortune? And do you understand, sir, that the scoundrel I suspect is married already?"

"Are you suggesting blackmail?"

"I am. And blackmail's a dangerous game to play with our lot! Overheard Hilary calling out to her aunt tonight, 'It's too late! We can't go!' Couldn't avoid hearing. Next room. Then she wouldn't see me. Tonight is some sort of climax. Know it in my bones. That girl's in desperate trouble. What can I do? Haven't the facilities to trace her. Can't go to Scotland Yard . . ."

Words, now, came in a torrent. This reserved, cynical man was moved to the depths.

"You know all the ropes. Find out where she is. I can get no reply from her aunt's number. For God's sake"—his voice shook—"find out where Hilary's gone tonight—and follow her. Save her. Tomorrow may be too late."

Storm Kennedy sighed—and stood up.

"It's a queer assignment, Lord Glengale, and a very tough one. But I'll do my best."

A hard, muscular hand grasped his as in a vise.

"Thank you," said the marquess quietly. "You see, Hilary's all I have. . . ."

2

A DANCE band was playing. But closed doors, closed and heavily draped windows, dimmed some of the sound. That which penetrated, however, appeared to be more than distasteful to the only occupant of the room. Seated in a corner of a massive oak inglenook, beside a fireplace designed to burn mounds of wood logs, but now empty, he glanced frequently at the clock—an impressive example of the grandfather school.

It recorded the hour to be twenty minutes after midnight; but, as it was an old clock, some slight inaccuracy might be looked for.

Yet the clock, although early Victorian, was a newcomer beside the relics which flanked its tall majesty. Ranged on open shelves, veiled in the shadows of the room, were figures, mostly imperfect, of the strange gods of the Nile: creatures part man and part ibis; part woman and part moon phantasy.

There were Sekhet boats, with grotesque little dolls, like marionettes, sailing to judgment in the ancient Egyptian Halls of Amenti. Anubis, the scribe of life's work, was there to hold the scales. Set, lord of the underworld, gaped in ferocious expectancy. Fragments of wall paintings, a reproach to modern pigments in the deathless freshness of their coloring, made a background for potsherds, enameled jewelry, scarabs . . .

Beyond, out of deeper shadow, loomed crowded, untidy bookcases. On top of these were piled brass Zem Zem cups from Mecca, incense burners, old Damascus ware. Above, hung scimitars, daggers and other examples of early Oriental arms—and in the inglenook there was the man who kept glancing at the clock.

He was, perhaps, in certain respects the most interesting exhibit of all. He had long, untidy, gray hair and had neglected to shave recently, so that a whitish overtone marked the angular yellow face. His skin, in color and texture, resembled old Persian calf, and he was built on cubic principles. A tall, stooping figure, his faded velvet jacket and narrow black trousers might have belonged to the wardrobe of Charles Dickens.

Pince-nez attached to a wide ribbon seemed highly appropriate. When not engaged in glancing at the clock, he was reading the *Times*.

A sound of smothered laugher, of swishing feet, drew his angry glance to the draped French windows. A girl and a man were dancing on the terrace, right outside. The band stopped suddenly, in the casual manner of dance bands, and whoever was outside moved away.

There came an outburst of high-pitched voices from some adjoining room, which gradually subsided as the dancers dispersed. . . .

The reader in the inglenook lowered his paper again.

A nervous hand was fumbling with the latch of a door immediately facing him. Slowly, hesitantly, the door opened, and someone looked into the room. Observing the frigid stare of its solitary occupant, he immediately retired, closing the door behind him.

The man in the corner glanced again at the clock, rolled the *Times* into a bundle and hurled it on the floor. Standing up, he opened a small cupboard in the wall. He took out a bottle, a glass and a siphon of soda water. Mixing himself a stiff whisky, he replaced bottle and siphon and resumed his seat.

He had just fixed his pince-nez in place and had unwrapped a copy of an archaeological journal, when something made him put it down.

Looking up sharply, he met the fixed regard of brilliant dark eyes. A slender figure stood before him, that of a brown-skinned Egyptian who wore evening clothes, with the somewhat unusual addition of a green turban.

"If I intrude"—it was a gentle, musical voice—"please do not hesitate . . ."

"I don't hesitate, sir! This room is private."

"Every room, like every man, is of glass, to him who can see. I was drawn here by your solitude, and"—he moved expressive hands—"the things about you."

"Indeed! Might I ask who you are?"

"I am a guest. I am called Mohammed. We are all guests in this world of shadows. Some meet with welcome. Others wander alone."

The man in the corner took a handkerchief from the breast pocket of his velvet jacket, breathed on the lenses of his pince-nez and began to polish them. His hands trembled.

"Your remarks, sir, appear to be poor paraphrases of indifferent poets."

"No one who seeks to share with others the beauty he perceives, merits indifference. These artists, scribes and craftsmen"—one long brown hand indicated the laden shelves—"some of them men of my own land, sought to give beauty to others. Now, you are sharing their dreams."

"Indeed?"

"Some of their dreams were unlovely," the somnolent voice continued, "of vengeance, of death. There is blood on those Damascus blades. I can see it, even after the passing of centuries. But some were beautiful, effendi. In such surroundings the poet refreshes his spirit."

The pince-nez being firmly set in place: "I am obliged to you," said the man in the corner, "for your informative observations. And now, if you are conscious of sufficient spiritual refreshment, no doubt you will wish to rejoin the other guests?"

"I will do so, *Khawâga*." The placid speaker crossed his hands on his breast and bowed. *"Es-selâm 'aleykûm."*

"'Aleykûm es-selâm," came the automatic response.

The Egyptian moved noiselessly to the door, opened it, and went out. As the door closed behind him, the dance band began to play again.

Muttering angrily and glaring at the clock, the man in the corner got up. His journal tucked under his arm and his whisky glass held in his hand, he crossed to a short, oaken stair leading to an arched opening above and went up.

A door banged loudly somewhere.

3

STORM KENNEDY ran into the first serious web of fog right on top of South Riding Hill. Knowing what this might mean, with five miles still to go, he was forced, nevertheless, to crawl. The hill was dangerous.

A picture, based upon scanty information given by Lord Glengale, was forming in his mind. With Lady Hilary as its central figure, it was not a pleasant picture. Kennedy had learned from experience to avoid deductions based upon insufficient data. But, all the same, he found it painfully hard to fit Hilary into the composition otherwise than in a poor light.

Her pale gold hair, graceful but almost ethereal slenderness, had inspired in him, the first time he had seen her, something more nearly adoration than desire. He had thought of her as a dream woman of Arthurian legend, as the stainless lady of some knight beyond reproach. Perhaps, on reflection, her unusual type of beauty had aroused submerged memories buried in the land of fairy tales.

For, as he realized now, she had several typical Bruton characteristics. Particularly, that firmly rounded chin which, he imagined, could harden into obstinacy. Her gray eyes, too, were not unlike her father's, except that they were softened and beautified by long lashes. But . . .

When Lord Glengale had gone, intending to spend the night at his club, Kennedy had squarely faced the responsibility he had accepted.

It was no light one.

In spite of his earlier scepticism, it had come to him as a sort of revelation, while Glengale talked, that Lady Hilary had reached some desperately dangerous impasse. Those scanty facts which her father knew, or had consented to tell him, supported his intuition.

Having failed, as Lord Glengale had failed, to get any reply on the phone, Kennedy sent Whittaker around to the Sloane Street flat where Lady Hilary was staying, to learn what he could of her movements since Lord Glengale had called. Sergeant Whittaker was an adept at this type of inquiry; and if, as was probable, the head porter proved to be a retired soldier, the matter might be counted as good as settled.

A freemasonry exists between Army veterans almost stronger than a blood tie.

Half an hour later, Whittaker called up. Sergeant Fawcett, late Coldstream Guards, had had orders to send certain baggage for the two ladies ahead to Victoria on the following morning. It was to be put aboard the Golden Arrow Paris express, in which their seats were already reserved.

This order had been canceled.

The two ladies had driven off, without baggage, in Lady Hilary's car, shortly after ten-thirty. Lady Hilary, who was driving, had asked the sergeant which was the best road to Lychgate, in Surrey, and he had advised her to go through Kings Riding, pointing out, however, that there was a threat of fog. . . .

What on earth did this mean? Why Lychgate—wherever Lychgate might be—at ten-thirty on a misty night?

Storm Kennedy found a possible explanation among

unanswered mail. Subconsciously, perhaps, he had been looking for it—an invitation card.

It was from Joan Faraway, whom he knew to be a particular friend of Hilary's, bidding him attend an "austerity birthday party" to be held that night at some strange address in Surrey. "All welcome any time between 8 and 8."

Kennedy had not intended to go. Joan's "austerity parties" were out of his line. Joan, American wife of the Honorable Peter Faraway, had far too much money. The town flat was unsuitable for the sort of affairs Joan loved.

She was out when he called the Mayfair number, as he had anticipated, but after some delay he heard Peter's voice, sounding comparatively sober.

"Hullo! Hullo! Is that old Bill Kennedy? Hullo, old Bill Kennedy!"

"Hullo, Peter. I want to ask you something in the strictest confidence. Do you know if Hilary Bruton will be at the party tonight?"

"Wait a minute. Can't hear you very well. Buzzing in my ear. Would you mind repeating what you said, dear old Bill Kennedy?"

"I said, will Hilary Bruton be at the party tonight?"

"What party, dear soul?"

"Joan's party, at some place in Surrey." He tried to lay his hand on the invitation card. "Birthday party."

"Good Lord! Is that tonight?"

"It is."

"Good Lord! So glad you called me. I'd forgotten!"

"Whose birthday is it?"

"Well, I'm a bit unsure, but I think it's mine. What day is it?"

"Thursday, the twenty-third."

"Oh, then it must be Joan's. Thanks awfully for reminding me, dear old Bill Kennedy. Did you say you were bringing Hilary Bruton?"

18

"I didn't say I was bringing her. I asked if she would be there."

"Oh, yes. I seem to remember Joan saying so. By Jove! I must buzz off! Expect you and Hilary about eleven, then. . . ."

But it was long past the hour suggested by the wooly-headed Peter when Kennedy came at last to Hangover House. . . .

The fog had grown steadily worse with every mile he covered. Such a blackout was wholly unseasonable, but by no means unprecedented in this neighborhood. In his methodical way, Kennedy, before starting, had traced the exact location of the house, to which careful staff work he owed the fact that he ever got there at all.

A number of cars creeping warily through the gloom had passed him during the last mile, which lay along an unfrequented road. He strongly suspected that they were those of Joan's departing guests.

In this suspicion he was confirmed as he picked a cautious way up an ascending and serpentine approach, winding, a crazy tunnel, through overhanging elms. Headlights materialized out of the murk, and a large sedan, narrowly missing him, swerved by. He had a glimpse of the occupants. One of them wore a light topcoat and a chef's tall white cap. He was singing.

The party had broken up. These were members of a caterer's staff. He was on a fool's errand. But he went ahead—for an unaccountable foreboding was settling down upon him, as if some elemental spirit of the fog—a malignant spirit—jeered at his futile efforts, muttered Lord Glengale's words in his ear, "tomorrow may be too late. . . ."

Once more the door of that strange museum-like room was opened, gently, and a woman looked in. Finding the room empty, she moved, with quiet self-possession, to a littered desk upon which a telephone stood.

Her movements had an Oriental languor, her backless gown displayed arms and shoulders having the gleam of mellowed ivory. A clear profile, its small nose and chin, petulant mouth, outlined against a fragment of wall-painting, closely resembled the profiles of Syrian captives depicted there, kneeling before Pharaoh. Her type was peculiarly attuned to her surroundings.

Composedly, she dialed a number. The light was poor, but she seemed to experience no difficulty. Then, listening, she waited, long, dark eyes turning sometimes toward the door, which she had closed, and sometimes toward the shadowy stair.

Evidently there was no reply. The tip of a silver sandal tapped the floor impatiently. She hung up, and then dialed again, with care.

The dance band in an adjoining room crashed into a perfunctory and abbreviated rendition of "God Save the King," so that the woman listening on the phone failed to hear a faint sound proceeding from the draped French windows. A sudden chill of colder night air entering made her shiver slightly. She glanced over her shoulder.

But she could see nothing to account for the draught.

Nevertheless, only a moment before, brown fingers had parted the faded velvet draperies, and dark eyes—eyes dark as her own—had looked in. A shaft of dim light, reflected from a lamp in the inglenook, touched, briefly, the folds of a green turban.

As, muttering impatiently, she put the receiver back and turned to go, the draperies hung undisturbed.

She actually had her hand on the door knob when the door began to open. She stepped aside—a swift, lithe movement.

A man came in, a man who peered shortsightedly

through the thick lenses of his glasses. He wore full evening dress and his white pique bow was slightly soiled. His fair hair lay plastered inertly back and he had a mustache so neat and narrow that it might have been drawn with a pen.

"Oh, I say!" He pulled up. "Am I intruding?"

"Not at all!" The woman flashed him a brilliant smile. "As a matter of fact, I think I am the intruder, in here. I was looking for—someone."

She had a faint, unusual accent.

"Perhaps I can help you."

"Well, I have been trying to find our hostess ever since I came. But she seems to have vanished."

The man adjusted his bow nervously, although it called for no attention other than that of a laundry.

"Someone told me—I forget who it was—that Mrs.—er—Faraway, had rushed off in a huff. Fed up with Peter. He's at his old tricks again."

The woman laughed. Her laughter, like her voice, had a husky, caressing quality.

"I should have thought Joan was used to it by now. But champagne always went to her head. Quite a lot of the crowd have left, though, isn't it so?"

"Undoubtedly." There was at times a pompous note in the man's manner. "I was looking for you. A heavy fog is coming on, and I was wondering—er—if I could offer you a lift back to town."

"That is very sweet of you. But I have ordered a car to call for me, Mr.—er . . ."

"Lovelace." The nervous tie habit was displayed again. "Allen Lovelace."

"I know the band has gone, Mr. Lovelace . . ."

"Bar's shutting down, too."

"That is tragic! Do you think, if we hurried . . . ?"

They went out, closing the door.

As if this had been a signal—which, in fact, to him, it may have been—the man in the velvet jacket materialized at the top of the stair. He came down, and crossed to the inglenook, his archaeological journal under his arm and an empty glass in his hand.

The glass he refilled, opening his small cupboard for the purpose and then carefully reclosing it. From somewhere outside, beyond, came a racket of starting engines, hooters, voices. He glanced once more at the clock, growled, and sat down.

Throwing the journal aside, and setting his glass on a ledge, he leaned back in the corner and closed his eyes. . . .

Someone was running along the terrace outside, shouting, "Sidonia! Where are you? We'll never make town! Sidonia!"

Evidently noting the opened French window and light shining through, the runner paused, pulled the draperies aside. The man in the corner never stirred.

"Sidonia! Are you there?"

Anybody seated in the shadowy alcove must have been invisible to one looking in, for the man dropped the curtains and went away. As his footsteps receded, a film of vapor floated across the room—and the hitherto motionless figure stood up.

Crossing, with his shambling gait, to the slightly billowing draperies, he jerked them aside, closing and fastening the window. Then, he turned, glaring about him. His expression was one of sheer ferocity. He moved slowly, from shelf to shelf, inspecting his treasures. A distant, diminishing male chorus became audible, singing, "Happy birthday to you . . ."

Returning to the inglenook, he picked up his glass and walked across to the stair. From a switch on the newel post he extinguished all the lights, excepting one standard lamp near the window, evidently not controlled from that point.

Then he went stumbling up the dark stairway.

A bombilation of motor horns and one shattering backfire made the night hideous. But no one intruded upon this sanctum of dead civilizations until a stealthy hand opened the door which Mr. Lovelace had closed.

Mohammed looked in, cautiously. Finding the room unoccupied, he entered. He walked silently to the draped windows, and, learning that they were fastened, unlatched them. He slipped out into the mist, and dropped the draperies behind him. . . .

Lady Hilary Bruton sat staring straight before her with wide-open, haunted eyes.

Her dress, a simple dinner frock, was dove-gray and harmonized artfully with her eyes. Only a woman blessed with Hilary's coloring and perfect skin could have made a success of such a frock. But, worn by Hilary, it was enchanting. She sat on a couch, where a few wraps and other feminine oddments still lay; for the small, oak-paneled room had been used for that purpose during the evening.

She had come in a moment before through a half-glazed and curtained doorway which opened on a corner of the terrace.

"Elfie, he isn't there!"

Elfie, more than discreetly robed, of somewhat grim appearance—except for an occasional twinkle in otherwise inscrutable hazel eyes—might suitably have posed for the duenna of tradition. Her dark-brown hair, dressed in a manner fashionable at the Court of George the Fifth, and untouched alike by time's blanching fingers or the magic of Bond Street, was still beautiful.

"It's the fog," she pronounced, on a note of stern finality. "It's fate."

Hilary's fingers clutched the worn leather.

"I never felt so—so desperate, in all my life. I had worked myself up for this interview—this—ghastly interview. Twice, now, I have been down, feeling more and more like a worm, and he hasn't been there." She sprang to her feet. "Is he—daring to—play with me? Like a cat with a mouse!"

"Be calm, dear. Try to relax." The deep voice was meant to soothe. "I tell you it's the fog. . . ."

"I say he's doing it deliberately!"

"Whichever it is, stick to your guns. Tell him where he gets off. And if he has the courage—which he hasn't—to do what he threatened, face the music. I'll face it with you."

Hilary's lashes glistened. She turned, on a swift impulse, and grasped both Elfie's hands.

"You're a grand old trooper, darling! Don't worry. I won't let our side down—whatever else I do."

"Atta girl!" said Elfie gruffly. "That's the talk I like to hear."

"You may be right about the fog," Hilary admitted, unhappily. "He may not have been able to get here."

"And *we* mayn't be able to get back, if we hang around much longer! Nearly everybody's pushed off. God knows what's become of Joan. And that ape, Peter, is all roped up with the singer from the band, who looks as though she bathed in permanganate of potash."

"I'll go down and take one more look. If he isn't there now, I shall have to give it up. How I hate the very thought of speaking to him!"

"Pity you didn't hate the thought earlier on, Hilary. Heaven be my witness, *I* tipped you the odds."

"I know, Elfie—I know. I suppose it was because I was so young and silly I didn't see through him in time."

"It's never too late to kick an outsider in the teeth."

"Elfie, it's sheer blackmail, now! Oh, *what* a fool I've been! I wish he were *dead!* I could *kill* him!"

Elfie nodded comprehendingly.

"Well, pop off and have a go, dear. I'll scout around again and try to keep anybody we know out of the way till you've done the deed."

Elfie went out. As she opened the door, the tinkling of a piano being played some distance away, became audible. Square-shouldered, with her almost mannish mode of dress, she had a raffish, rolling walk perhaps inherited from her father, a former commander in the Navy.

And she had been gone no more than ten seconds when the half-glazed doorway behind Hilary opened, and a man came in out of the fog. Hilary twisted around and faced him.

"Larry!" he whispered, and held his hands out, beseechingly. "I have found you."

He was, by crude standards, a strikingly handsome man, in the late thirties: a tall, athletic figure, a face deeply browned by the sun. His closely curling dark hair, attractively silvered at the temples, his regular features, must have satisfied a Hollywood casting director. When he smiled—and it was a half-fearful, pathetic smile—dusky skin enhanced the whiteness of his teeth, the light blue of his eyes.

Hilary, breathing quickly, stood watching him, a small, gray and white handbag tucked under her arm. She had grown pale.

"I had given you up," she said coldly.

The smile faded from the brown face.

"It seems to me, Larry, that you want to give me up altogether. . . ."

"I have said so. Apart from anything else, even you

must admit I have good reason. There's only one thing more you can do for me. Go away."

The man took a step forward. Hilary stood still, her gray eyes blazing.

"Larry! After all you have meant to me! There's nothing I can't explain. . . ."

"There never was anything you couldn't explain. Please don't drive me too far. I have grown up. I was a silly, vain, stupid schoolgirl when you told me those tales. Don't you understand—*can't* you understand—that I *know?* I know all about you—and now that I know, friendship of any kind between us is simply impossible."

"But, darling . . ."

"Stop!" Hilary's hands were white-knuckled fists. "I shall *not* listen to you. You forced this meeting upon me. I have nothing to say except that I never want to see you again. Carry out your despicable threats—if you have the courage. And now, go away."

"Larry! Larry! You shall, you must listen!"

He took another step forward and threw his arm around her shoulders. She grew rigid.

"Let me go!" Hilary spoke through clenched teeth. "Do you hear me? I warn you, if you don't, there will be a scene. . . ."

The man released her. But his expression was dangerous. . . .

Footsteps approached the door.

"I believe," came a girl's voice, "I left my wrap somewhere."

"Come out here!" said Hilary, sharply. "Quick! You mustn't be found in this room with me."

She went swiftly through the curtained doorway, which now admitted slowly curling fog wraiths. The man followed. . . .

4

Two other cars had groped past Storm Kennedy before he came out upon a sort of neglected, weed-grown courtyard into which, from a porch, light streamed bravely. It was absorbed, deadened, by a curtain of slowly moving vapor which it failed to pierce.

Several parked cars were visible in the mist.

He hurried into a barely furnished entrance hall. It was hazy with fog. Uncarpeted stairs swept upward to shadows. Somewhere, a piano was tinkling. There was no one in sight until a door opened and Peter Faraway came in, one lock of reddish-brown hair hanging down on his forehead, his face pale and his eyes looking out of focus.

Peter had his arm around a tall, well-modeled young woman, wearing an unobtrusive green frock designed to show that she was artistically and expensively sun-tanned all over. In Storm Kennedy's mind she was immediately and irrevocably ticketed, no matter what name might later be revealed for her, as "the bronze."

"Hullo! Hullo! Hullo!" he hailed. "Here's dear ol' Bill Kennedy."

"Hullo, Peter. Have you seen Hilary Bruton?"

"I'll r'peat former remark. Hullo! Hullo! Hullo! Would

you mind, dear ol' Bill Kennedy, r'peating *your* former remark?"

"Have you seen Hilary Bruton?"

"Have I seen her? Certainly—seen her. Five minutes ago. You should keep 'n eye on girl friends, ol' soul. Have you seen m' wife?"

"No."

"No' seen m' wife? Well, meet fiancée." He towed the bronze forward. "This is Sidonia."

"How d'you do?" said Kennedy, shortly.

"She's very sidonious—don't you agree? Come on, Sidonia." He dragged her away, then turned. "If you *should* see m' wife—Jo-Jo-Joan, that is—lemme know, dear old . . ."

But Kennedy had turned abruptly. He headed in the direction from which came the sound of the piano, beyond the door opened by Peter.

He discovered a long, lofty apartment, beamed and paneled with time-blackened oak. At the further end he saw a gallery supported by massive pillars. Trestle tables piled in one corner showed where the temporary bar had been, and under the gallery stood a grand piano. Four tall French windows, wide open, admitted fog from a weed-grown terrace.

A square woman wearing a dress not unlike some sort of uniform, was smoking a very long cigarette as though it had been a cigar. She leaned on the piano beside a blond, bespectacled young man, listening, without enthusiasm, to the appalling playing of a brunette who, from where Kennedy stood, was apparently naked.

Recalling Sidonia, Kennedy concluded that Joan's guests had ideas of their own on the subject of "austerity."

There was no one else in the long gloomy hall, in which most of the lights had been switched off.

Kennedy withdrew, unnoticed. Peter and the bronze

had disappeared, presumably in the fog. He paused for a moment, irresolute. The piano player ceased upon an excruciating discord. Glancing about the lobby, he crossed and looked along a dim passage. He decided to explore.

He passed a door marked "Private" and then another bearing a notice, "Powder Room." He went ahead, opened a third door at the far end, and was met by a barrage of fog. He found himself out on a narrow terrace.

No one was in sight. But he thought that a vague shape, real or imaginary, merged into the shadows of an arched opening on his left. He dismissed the idea as a fog mirage, but walked along quietly and looked through the arch. It led to some steps, which he descended, to find himself at the end of the main terrace.

Near by he saw a partly open, draped window. He pushed it wider and drew the drapes aside, looking into that strange museum-room where shadows of the past mocked shadows of the present. Only one lamp was alight. There was no one in the room.

Proceeding farther, he paused by the first of the big windows and looked into the paneled hall. The musical trio had dispersed. Both women were gone. The blond man was inspecting a brigade of bottles paraded on a trestle table, evidently hoping to find one that had something in it.

Storm Kennedy swore under his breath. Whatever had brought Hilary to this lunatic party on such a night, had already happened, and she was gone. He was too late. He stepped into the room. The blond man turned and peered at him.

"Can you tell me if Lady Hilary Bruton is still here?" Kennedy asked.

"Er—I'm afraid, sir, I don't know Lady Hilary Bruton."

"Sorry."

Kennedy crossed the floor and went into the now empty

lobby. He glanced up uncarpeted stairs. Landings to right and left, above, were unlighted. He was about to go outside, when a sound of firm, approaching footsteps made him change his mind. He turned, and saw the square woman bearing down upon him like a destroyer at full speed.

"I don't know who you are," she announced gruffly. "But have you seen Hilary?"

"Why—this is fantastic! The very question I was about to ask *you!* My name is Storm Kennedy."

"Elphinstowe," snapped the lady. "Amelia (Miss) Elphinstowe. Heard Hilary speak of you. Where the devil is she?"

Kennedy's face grew grim.

"But surely she came with you, Miss Elphinstowe?"

"Quite. But where's she gone?"

"Suppose," said Kennedy, quietly, "you tell me when and where you saw her last?"

"Powder Room. Along that passage. We were getting ready to push off. Ten minutes ago."

There was urgency, sternly repressed, in her manner. Storm Kennedy felt quite sure that she had some other more valid reason for alarm.

"Let's go and look again," he suggested; then, recognizing the necessity of covering the real purpose of his visit, he added: "I turned up very late, and when Peter told me you were here I thought I might be useful as a fog guide."

The small, oak-paneled room was empty. That doorway which opened on a corner of the terrace was closed. As they returned to the dark passage:

"What's in here?" said Kennedy, sharply.

He stood looking at the notice "Private"—and the door upon which the notice was pinned burst open and Hilary ran out!

Even in that half-light, he could see that she was unnaturally pale. She stopped dead, looking from face to face.

"Thank God!" said Miss Elphinstowe in a deep voice. "You gave me a shocking fright, dear. Mr. Storm Kennedy has come to rescue us."

To Kennedy the fact became unmistakable that Hilary was taxed to the limit of her endurance. Therefore, he admired the way in which she held out a quivering hand and spoke in a controlled voice.

"I'm so glad to see you. Will you excuse me for just ten minutes? Come with me, Elfie."

Kennedy stood aside to let them pass. What had happened? And why had Hilary come out of that room? He opened the door and glanced in. The interior was quite dark. He flashed a pocket torch momentarily.

It was the room into which he had looked from the terrace—the room which resembled a museum.

There was no one there.

He walked back to the long hall and found it deserted, fog floating among its high beams. Lighting a cigarette, he went outside—and learned that visibility was now reduced to about fifteen feet.

Desperately, he wanted to think, to think calmly. He had a number of things to think about.

But his meditations were interrupted by a muffled voice, coming from somewhere beyond and below:

"Tallyho! Fog warning! All out! All out!"

It was Peter Faraway, down in the garden, presumably endeavoring to round up possible stragglers.

And presently, through a moving curtain of mist, he saw the erratic movements of a flashlamp. The light drew nearer. Peter was coming up the steps from the lower terrace.

Suddenly, he stopped.

"God's mercy!"

The words suggested that something had sobered Peter like an icy shower. Dimly, Kennedy could see that he had set his lamp on a step and was kneeling down. He ran to him.

"What's up, Peter?"

"Is that Bill Kennedy?" Peter Faraway raised frightened eyes. "I say! Look here!"

Storm Kennedy looked.

Lying half on his side on the bottom step, so that the light shone upon a ghastly, contorted face, was a man whose limbs were drawn up as if in agony, whose fists were clenched. A red patch showed on his shirt front, and lying near—so near that he might have plucked it out in his death struggle—Kennedy saw a small dagger, its jeweled hilt glittering in the rays of the lamp.

5

"Don't touch him!" said Storm Kennedy sharply. "Touch nothing."

He stood up and met Peter Faraway's stare.

"The poor cove *is* dead, isn't he?"

Kennedy nodded.

"Very dead—within the last few minutes."

"But . . ."

"My God! That explains it!"

The frightened, intruding voice brought them both about. The blond young man who wore spectacles stood there staring down.

"Explains *what?*" Kennedy demanded.

"The row I heard. Sort of gabbling, and—er—loud breathing. It was just after you came in and asked me if I'd—er—seen somebody or other. Then I heard a kind of choking cough. But I thought—er—it was some chap being sick."

He sounded as though he might be sick himself, at any moment.

Kennedy flicked his flashlamp alight and looked at his wrist watch.

"That would make the time of the attack approximately

one-thirty." He glanced down again at the contorted figure. "One of your guests, Peter?"

"Good Lord, no! Never saw the cove in my life. But, wait a minute. He might be. Joan got this party up, and she knows all sorts of queer birds I don't know."

They fell into silence, one of those strange silences which come at the most unlikely moments. Three pairs of eyes stared downward.

Kennedy found himself listening—he could not have said for what. There was a sustained whispering, like a sigh, and a drip-drip as of tears. He knew it to be caused by mist condensing on the leaves, but it depressed his spirit. Almost overhanging the steps, some kind of willow drooped spectral arms, a ghost tree. Beyond, in hidden acres, fog-sheeted, the assassin might be stealing away.

"Stay here and keep the women clear. I shan't be a minute."

Kennedy ran up the steps and along a few paces to the window of the room harboring many relics. He had seen a telephone on a table there. He found the window wide open now, but the room in darkness. He pulled up for a moment, assailed by a sudden thought.

When, a few minutes earlier, he had looked into this odd sanctum from the terrace, a floor lamp had been burning. When Hilary ran out into the corridor the room had been in darkness.

Who had switched the light off? When—and why?

He snapped his flash on and stepped inside.

Sixty wasted seconds satisfied him. The line was dead.

He was about to run back along the terrace, when a faint sound checked him. He switched his light off.

Someone very quietly opened a door on the other side of the room. Kennedy knew it was that room from which Hilary had come out. A slender figure whose head seemed to be of disproportionate size showed silhouetted against faint light from the corridor.

"Is anyone there?" came a soft voice.

Kennedy shot a ray onto the man's face. The illusion of the deformed head was explained. He saw an Egyptian who wore a turban. His large, deer-like eyes never blinked; he merely stared, inquiringly.

"Whom were you expecting?"

"The wise man expects nothing, sir."

"Is this your house?"

"I have no house, other than the house of clay which the All-Knowing, the Omnipotent fashioned to imprison my spirit."

"Not too helpful. Have you been in here before?"

"Twice, sir. Once, to converse with a student and philosopher, and a second time in search of the Honorable Peter."

"When was the second time?"

"Perhaps some ten minutes ago."

"What lights were on?"

"This light, only."

Mohammed indicated the lamp by the open window.

"Anybody in here?"

"No one, *Khawâga*."

"Did you switch the lamp off?"

"Why should I disturb the arrangements of others?"

"You mean you didn't?"

"Such is my meaning."

Storm Kennedy challenged the gentle eyes, but they met his regard unflinchingly. He went out and back to where two shadowy figures loomed, phantomesque, through the fog. Peter had switched the flash off.

"Phone's out of order, Peter," said Kennedy rapidly. "But there's a call-box at the end of the lane leading to this place. I know, because I ran into it when I came. There are one or two things I must check up on, immediately. So it will have to be you. Feel up to it?"

"Positively. Never soberer in my life, dear soul. Astonishing. What do I say?"

"Police. Surgeon. Murder. Hangover House. Hurry."

Peter Faraway considered this, then:

"Got it," he replied, turned, stood still and combed his fingers through disordered hair. "But wait a minute. Let me think. Joan has pinched the car!"

Kennedy, impatiently, spun around on the blond and now pale young man.

"Got a car?"

"Yes—yes, I have."

"You drive him, then. Come on, Peter."

He was feverishly anxious to get these witnesses away from the scene of the crime—to conduct a private examination before the police arrived. Grasping Peter Faraway's arm, he hurried him along past the open windows of the big hall, around the angle of the house and into that weedy courtyard where cars were parked.

"It's not going to be easy, you know," said the fair young man as he switched on the headlights of a Morris Eight.

"You'll manage. It's no distance. Push off."

He waited until the Morris crawled past the open gates, then he turned back. . . .

Who else was in the house, apart from those he knew? Who was the softly spoken Egyptian, and where had he been at the time of the crime? Who was the "student and philosopher" to whom he referred?

Paramount perplexity: why had Hilary Bruton come running out of the darkened room, and how long had she been in there? For, during the short interval which had elapsed between the time when he first spoke to the blond fellow and the time when he met Miss Elphinstowe in the lobby, a man had been stabbed to death on the terrace outside!

He checked up quickly on the cars.

There were four, including his own and the Morris in which Peter had gone. He could still hear the latter stuttering through darkness on its way down that serpentine elm tunnel which led to the main road and the call-box. No other had left Hangover House since he had arrived. Of this he was sure.

Apparently there were no servants in this singular establishment. Not a living creature appeared in the weedy courtyard. Kennedy wondered to whom the place belonged and how it had come to be selected by Joan Faraway. He went inside again, and found no one in the gloomy lobby. The paneled hall was similarly deserted. Fear of being fogbound accounted for the break-up of the party, the desertion of the caterers; but what of the inhabitants?

It was more than peculiar. It was uncanny. *Somebody* must live in the place, as evidenced by the furnishing of the room marked Private.

He went out onto the terrace and down the steps, but paused above the one on which the body lay. Peter had left his lamp there, and Kennedy switched it on.

The dead man's face was so horribly and unaccountably contorted that he avoided looking at it. There was more blood than he had noted at first. A red, sticky rivulet had touched the dagger. Stooping, Kennedy checked an exclamation.

He had seen something else.

Footprints—marks of high-heeled shoes—showed clearly in the lamp ray!

"My God!" he groaned.

Using his torch, he circled gingerly around the body

and examined the lower step. A certain amount of blood had trickled over. There were other, larger, footprints here. Peter's, no doubt.

But there was something else.

There was a tiny lace handkerchief covered with red stains!

Certain of Lord Glengale's words assumed an ominous significance.

Yet—it was unthinkable.

Storm Kennedy found himself face to face with the most vital decision he had ever been called upon to make. He switched off his torch and put it back in his pocket. Then, stooping, he also extinguished Peter's lamp. . . .

The sound of a slammed car door brought him running around to the courtyard—but not before he had completed his task.

He found the turbaned Egyptian preparing to drive away in a smart-looking Packard. Raising his hand, he stepped to the open window from which the man was looking out questioningly.

"Just a moment, if you please."

"Can I assist you in any way, sir?"

"Yes, you can. Be good enough to get out again."

"Perhaps, sir, I misunderstand you?"

"No, you don't. There has been an—accident. I'm afraid no one must leave until the matter has been cleared up."

Mohammed mutinied for a fractional moment. The gazelle eyes flashed a glance which was neither gentle nor genial. Then he obeyed.

"I am at your service, *Khawâga.*"

"Thanks," said Kennedy drily. "If you will wait in the big room, the rest of the guests will be joining you there."

He followed the Egyptian, and as they entered the half-lighted, paneled hall, with piled-up trestle tables, chairs and rolled rugs left behind, some under the gallery once designed for minstrels, he saw the glittering brunette coming toward him. She came from that passage which led to the powder room. A mink wrap covered her bare shoulders.

She smiled a vague greeting.

"As you have just been outside"—she addressed Kennedy—"please tell me—is there any sign of my chauffeur?"

He noted the accent, the husky voice, easy acceptance of an awkward situation.

"I'm sorry, but there isn't. Where did he go?"

"I lent him to somebody, local, earlier."

"Bad luck. He's probably fogbound."

"But that is terrible! Is someone else going back to town?"

Mohammed crossed his long hands on his breast and bowed.

"I am at madame's disposal—directly this gentleman gives his consent."

"His consent?"

Dark eyes were raised to Storm Kennedy, penciled brows slightly lifted.

"I am quite without authority in the matter. There has been—a little trouble."

"Can I help?"

"Thank you. But all you can do will be to wait until the doctor comes."

Kennedy glanced at the Egyptian. He learned nothing.

"The doctor?" It was fascinating, this woman's husky voice. "Then, someone . . . ?"

"Someone has been hurt—badly. I'm sorry to be a nuisance, but I'm just acting for Peter Faraway, who has gone to the call-box."

"Who—is it?"

"No one any of us knows."

Big eyes searched his own. A slight breeze had sprung

up and fog was moving like floating cobwebs outside the open windows. The dark woman smiled, pathetically, and shrugged her shoulders, turning away, as Hilary and Miss Elphinstowe came in.

"Well, troops," Miss Elphinstowe remarked gruffly, "what about heading back to camp?"

Hilary's face was unreadable—a pale mask.

"I'm afraid," Kennedy told her, "we shall all have to stay here awhile." But he was watching Hilary. "Someone —a stranger to Peter and to me—has been killed out there on the terrace."

"Killed?"

The last remnants of color deserted Hilary's cheeks. There was terror, undisguisable, in her widely opened eyes. Storm Kennedy glanced aside to where the Egyptian was talking to the brunette.

"Yes." He restored his attention to Hilary. "Peter has gone to call the police. The phone here is off duty."

He had looked aside deliberately, but now he detected an exchange of glances between Hilary and Miss Elphinstowe, laden with understanding. Hilary was biting her lip. She lowered her lashes swiftly. It was the elder woman who spoke.

"Male or female?"

"A man. Dark, sunburned. Might have been a good looker. Wavy black hair, with a fleck of gray."

Hilary, performing one of those amazing feats of self-control in some way reminiscent of her father, looked Kennedy squarely in the eyes.

"Someone Peter doesn't know? Someone who wasn't at the party?"

"Yes."

Hilary glanced again, a swift glance, at Miss Elphinstowe, then: "How was he killed?" she asked quietly.

"He was stabbed—with a rather unusual weapon. A

small, silver-hilted dagger, the hilt set with amethysts—or they look like amethysts."

She was silent for some moments. She wore a sort of light, fleecy wrap over her frock and her fingers played nervously with the clasp of her gray-and-white bag which she held tightly in her left hand.

"How horrible!" she whispered. "I suppose it means we are all prisoners here until the police have . . . ?"

"I'm afraid so. I arrived late, myself, and I was going to offer my services as a pilot back to town."

Hilary thanked him with a smile which was, at once, an acknowledgment of the fact that she liked him and a miracle of courage.

"Looks as though we are all in for a cheery evening," said Miss Elphinstowe. "So the sooner we get matey the better. I'm Miss Elphinstowe to my tradespeople—Elfie to my friends. You know Hilary. What's your name for short?"

"Bill."

"Now we can get cozy. There isn't a spot left in the bar, there's nowhere to sit down, and I've run out of cigarettes. I suppose"—as Kennedy produced his case—"the next part of the entertainment will be viewing the corpse?"

"I suppose so."

He offered his case to Hilary.

"Thanks, no. I won't smoke."

"I should have hated to miss such a gorgeous party," said Elfie.

And as Kennedy lighted her cigarette, his esteem for Amelia Elphinstowe grew; for he knew that all this was a brave façade which she had built up to shield Hilary from danger foreseen.

What were these two women hiding? It was a maddening situation.

Assuming (and he had little data to help him) the dead

man to be Hilary's persecutor from whom Lord Glengale had briefed him to protect her, what, in heaven's name, had happened? Granting (again, hypothetically) Hilary to be capable of killing a man in just anger, would she have chosen so strange a weapon?

A woman with Hilary Bruton's background doesn't carry a stiletto. Further, where could she have come upon such a thing? It was an Eastern dagger—a short-bladed, ornamental trifle. A powerful blow, skilfully directed, would be necessary to inflict a mortal wound with such a toy.

Against all this, why had she canceled her journey to Paris and driven on a foggy night to Hangover House? Why had she burst out of that room in a state of wild agitation only a few minutes after the crime had been committed? And whose were the footprints in the dead man's blood?

Whatever had happened—Elfie knew.

He wondered how long it would be before the police and the doctor arrived. . . .

6

Dr. Smithy stood up, an arresting figure in an island of many lamps around which swirled waves of fog. He was a big man, bald and paunchy. He wore uncommonly large, owl-like glasses and he was dressed in a green pajama jacket, creased white flannel trousers and bath sandals.

He looked from face to face with a sort of snarling smile; he had very prominent teeth. The stone steps and a space above and below, had been roped off by the police. At the moment, Dr. Smithy was the only member of the party inside the ropes. Outside, Storm Kennedy stood with Inspector Hawley (chief detective officer from Lychgate) and a uniformed police sergeant.

"Some heavy-footed oaf," said Dr. Smithy with a wolfish grin, "has been paddling about in the bloke's blood. He ought to be shot, whosoever he is."

"Possibly myself, or Peter," Kennedy admitted.

Dr. Smithy ignored the remark.

"All this blood, you know," he went on, "means that there's probably no internal hemorrhage. The blade doesn't seem to have gone far in. Diverted by this rib"—he stooped and prodded his finger into the stripped torso—"I imagine. Damn funny."

Peeling off his rubber gloves, he took a packet of cigarettes and a lighter from a hip pocket.

"Do you mean, Doctor, that the wound didn't kill him?" Hawley asked.

"Yes, possibly I do."

He lighted a cigarette.

"Complicates things a bit," Kennedy murmured.

"It does," Dr. Smithy agreed, enthusiastically. "It does, my dear sir. It's a frightful muddle. I mean to say, the bloke's all drawn up—tensed. That's damn funny, too. A bloke with a knife in his midriff doesn't act like that. It's not done. It's unethical. Then, there's the ghastly expression on his mug. In fact, he looks more like an angina than a stabbing. But we'll know better when we get him on the slab. And now I'll cut back to bed."

Kennedy turned and walked toward the house.

"When your fingerprint man arrives, Inspector," he said, "he will probably find evidence on the hilt of the knife."

"He won't, my dear sir!" Dr. Smithy assured him. "It looks as though the defunct had plucked it out of his own chest. It's bathed in blood. The thing's in a frightful mess."

He was struggling into a topcoat which appeared to be much too small for him and bestowing a leering grin upon Inspector Hawley.

Hawley called back to the sergeant: "Stand by there, Martin, until the Super arrives."

Inspector Hawley, a pale, cadaverous man who rarely took his hands out of the pockets of a depressed-looking Burberry, took them out now and removed a depressing felt hat.

"I'm afraid footprints will be muddled up, too," he remarked. "A lot of people seem to have been trampling about there."

Storm Kennedy glanced aside at the Inspector, but his expression conveyed no more than his tone.

The three passed along the terrace in front of tall French windows closed and draped by Hawley's orders. Kennedy said nothing, but he was thinking much.

"You can send for the hearse whenever you like." Dr. Smithy flicked ash from his cigarette. "I'll put my report in."

"Waiting for the Super," Hawley replied gloomily. "I called him at King's Riding."

They went around the angle of the house and through the arched opening into that weedy courtyard, where the doctor's veteran but self-respecting automobile awaited him. As he plumped his bag inside:

"I mean to say," he remarked, grinning fiercely, "I always thought I should be called here some dirty night." The breeze had freshened. Fog wreaths swept across the porch lights. "This bally old ruin dates back a bit, you know. Must have been lots of murders here. Just the place for that sort of thing."

He ducked into the car and slammed the door.

"Can you find your way in the dark, Doctor?" Hawley called.

"With my eyes shut." Dr. Smithy stuck his bald head out. "A general practitioner has to. Babies have a nasty trick of getting born in the middle of the night. What's more, they favor foggy nights. Vindictive little brats. Cheery ho . . . !"

He drove off into swirling mist.

Storm Kennedy had urgent need of private conversation with Hilary Bruton. It would be a difficult conversation, for she mustn't suspect that he was anything other than a stranded guest, like herself. But, now that he was deeply committed, he must find out the truth, whatever the truth might be. Something more than his reputation, his very liberty, was at stake.

But, since the inquiry had been taken over by Superintendent Croker, opportunities were fewer than ever.

Superintendent Croker, although aroused from his bed at nearly two o'clock in the morning, had, nevertheless, turned up in uniform. He had gathered that there were ladies at Hangover House, and the Superintendent was a gallant officer.

He had arrived in a car equipped with a searchlight, preceded by two motorcyclists, and accompanied by a photographer and a fingerprint specialist.

Having established contact with Sergeant Martin, on duty beside the body, conducted a brief personal inspection and set the technicians to work, he made a spectacular entrance into the long paneled hall where most of the guests trapped in the net were assembled.

He wore his uniform smartly, his silver-edged peaked cap at a jaunty angle. Superintendent Croker had all the self-assurance, and some of the appearance, of the lamented Benito Mussolini.

Conversation was arrested when he opened the door and raised a gloved hand in a military salute.

"I am sorry to have to trouble you, ladies and gentlemen, but I'm afraid I must take statements from all those present. . . ."

More than half an hour had elapsed, since then. Storm Kennedy had signed a statement—which sorely troubled his conscience. Peter Faraway, the blond man, and the Egyptian had been called to view the body, and then into the study, requisitioned by the superintendent for this purpose. He was dealing first with the men and reserving the women for dessert. A police sergeant had just summoned the brunette, whose name, Kennedy had learned, was Mrs. Muller. He thought she looked pale as the man led her out onto the terrace. No wonder . . .

Hilary, he could no longer doubt, was deliberately avoiding him.

She and Elfie had disappeared some time before, Elfie having thwarted his several attempts to talk to Hilary alone. He knew they couldn't have left the house, for constables were on duty back and front. Yes—Hilary's absence was deliberate.

But he *must* see her, if only for a moment, before Superintendent Croker got her into his clutches. He made a quick survey.

The Egyptian, who had been interrupted while reading Mrs. Muller's palm, was talking earnestly to the blond man. Peter had vanished—no doubt to some dark corner with Sidonia. Inspector Hawley, he knew, was carrying out investigations in the garden. One of the police cyclists had been dispatched for the wagon to remove the body directly after remaining witnesses had viewed it.

Kennedy walked briskly along the dim passage and knocked on the door marked Powder Room. Two excited voices ceased instantly, then:

"All right. I am ready," Hilary called.

She opened the door—and stood stock still.

"You weren't expecting me," he said. "But I particularly wanted a few words with you before the interview with Superintendent Croker." He took her arm and drew her quietly out into the corridor. "You see, he will make you sign a statement, and we all have to be careful what we sign."

It was dark out there, but Storm Kennedy could see that firm set of the chin as Hilary averted her face.

"I intend to be careful." She spoke in a low, composed voice. "I have no more to be afraid of than—anyone else." She glanced at him swiftly. "Have I?"

"I don't suppose you were ever afraid of anything in your life. But our various statements will be expected to add up. What I have in mind is this: Can you explain, to the Superintendent's satisfaction, what you were doing in that study, with all lights out? Because, if the explanation is likely to confuse him, say nothing about it."

Hilary was silent for ten seconds, then: "Did *you* say you met me coming out of that room?" she asked.

"I didn't refer to it."

"Why?" she demanded, turned and faced him.

"Because I thought it was unnecessary."

"You mean you thought it was suspicious!" she challenged.

And Storm Kennedy sensed the fact that Hilary Bruton, under that forced composure, was overwrought to breaking point, incapable of calm reasoning; that he could hope neither to learn anything from her, nor to guide her in any way.

"I'm sorry you misunderstood me," he said quietly. "I realize we have all got let in for a very nasty business. I only wanted to help, but"—he patted her hand—"think no more about it."

Hilary's lip quivered. She turned aside quickly. But when she spoke, she had her voice well under control.

"Please forgive me. I'm stupidly irritable at times. One doesn't expect to come to a party and become involved in —a murder." She gave him a fleeting glance. "You are very kind."

It was a generous apology. Whatever Hilary's faults, pettiness was not one of them. Kennedy would gladly have risked more than he had risked already to help her. But he knew that this was the wrong moment. In any case, it was too late.

The door marked Private opened and Mrs. Muller came out, followed by a police sergeant. She turned quickly in the other direction. The sergeant saw Hilary and beckoned to her.

"Good luck," Kennedy murmured.

His glance followed the slight figure, almost ethereal beside that of a stocky policeman, as Hilary was taken to view the dead man. . . .

Could he hope to get any sense out of Miss Elphinstowe? He was considering the possibility when Peter Faraway came along the corridor. Kennedy went to meet him.

"I say, Bill—have you seen Sidonia?"

"No. Why?"

"Because she's vanished!"

"Vanished? Since when?"

Peter combed his hair with his fingers.

"Let me think. Where was I just before I found the dead cove?"

"I haven't the slightest idea."

"No? Oh! Devil of it is, nor have I! But, wherever it was, that's the last I saw of her."

"But, damn it! That's more than an hour ago!"

"I know. Odd thing, isn't it?"

Storm Kennedy hesitated for a moment, and then: "We had better see Inspector Hawley," he muttered. It's rather more than odd."

7

Miss Elphinstowe signed her brief statement. She had concluded that a peculiarly musty odor which characterized this room was the smell of ancient tombs. Superintendent Croker, who had had the big, untidy desk cleared, and sat there interviewing witnesses, was glad to get rid of this one; a very awkward subject, resentful, and difficult to the verge of truculence. Laying her pen down, she inquired:

"Do you think, Superintendent, I could hope to go home now?"

He stood up. He had removed his cap, and with it much of his dignity.

"There is only one more witness to see, Madame. Nobody regrets the unpleasantness of this affair more than I do. As I have names and addresses of all present—with this one exception—and as none of you seems to know anything about the matter, I think I may answer, yes."

"Thank God for small mercies! Who's the one exception?"

Miss Elphinstowe was desperately anxious to rejoin Hilary, who had returned from her interview even paler than before. But her curiosity temporarily conquered her anxiety. The Superintendent glanced at some notes.

"Someone called Sidonia. Do you know her?"

"I saw her, during the evening. She makes unpleasant noises into a microphone."

The Superintendent's reply was interrupted. The phone bell rang.

"According to evidence," he muttered, "this line is out of order."

"Service suspended, sir, no doubt," said the sergeant in attendance, respectfully. "Doesn't apply to incoming calls."

"Is that so?"

Superintendent Croker glared at the man, sat down, and took up the receiver.

"Yes? Superintendent Croker, King's Riding, here."

A moment later, his entire manner changed; his voice became subdued.

"Yes, sir. Superintendent Croker here. I see, sir. . . ." He listened attentively for some time. "I will make all arrangements. . . . Quite clear . . . You may leave it to me."

He hung up. He glanced at the sergeant and then at Miss Elphinstowe.

"Scotland Yard," he explained. "That was the Assistant Commissioner. I don't know who called the Yard. I didn't. But I'm instructed to hold all material witnesses and keep the body on the premises until the C.I.D. officers arrive. . . ."

"Meaning that I can't go home?" Miss Elphinstowe challenged.

"My regrets, Madame. Yes, meaning that none of you can go home until . . ."

He stood up again. Miss Elphinstowe turned sharply.

Someone was descending the short stair which led up to an arched opening. Amid a hushed silence, the figure became visible; that of a tall, thin, parchment-faced old man, who peered through pince-nez, who wore an untidy dressing gown over wrinkled pajamas. He paused on the last step, looking down from one to another.

"What the devil is this?" he demanded. He fixed an angry glare upon the Superintendent. "Who the hell are you? What are you doing at my desk?"

The sergeant whispered, "Larkhall Pike, sir."

"I am Police Superintendent Croker of King's Riding. Are you the owner of this house? If so, I must ask you where you have been all night."

"I have been asleep, sir, a fact it is possible to deduce from my attire. I was awakened by the telephone. I demand again—what is this?"

Before the Superintendent (whose fresh color was mounting) could reply, there came a rap on the door, and Inspector Hawley entered.

"Ambulance from Lychgate is here, sir," he said. "But I have to report the disappearance of a witness wanted for interrogation."

Superintendent Croker swallowed. His baneful glance lingered on the figure of Larkhall Pike.

"What name?" he snapped.

"The only name I have is Sidonia."

"Who saw her last?"

"Mr. Faraway—just before the crime was discovered."

"Has she been searched for?"

"Men searching now, sir."

"Another question: Am I indebted to you for notifying Scotland Yard of this affair?"

"Yes, sir. The name of the gentleman who called us at Lychgate made me think it was a Yard case."

"Why?"

"Well, sir, the Honorable Peter Faraway is Lord Deem's son, and those are our instructions where . . ."

"Quite so!" The Superintendent turned to Miss Elphinstowe. "I need not detain you, Madame. But no one must leave the house."

As she came out, Miss Elphinstowe heard the Superintendent say, acidly:

"Mr. Pike, what rooms are available upstairs . . . ?"

She heard no more. The sergeant closed the door behind her. But that part, at least, of the hateful business was over. Perhaps there was worse to come.

When she went into the little white-paneled room where she had left Hilary, it was empty. But Hilary's bag and wrap lay on the worn leather sofa. The glazed door was half open, and the air of the room damp and misty. Miss Elphinstowe stepped outside.

"Hilary!" she called, softly, "where are you?"

"Ssh! Pull the door to, Elfie! There's—something going on . . !"

Hilary stood just outside, on the corner of the terrace. And now Miss Elphinstowe heard subdued voices and, somewhere below, saw moving lights. She joined Hilary, putting a protective arm around her shoulders.

"What is it, dear?"

"I don't know. I heard Mr. Kennedy's voice. Look! There's a flight of steps here and some sort of pond at the bottom. Police down there!"

"So I see," Elfie remarked grimly. "Let's get a bit closer."

They stole to the head of the steps, which neither had noted before. The breeze had begun to disperse the fog. It was possible to see a neglected and slimy lily pond below, surrounded by mossy paving. A number of men were moving about, and the scene was lent macabre lighting by their flashlamps.

Storm Kennedy was bending over a dim shape which lay beside the pool.

"Oh, my God!" Hilary spoke in a tremulous whisper. "I believe someone else—has been killed!"

Lights were focused on the hitherto shadowy figure—a woman's body.

It was that of Sidonia . . .

"There has been a sort of formal garden down there," Storm Kennedy explained rapidly. "It's a wilderness now, and the steps are dangerous. We found her lying under a lavender bush which had grown into a young tree."

Superintendent Croker nodded, shortly. Some ten minutes had elapsed since the discovery of Sidonia, and he was in an evil humor. What with the insolent behavior of the man, Pike, and those peremptory orders from Scotland Yard, he felt that his official standing had been challenged. He turned to Inspector Hawley.

"Have you sent for the doctor?"

"No, sir." Inspector Hawley shook his head in gloomy resignation. "The lady—Miss Elphinstowe—tells me she had six years with the Red Cross and can manage very well herself."

"But, look here," Peter Faraway broke in. "I mean to say—let me think . . ."

"One moment, Peter!" Kennedy spoke urgently. "I want a word with you."

They had been standing in the shadow of the old minstrel gallery. Kennedy took Peter's arm and led him into the courtyard. A constable was posted on the terrace with orders to permit no one out there. As they moved away, Inspector Hawley removed his depressing hat and scratched his close-cropped head.

"That gentleman seems to have taken charge here, sir," he remarked.

"Anyone can take charge as far as I'm concerned," the Superintendent snapped. "I make the Yard a gift of this case. They're welcome to it. A man's murdered, a man none of the witnesses has ever seen before, with nothing on him to establish his identity. And now a woman's attacked in the garden. Some homicidal maniac is hiding out there."

"The fog makes it more difficult. There are about eighteen acres of ground around this house, mostly wilderness. I have six men on the job, but they've found nobody so far."

"I leave the case in your hands, Inspector Hawley; the fingerprints and the signed statements. My instructions are to proceed no further with the inquiry. Therefore, I'm retiring from it. The photographs will be here shortly. I shall only wait to learn what this woman Sidonia has to tell us, and then go home."

Superintendent Croker portrayed a monument of offended dignity.

But only a few minutes had elapsed when Miss Elphinstowe walked briskly into the echoing, misty room.

"I've pulled her around," she announced. "Anybody got a cigarette?"

The Superintendent produced a silver case and lighted a cigarette for her.

"Can I interview her, Madame?"

"I'll tip you when she's ready."

"What is her explanation?"

"Well—different from mine. Mine's chiefly booze. She seems to have been down the garden with Peter Faraway and lost him, somehow. Coming back, she blundered onto the body—stepped right in the blood. Bit of a shock. Tottered along to the door of the Powder Room opening on the terrace and then came over faint. She stayed out there for some time, I gather, being sick and what not. Finally, she fainted in earnest—and fell down the steps. Crack on the napper. But it hasn't done her much harm."

"Is there any evidence to support this story?" Hawley inquired.

"Well"—Miss Elphinstowe fitted her cigarette into a holder and stuck it in her mouth so that it projected upward—"there's plenty of blood on her shoes."

Storm Kennedy quietly opened the door of the small, white-paneled room and peeped in. Nobody was there but Sidonia.

The bronze, now slightly disheveled, lay on the sofa, a bandage round her head. She appeared to be asleep. Only one shaded lamp remained alight. There was a smell of eau de cologne. The half-glazed door had been opened. He crossed, on tiptoes, and stepped out onto the corner of the terrace.

He had made next to no sound. But Hilary turned and faced him. She held a smoldering cigarette between her fingers. In that dim light, her gray eyes were dove-soft and very lovely.

"Did I alarm you?" He spoke in a low voice.

"No. I was expecting you."

"Why?"

She put the cigarette between her lips and moved to the parapet overlooking the lily pond, now invisible.

"Because you are almost as obstinate as I am, and I knew you meant to talk to me, alone."

There was a momentary silence. Kennedy moved over to her side.

"Does that mean you didn't want to talk to me alone?"

Hilary raised her chin, but didn't look at him.

"Not necessarily. But you don't really know a lot about me, and so it's very, very kind of you to bother at all. You have an idea that I'm involved in some way in what happened here tonight. You want to help. I appreciate that—

tremendously. But, just supposing I were in a jam, why should *you* get mixed up in it?"

Storm Kennedy grew suddenly hot. Hilary had all of her father's directness of approach. Whatever she had done, wherever she had gone wrong, there had been no ulterior motive, no meanness. If she had sinned, she was ready to pay the price.

And he? He was an impostor. He had been retained to "get mixed up in it!" She had no suspicion of his present profession. Instinct warned him that if he would serve her, no such suspicion must arise. But he hated to sail under false colors with Hilary. Later, but soon, he was to ask himself why.

He considered his answer with care.

"Perhaps," he said, "I'm in it already."

She turned to him swiftly. He had learned that she was essentially a creature of impulse.

"I don't understand. What do you mean?"

He stood close beside her, for he must speak softly. He found her nearness disturbing; she was intensely vital.

"When—Elfie—and I came to look for you earlier tonight, and you ran out of that room, I could see that there was something wrong." He spoke with studied slowness. "When, only a few minutes later, Peter found a dead man outside, I argued like this: There's going to be a police inquiry. Unless the facts are plain, everybody is going to become a suspect. And Hilary has no alibi."

He glanced aside at his companion. But she was staring straight ahead into the mist.

"Do you see?"

"Yes, I see."

"I argued that you might have blundered onto the body and run on into the house. So, when I found the prints of a woman's shoe in his blood . . ."

"A woman's shoe?" Hilary's clear voice had become a strained whisper; then: "Oh! Sidonia?"

"Yes. It doesn't matter that I know now whose shoe it was. At the time, I didn't know. And so—but this is not for the police—I defaced the footprints with my own. You see, I *had* an alibi. I was with Peter when he found him."

Hilary tossed her cigarette away and bent forward, resting her hands on the low stone parapet. She said nothing.

"That's why I didn't mention meeting you coming out of the room. But"—his words became deliberate—"I don't know what you told the Superintendent."

Hilary turned to him again. She rested her hand for a moment on his arm then withdrew it. The gesture was that of a lady of old throwing a rose to a knight in recognition of achievement. No less. No more.

"Thank you," she said softly. "I thought chivalry was dead." She paused for a moment. "But I'm afraid I have undone all your good work."

"In what way?"

She did not reply at once, but presently she said, "Supposing"—she spoke quietly—"supposing, foolishly, that if only I could get clear of this ghastly house tonight, I might hope to be free of it all, I took—certain liberties— in answering the Superintendent's questions. Now, I'm told, we are being held here for somebody from Scotland Yard?"

It was Storm Kennedy's turn to be silent. Hilary had accepted him as an ally, but had given him less than half her confidence. He had hoped for more. It was one thing to make a reticent statement to Superintendent Croker, but the "somebody" from Scotland Yard presented a proposition of a different color. He had learned from Hawley that Chief Detective Inspector McGraw of the C.I.D. had been assigned to the case.

And Chief Detective Inspector McGraw was not only a

highly competent investigator, he was also the officer who had handled the Mallory jewel robbery. It was McGraw who had been cheated of his triumph by Storm Kennedy's recovery of the missing heirlooms from the young scoundrel who had stolen them!

Hilary rested her hand on his arm again, and let it remain there.

"Do you think we're in for a bad time?" she whispered.

He turned to her.

"Yes, I'm afraid we are. . . ."

8

Restful slumber was not to be looked for that night. Nevertheless, Storm Kennedy dozed off several times.

He had tried to talk again to Hilary, but she had retired with Miss Elphinstowe to the Powder Room, saying that they hoped to rest there. It was, in fact, a large dressing room with bath and lavatory accommodation attached, so that, even though Sidonia occupied the only couch, it had advantages not possessed by the paneled hall.

It was a dismissal. Intuition and observation alike told him that the older woman had urged enlisting him as an ally, but that Hilary, for some obscure reason, had declined.

He found an old canvas chair in a shed adjoining the courtyard, carried it into the long hall and placed it near one of the draped windows. At this time he was the only person in the room. He dozed, and awakened to find that Miss Elphinstowe had set up camp on the other side, and was already sound asleep.

Out in the courtyard, Mr. Lovelace slumbered musically in his Morris, but none of the other cars was occupied. A constable stood on duty at the gate.

Returning, he went quietly along the corridor, in which someone had turned the light off. There came a sound of voices from the women's room, which he thought he recognized as those of Hilary and Mrs. Muller. Possibly Sidonia was there, too. Of the Egyptian and Peter Faraway he found no trace. He assumed that Mr. Pike slept in unchallenged solitude in the study. . . .

When he awakened next, it was a creaking door which disturbed him. He sprang up in a moment, peering into the dark corridor.

A vaguely discernible figure was stealing out of the study!

By the time that he had found his pocket lamp and pressed the button, this figure had disappeared. He realized that he must have been clearly visible against the dim glow of one light left on in the paneled hall.

Miss Elphinstowe never stirred. And daylight was not far away when Kennedy dozed off again. . . .

He was awakened by the sound of distant voices. He got up and parted the draperies of one of the long windows of the paneled hall and stood there looking out.

Points of light moved about the misty acres of Hangover House. Some hurricane lanterns had been pressed into service to reinforce the police lamps. Whatever Scotland Yard may have directed, Inspector Hawley was pursuing his own investigations.

Kennedy could see that the fog was dispersing, for even more distant lights were becoming discernible.

"I cannot imagine what they are looking for. Can you?"

He turned to find Mrs. Muller beside him, swathed in mink.

"No," he confessed. "It isn't particularly clear to me."

"Unless," she suggested, "for the murderer?"

Kennedy smiled. It was a rather forced smile.

"If the crime was the work of someone from outside, it's not likely he would be hanging about now."

Mrs. Muller stifled a yawn, and turned it to a faint laugh.

"I am almost asleep on my feet! I explored upstairs awhile ago, in the hope of finding somewhere to lie down. But every door is locked."

Storm Kennedy pointed across the room.

On an extemporized divan, composed of several folded rugs, Miss Elphinstowe slept peacefully. She had a scarf tied over her hair, and her shoes were placed neatly beside her on the floor.

"Old campaigner!" Kennedy murmured. "As far as I can make out, there's only one furnished bedroom in the place, and the superintendent had the bed stripped and the body put there!"

"Yes," Mrs. Muller nodded. "He seemed to be very angry with that strange old character. I don't know why!" She paused, sighed, and then, "Oh, dear!" she added, "here comes Lovelace again!"

Kennedy followed the direction of her glance and saw the blond man peering in from the door which opened onto the vestibule. "Oh, there you are!" Lovelace exclaimed, coming forward. "I have been looking all over for you."

"Have you?"

Mrs. Muller smiled pathetically at Kennedy.

"Yes—er—I wondered if I could get you anything."

"Many things—if you know where to find them!"

"Well—er"—he peered around vaguely—"I could ask somebody, if you told me what you wanted."

"A cup of coffee would be a godsend."

"Yes. I'll see what I can do."

He wandered off toward the corridor, to become lost in shadow.

"No doubt," Mrs. Muller said, "Mr. Lovelace means well but, frankly, he is rather a nuisance!"

"Bit of a mystery, too. I suppose he's one of Joan's discoveries."

"He must be. He writes songs. The lucky ones were those who left early. Unfortunately for me, I ran into Joan only yesterday, and she invited me to the party. I happened to find myself at a loose end, and . . ."

She finished on an eloquent shrug.

"Bad luck!"

"It was, indeed."

A sudden uproar arose from somewhere not far away.

"Be good enough to get out of this room—and stay out! I can offer you neither coffee, tea, nor any other type of beverage. There is a pump on the premises."

A door was banged loudly.

Kennedy presently drifted into the courtyard. Dim, eerie light began to displace misty darkness, for dawn was breaking. He could just see Hilary, curled up on the back seat of a Bentley, her bright hair buried in a fleecy cloak. He stood there watching her for a long time. She looked like a gray squirrel.

That extra sense which warns us that we are observed, prompted him to turn suddenly. He met the placid gaze of dark eyes. The Egyptian sat at the wheel of his Packard.

"The sun rises in the East, Effendi."

Kennedy stared hard.

"Yes, it does as a rule, I believe."

He went in and almost upset Mr. Lovelace, carrying a tumbler full of water.

"Er—pardon me," he said, "but have you seen Mrs. Muller?"

"Not recently. But she must be somewhere about."

In the ghastly battle of dawn versus electric bulbs, Mr. Lovelace, in his tail coat and near-white tie, presented a strange spectacle. Storm Kennedy fingered the stubble on his own chin, and wondered what *he* looked like. . . .

Miss Elphinstowe woke up shortly after dawn and began to put her shoes on. She was engaged in doing so when a Flying Squad car was driven into the courtyard and a man got out stiffly and stretched his cramped limbs; a tall man, physically unsuited to long hours cooped in confined spaces. He removed a topcoat and threw it in onto the back seat as a second passenger alighted.

"Case, Sergeant."

The second man, who wore a blue raincoat, took a leather portfolio from the uniformed driver, as Inspector Hawley, who had heard the Yard car approaching, came through the arched opening.

"Chief Inspector McGraw?"

"My name."

The tall man, who had a gaunt, aquiline, clean-shaven face, and tired-looking eyes under drooping lids, chewed as he spoke. His words were few, and tired, like his eyes.

"Inspector Hawley of Lychgate."

McGraw extended his hand. "Called us, didn't you?"

"Yes, sir."

"Got stuck on the hill. Wrecks ahead. Murder?"

"A clear case, Chief Inspector."

"Site roped off?"

"Every area believed to bear on the crime is isolated. The body of the dead man is in the house. Fingerprints of all present were taken after they had viewed the body and the weapon used. Some new evidence has come to hand. . . ."

"Own impressions first. This is Detective-Sergeant Sample. Begin with scene of murder . . ."

Three-quarters of an hour had elapsed before Chief Inspector McGraw and Sergeant Sample entered Hangover House. When they passed through the long hall, McGraw merely glanced at that gray company wearing creased evening clothes. Inspector Hawley led the way to the relic-crowded study, rapped on the door and entered.

Storm Kennedy stood by an open French window, and half-light seeped in. A desk lamp was switched on and one in the inglenook. The shelves, with their dead gods and fusty volumes, lay in haunted shadow. No one else was in the room.

McGraw pulled up on the threshold as Kennedy turned. "Hullo!" he said. "*You* here?"

"Good morning, Chief Inspector. Glad to see you again, Sergeant Sample."

McGraw chewed thoughtfully. Hawley watched.

"This is homicide, not larceny. Who're you covering?"

Kennedy smiled and came forward. He had planned to have as few witnesses as possible to his meeting with the C.I.D. men. He offered a slip of cardboard to McGraw.

"I received this a week ago. Socially, I'm a gentleman at large. Don't give me away. I'm just one of the guests."

Chief Inspector McGraw glanced at Joan Faraway's invitation and then returned it.

"Oh," he said, "is that so?"

"I may add that if I can help in any way, I am entirely at your service."

"I'll bear it in mind." McGraw spoke over his shoulder to Hawley. "Where's the body?"

It was a fact which should have interested a psychologist that whereas most of the men in this ill-assorted company were badly shop-soiled, the women, by means of some feminine magic, had contrived, with no resources other than those contained in their handbags (aided, possibly, by cold water) to make a fair showing. Even Sidonia had transformed herself. All looked as presentable as any woman can hope to look who wears evening dress in the grey light of early morning.

Chief Inspector McGraw, seated at the desk in Larkhill

Pike's study, gazed around. Only Peter Faraway and Mohammed were absent. His open portfolio lay before him. Detective-Sergeant Sample stood behind his chair. McGraw glanced at a number of papers neatly pinned together.

"I regret," he said drowsily, "inconvenience to those present, particularly the ladies. When the case was placed in my hands, I ordered parties then on the premises to be held until I arrived. Fogbound on the way. Sorry. All know the serious nature of the case. Murder. I have examined the scene of the discovery—dead man—photographs—fingerprints. Have not yet established identity of victim. Here's a list of names of those present. Call out, Sergeant."

He detached a page from the pinned papers and handed it to Sample.

"Yes, sir."

"Glad if you will answer when you hear your names."

Inspector McGraw lay back in the chair and closed his weary eyes as he chewed.

Sergeant Sample, who had not removed the blue raincoat, looked more like a sailor than a policeman. He had a rugged, weatherbeaten face, a resigned expression, and a mode of speech so completely resigned that it had no expression at all.

"Mr. Storm Kennedy."

"Here, Sergeant."

"Mohammed"—he paused, peered down at the notes—"Mohammed Ibn—La . . ."

"I am Mohammed Ibn Lahûn," said the Egyptian, who had just walked silently in.

Sergeant Sample stared suspiciously. Inspector McGraw didn't open his eyes.

"Mr. Allen Lovelace."

"Er—yes."

Mr. Lovelace looked furtively around, tried to catch the

glance of Mrs. Muller, failed, then went out. He left the door partly open.

"Honorable Peter Faraway."

There was no reply.

"Honorable Peter Faraway!"

Came a sound of hurried footsteps, and Peter appeared. He wore creased dress trousers and a silk vest and was mopping his wet hair with a handkerchief.

"I say"—he glanced vaguely about him—"did I seem to hear my name?"

McGraw spoke, without bothering to open his eyes.

"What does your name seem to be?"

"Faraway, I believe." He was suffering from delayed-action-alcoholic shock. "Let me see. I must think."

"Where have you been, sir?" Sergeant Sample asked, his voice conveying that he didn't care a hoot where he'd been.

"I've been asleep."

"Understood there were no beds," McGraw muttered.

"Oh, I wasn't in a bed. I was in a bath. And the beastly tap leaks."

"Go ahead, Sergeant."

"Miss Elphinstowe."

"I am Amelia Elphinstowe," came a crisp response.

"Mrs. Muller."

"Yes."

"Miss Julia Sidney, professionally known as Sidonia."

"I'm here."

Sidonia, lolling in a chair, nodded and smiled, then resumed a whispered conversation with Peter, who had seated himself on an arm of her chair.

"Miss Mary Bruton."

Storm Kennedy clenched his teeth and stared hard at Hilary—then at Miss Elphinstowe. Both avoided his glance. Hilary, flashing a swift look in Peter's direction, answered steadily:

"Here."

"Mr. Larkhall Pike."

But Mr. Pike, arrayed in pajamas and old dressing gown, who had returned to his favorite seat in the inglenook, remained absorbed in a book he was reading.

"Mr. Larkhall Pike!"

He looked up.

"What d'you say? Pike? Yes."

He went on reading. In a momentary lull, Peter's voice became loudly audible.

"I wish I could remember what happened last night. I feel very cross about all that has occurred. Let me see— what day is it?"

Inspector Hawley came in. He crossed to the desk.

"I have sent for Dr. Smithy, Chief Inspector. The Post Office say they can't restore phone service until the subscriber has complied with demands."

McGraw raised his lids partially.

"Told 'em *I'm* here? Who does this house belong to?"

"Mr. Pike."

The man in the corner glanced up.

"Not at all."

McGraw slowly turned in his direction.

"Telephone account not settled?"

"Quite. It isn't."

"If this is not your house, whose house is it?"

"My brother Benedict's."

"Can I interview your brother Benedict?"

"I presume so."

"Where?"

"Australia."

But no one laughed except Peter Faraway, who had not yet found out what day it was. Mr. Pike went on reading, and McGraw stood up, walked around the desk and then leaned back against it.

"Inspector Hawley, want this line working. Go and tell 'em so."

Inspector Hawley departed. McGraw surveyed all present, one by one.

"In the first place, now that you have had time for reflection, does anyone here know the name of the murdered man?"

Mr. Lovelace entered, carrying with care a tumbler of water. He conveyed it to Mrs. Muller, who leaned against a bookcase. She took it, forced a grateful smile, and put it down. There was silence.

"Nobody? Is that so?"

Storm Kennedy watched Hilary, who had joined Miss Elphinstowe. She had her back turned to him. McGraw proceeded:

"Now—after the murder had taken place, who first entered this room?"

Kennedy had been expecting the question. Nevertheless, he flinched under its impact. It was the question he, himself, would have asked on the evidence, had he been in charge of investigations. His glance searched the company. Hilary didn't turn, and he couldn't see Elfie's face. Mohammed's velvet eyes met his glance disinterestedly. Peter Faraway was combing his hair with a comb borrowed from Sidonia, who looked frightened. Mrs. Muller was smiling at Mr. Lovelace—and Mr. Pike was reading.

"*I* did," Kennedy replied.

Something in the tone of his voice, quiet though it was, struck an instant, vibrant chord. All sensed tension. Even Mr. Pike looked up.

"So you said." McGraw drawled, and turned his veiled regard in Kennedy's direction. He continued to chew. "Just thought maybe someone else might have been ahead of you. People are so forgetful."

"Elfie," Hilary whispered. "We must slip away, somewhere, somehow, and think! This man frightens me."

McGraw leaned farther back, but his half-closed eyes continued to study the faces of those in the room.

"All wait outside. Needn't stay indoors. Avoid roped-off spaces. Going to try a little experiment. As I hear no one has had anything to eat, shall do my best to arrange for refreshments."

Elfie and Hilary left first, hurrying out into the corridor. Mr. Lovelace conducted Mrs. Muller onto the terrace. It faced west, and already a shadow of the house lay over neglected lawns, for the sun was rising. Sidonia took Peter's arm and led him through the doorway. Mohammed approached the Chief Inspector, crossed his hands on his breast and bowed.

"Sir, as this matter concerns me not at all, as I have no evidence to offer, is it not proper that I depart about my affairs?"

"It isn't," said McGraw. "Wait outside."

Mohammed bowed again, and retired silently. Storm Kennedy walked to the door, and then turned.

"My offer holds good, Inspector McGraw."

"Haven't forgotten it."

Kennedy went out. The thing was taking even worse shape than he had anticipated. Every move she made increased the difficulty of screening Hilary. He was so angry that he knew he must avoid her until he had himself well in hand again.

Chief Inspector McGraw turned to Mr. Pike.

"Possibly didn't hear what I said." Mr. Pike looked up from his book. "Want everyone out of this room."

Mr. Pike allowed his pince-nez to drop down onto his dressing gown, where the glasses swung on their black ribbon as he sprang to his feet.

"Sir!"—it was a choking voice—"this behavior is disgraceful! The *Times* shall have the full facts at once. First, some blundering policeman from King's Riding turns me out of my own bedroom. Now, you propose to turn me out of my study! Your methods, sir, are those of the Gestapo. If this is British justice, God help Britain!"

McGraw chewed reflectively.

"Sorry. But there's been a murder."

"I wish sincerely every damn fool who was here last night had been murdered! My only regret is that the assassin confined himself to one."

He snatched up his book and stalked to the door. He paused.

"May I hope to remain undisturbed in the kitchen?"

"You may. Call you when you're wanted."

"Pshaw!"

Mr. Pike went out and banged the door. Sergeant Sample stared at Chief Inspector McGraw.

"You know, sir," he said, "he's another of 'em who has no alibi."

McGraw nodded. "Let's go upstairs again."

He led the way up the short stair, opened a massive door and entered a room not much larger than a monk's cell, sparsely furnished as a bedchamber. Leaded windows overlooked neglected gardens, for the room was built out on an arch which spanned the terrace. A form covered with a sheet lay on the bed, and on a small table beside it were a few exhibits—articles found in the murdered man's possession. A wrist watch; silver cigarette case; lighter; a leather wallet which contained twenty-odd pounds, but nothing else; a bunch of keys; and a gold object resembling a fountain pen, the top attached to the base by a thin metal chain.

McGraw picked it up and fumbled with it for awhile; then shook his head and replaced it on the table.

"Got us all whacked, sir," said Sample. "Inspector Hawley couldn't unscrew it, either. Some sort of trick fastener."

McGraw merely chewed, and switched his attention to a number of garments set out on two chairs. Presently: "Shirt was bought in Paris," he muttered. "Laundry marks aren't English. Suit is a hand-me-down, but good quality. Label says 'Simon Artz,' but no address. Ever hear of a tailor of that name?"

"No, sir."

"Light-weight material; probably tropical wear. Looks as though he'd lived in a hot climate."

Finally, McGraw turned to a deep window ledge and considered what lay there.

On a sheet of white paper was the blue-bladed, silver-hilted dagger, the hilt finely chased and inlaid with a design in amethysts. It had yielded no identifiable fingerprints. A shagreen sheath, evidently of great age, lay beside it. This had been discovered by Inspector Hawley at some distance below the terrace.

But there was one other exhibt—found by the same patient searcher not far from the sheath. It was an ancient Egyptian necklace representing a winged disk, fashioned in delicate enamel on gold.

And the only fingerprints upon the shagreen and the necklace were those of the dead man!

McGraw pushed the leaded panes open and looked out. Mrs. Muller and Mr. Lovelace were walking slowly along the terrace; fantastic in their dress clothes. No one else was in sight. A choir of birds saluted the rising sun.

9

Storm Kennedy made a complete circuit of the rambling building. Part of it was of great age, but there were comparatively recent additions. Some of the walls he saw smothered in untended ivy. Windows were broken. The outbuildings, comprising a dairy, a huge stable and coach house, storerooms, a steward's cottage, stood practically in ruins. The gatehouse looked as though no one had inhabited it for several generations.

He came to a smaller courtyard, on the east side, surrounded by more outbuildings. A provocative smell drew his attention to an open window. He looked in, and saw a vast kitchen, dimly lighted. He saw, also, at a very small gas stove, Mr. Larkhall Pike brewing coffee.

"Good morning!" he called, cheerily.

Mr. Pike turned, his pince-nez swinging pendulum fashion over his faded dressing gown.

"I don't know you, sir. And I labored under the delusion that this part of the house, at least, might be regarded as private."

"May I introduce myself? Storm Kennedy is the name. I don't want to intrude, and I don't want any coffee. But I think you have had rather a shabby deal, and I merely looked in to say so."

"My thanks, Mr. Kennedy."

Mr. Pike turned again to his coffee making. But Kennedy stayed—for he had found the man he was looking for.

"I'm here by accident, myself. Wouldn't come to such a jamboree for choice, and I'm dead sick of being bullied by these blasted policemen. . . ."

"In that, sir, I agree with you."

"Had no sleep. Don't know if you had?"

Mr. Pike's coffee was ready. He turned.

"I am amazed, sir, to learn that there is a sane man present—and one who knows how to behave himself. You are the first of this type I have met since the socialist government came into power. May I offer you a cup of coffee?"

"Well, are you sure there's enough?"

"Quite sure." He took down two cups from a dresser designed to accommodate two hundred. "The milk is canned—unless you prefer *café noir?*"

"*Café noir,* if I may."

"Spoonful of sugar?"

"Thanks."

"Come in and sit down, Mr. Kennedy."

They sat on two unpainted chairs, and presently Mr. Pike unbent. He declined a cigarette.

"You asked me if I slept? How can a man be expected to sleep, sir, when he has been turned out of his bed to make way for a corpse? I tried to compose myself in the study. But on two separate occasions I was aroused by someone stealing into the room."

Storm Kennedy grew keenly alert. But he gave no sign.

"Looking for somewhere to sleep, no doubt?"

"Stuff and nonsense, sir! Rot, sir! I had, naturally, extinguished the lights, and therefore was unable to see clearly. So that on both occasions the intruder escaped before I could reach the switch. But her objective . . ."

"*Her* objective?"

"I said 'her objective'—the prowler was, unmistakably, a woman—seemed to be the stair leading to my bedroom."

"In which the dead man lay?"

"Unless he is a vampire, an unclean nocturnal, in which, as you say, yes, the dead man lay. My visitor was wrapped in a cloak or cape. So much I learned in one glimpse I had of her retreating to the corridor from which she had entered."

Storm Kennedy knew that his pulse had quickened, but he spoke calmly.

"Have you informed Chief Inspector McGraw?"

"Pshaw!" Mr. Pike had not quite emptied his mouth of hot coffee. A faint spray might be detected. "If that man wants any information, sir, he must subpoena me as a witness and put me under oath."

"H'm. Most extraordinary incident, Mr. Pike."

"Two incidents, Mr. Kennedy. Both equally extraordinary."

"Have you any idea of the color or texture of the cloak this woman wore?"

"No idea whatever. She appeared as a dim silhouette."

"You didn't attempt to follow her."

"I did not."

"Nor lock the door?"

"The lock is broken."

Storm Kennedy lighted another cigarette. He recognized the fact that he stood on dangerous ground. This remarkable man was liable to become jet-propelled on the slightest provocation. But he determined to risk it.

"You have traveled extensively in the East, sir, I gather?"

"Extensively, sir. I formerly held His Majesty's commission, Indian Army. I am entitled to describe myself as Major; but the liberties these socialist fellows have taken with pensioned officers so disgusted me that I laid aside my rank with my equally useless medals. After my retirement, I joined several expeditions—excavating in Egypt, Syria, and so on. Expensive hobby. Lost all my money since those days."

Kennedy inhaled deeply, and then:

"The weapon employed in this mysterious affair," he ventured, "is of a type with which you may be familiar?"

"Quite familiar, even out there in lamplight. Damascus blade. Best period. Hilt of poor Baghdad workmanship. Decadent. Late Abbasîd. Harem toy. Not a bad piece—though I have seen better."

"Did Superintendent Croker invite your opinion, Major?"

"Forget my Majority, sir, unless you wish to be offensive. Superintendent Croker is a damned outsider! Ex-noncommissioned officer—Sappers. Risen by impudence and petticoat influence to his present job in the police."

Kennedy stood up. He sensed Major Larkhall Pike's rising temperature—and he had learned much.

"It has been a pleasure to chat with you, sir. A very unsavory business. You have my sincere sympathy. . . ."

But Kennedy reserved a quota of sympathy for himself.

His inquiries had been prompted by that curious occurrence which he had noted during the night.

Now, according to Mr. Pike, the figure he had seen was that of a woman.

And this woman could only have been one of four!

The problem grew deeper, darker, more terrifying. . . .

At which point in his unhappy reflections, Storm Kennedy found that he had circled the northern elevation of Hangover House, ploughing through thickets where green lawns had spread and stumbling over remains of former rock gardens; that he was on a gravel path of sorts which led to a tumbledown rustic summer house; and that Hilary was walking toward him.

His mind was made up in a flash. This time she should hear a few hard truths. But he recognized for a fact, and experienced a sort of helpless anger, that his heart was misbehaving.

She wore the fleecy wrap, and a morning breeze played with her bright hair. But when they met she was smiling.

"Good morning, fellow prisoner!"

"Good morning, Hilary. Did you sleep well?"

"Don't be too wildly absurd! How could anybody hope to sleep well cramped up on the seat of a car?"

Kennedy loved those smiling lips. But Hilary's eyes were not smiling.

"No, hardly. Well, this is at least a breathing space before the next ordeal."

Hilary glanced down at a jungle of wild briar which at some time had been part of a rose garden.

"I dread it," she said simply.

"So do I."

She flashed him a swift, searching look.

"Why should *you* dread it?"

"For the good and sufficient reason that I don't know how the devil you are coming out of it."

Hilary was silent for a while, picking at a stone imbedded in the gravel, with the toe of a fragile evening shoe, then she said, "I'm afraid," she confessed. "I have acted like an incredible fool."

"You have! I don't know what to do about you."

The gray eyes blazed for a moment, but Kennedy met their anger with a quiet stare, and Hilary dropped her lashes.

"I know I *am* a fool," she said; "but I hate to be treated like one!"

"Listen, my dear. I quite understand that you gave Croker your name last night as Mary Bruton, because . . ."

"It *is* my name. I was christened Hilary Felice Mary."

"Very likely. But you hoped it would enable you to pass unnoticed. You thought, then, that you might be dismissed from the case and nobody be any the wiser. Isn't that true?"

"Yes."

"But Elfie didn't know until your name was called out by Sergeant Sample?"

"No. I hadn't told her."

"Of course, I realize that having done it, you had to stick to it. But, as things have turned out, well, it makes matters look so much worse. You see, unfortunately this was only one of many indiscretions."

Hilary didn't meet his eyes, but some of her color faded.

"You seem to know almost too much about me."

"Too little, Hilary. If I knew all, I should know what to do. Just moving in the dark, I have done what I could. . . ."

"I know!" Impulsively, she grasped his arm. "Don't think I have forgotten. No one could have done more. But, you see, truly, I'm not worth it."

"Don't talk damn nonsense! You can't frighten me off like that. You are worth far more than it's in me to give. But you have been behaving like a perfect lunatic, and I don't know how you are going to avoid the consequences. I have told you that I understand why you gave the police a wrong name. What I don't understand is why you said you had never seen the murdered man before, when, in fact, you knew him quite well."

It was a body blow, delivered quite deliberately. Hilary flushed hotly, and then grew alarmingly pale. Her gray eyes, when she raised them to him, were like those of a wounded thing pleading for mercy.

"How do you know?" she whispered.

"How I know doesn't matter. What matters is that McGraw is certain to find out—and draw an inevitable conclusion. Hilary, for God's sake, help me! Or how can I hope to help *you*?"

Kennedy had his arm about her. He had not intended it to be there. The thing happened automatically, inevitably. And Hilary rested her bowed fair head on his shoulder for a magical, timeless instant, then drew away, very gently.

"But you haven't answered my question," she said.

Kennedy clenched his teeth. To torture Hilary was the hardest task life had ever forced upon him. But he knew he must do it.

From his pocket he took out an old envelope—one he had found there—it was addressed to himself. And from the envelope he extracted a square of stained, embroidered cambric. In one corner the initials H.B. had been worked in silk.

"This handkerchief lay beside the dead man, Hilary. I committed a serious felony in removing it. It's yours, isn't it?"

10

Yes—it is mine."

Hilary's voice, low-pitched, was quite steady. Now that danger was no longer merely apprehended, but here, she betrayed no trace of fear. Her eyes met Kennedy's glance calmly. Her chin was firm. She had achieved, again, one of those feats of self-control which always won his admiration.

He stood watching her in silence. Afterwards, he remembered that a thrush called, perched on a branch of a Japanese cherry tree nearly overhead, and was answered from far away. At last he said, "No one else knows. But I think it would be better if I kept it." He replaced the handkerchief in the envelope and the envelope in his pocket.

Then, Hilary spoke. "Are you going to ask me how it came to be—where you found it?"

"Not if you don't want to tell me."

"I can't tell you—because I don't know."

"Had you missed it?"

"No." She shook her head slightly. "Not until I saw it in your hand. I had another one with me."

"Hilary"—he spoke earnestly, appealingly—"if I say

that I am deeply concerned about you, won't you give me your confidence?"

She watched him with steady eyes.

"Why are you so concerned about me? I have told you I'm not worth it."

Again that direct approach, that challenge! But Storm Kennedy's conscience was clear when he answered; for, now, he was not interested in a merely professional way.

"Because I like you very much, and I can't bear to see you getting deeper and deeper into this ghastly business."

Hilary knew, then. But what she knew merely made things harder. She glanced away, and he saw her hands opening and closing in indecision. The impulse was there, an impulse to cast the burden of her despair onto the shoulders of this capable man who—she gave him a swift glance—who cared for her, who, perhaps . . .

But impulse lost the battle. How *could* she tell him? See that look in his eyes, which had begun to disturb her in a new way, turn to one of contempt?

She shook her head again. Her lashes were wet, for, suddenly, Hilary wanted to cry. Kennedy waited. Slowly, painfully, he was beginning to understand her moods. This thing had struck deeper than Lord Glengale suspected—or had cared to admit.

When he thought he might safely speak, he said, "Take your own time, Hilary. We have no choice but to see this affair through together. It's just a matter of luck that McGraw hasn't found out yet how you tried to conceal your name. He is sure to find out, and that one slip will lead him to suspect the truth of everything else you have told them."

"I know." Hilary was composed again. "I have been an awful fool. And you"—the gray eyes were raised momentarily to his—"have been so patient, so wonderfully patient, with me. I can never hope to thank you for what you have done."

He found her hand in his, felt its firm clasp, and knew that his heart was beating too rapidly. He raised the clinging fingers—then grimly restrained himself. This was madness! ·

Hilary turned away quickly when he released her hand and began to walk back toward the house. Storm Kennedy walked beside her. . . .

Miss Elphinstowe met Hilary as she came running up the steps to that corner of the terrace which overlooked a weedy lily pond.

"Is there anyone in that beastly little room, Elfie?"

"No, dear."

Hilary ran in. Elfie followed.

She found Hilary prone on the worn leather couch, her face buried in her hands, sobbing wildly. In a moment she was beside her, an encouraging arm around the shaking figure.

"My dear child! What is all this about?"

"It's about myself!" Hilary whispered, between sobs. "I'm a rotten little outsider! I'm not fit for any decent man—to look at. . . ."

Elfie held her tightly, but didn't speak at once; then, "Shut up!" she said, gruffly. "Shut up!"

"I won't. It's true. That devil—he's dead now, but still a devil—has ruined my life. . . ."

"Be quiet, Hilary, if you don't want me to give you a good hiding!"

The sobs subsided.

"Just when—at last—after all the wrong kind—someone turns up who . . ."

Elfie nodded; and her smile—invisible to Hilary—was an understanding smile.

"They do, you know. It was the same with Ronnie and Agatha. I'm talking about your father and mother. Poor Aggie was all lashed up with a Marine. My dear! The trouble she had to shake him off when she met Ronnie! In the strictest confidence, dear, things had gone pretty far. We belong to a seafaring family, and stand by Nelson's motto: 'Engage the enemy more closely.'"

Hilary half-turned a tear-stained face to look up at Elfie.

"Was Mother really as racketty as I am?"

"Pretty nearly. She'd weathered a few storms before she made port."

Hilary began to dry her tears, and then she asked, swallowing hard, "How long have I known Bill Kennedy?"

"The first I ever heard of him was after a theater party last November, with the Elwingtons. You came in next morning and raved about him. . . ."

"I didn't!"

"Very well. You didn't. But that's the first I heard of him."

"Then we have really known one another quite a long time."

"Depends how often you've seen him since."

"Only twice, until—now."

"Hilary!" Miss Elphinstowe raised Hilary to a seated position. "I tipped you to tell him the whole story, chance what he thought, and ask him to do all he knew how to . . ."

"How can I?"

"You'll have to, sooner or later. If you don't, this damned policeman will burrow down to it. He's dangerous."

"I know he is."

"We're in up to the eyebrows—you and I. If ever two silly women needed help, *we* do!"

And Storm Kennedy, had he been present, would have shared Elfie's opinion. He walked slowly back down the sloping, neglected garden, wondering how he had succeeded in offending Hilary again. That abrupt parting, by the lily pool—the way she had averted her face and run up the steps . . .

Perhaps, in any event, it was as well. The sooner he went to work to forget Lady Hilary Bruton, only daughter of the Marquess of Glengale, and a wealthy woman in her own rights, the better for him. He would start the very moment that she was cleared of this sordid affair. Only those cynical gods who control human passions could inform him how deeply she was involved; and this being so, he could never hope to find out, unless Hilary told him. But, even against her infuriating reticence, and however irreparably he offended her, he would fight to save Hilary from the penalty of her own folly. . . .

His reflections were interrupted by a curious sight.

He had reached that dilapidated summer house, which, once, had fronted onto velvet lawns but which, now, lay half-buried in undergrowth and smothered in creeping weeds. On the step, soles upward in early morning sun, he saw a pair of high-heeled shoes!

Walking to the doorway, he looked in—and there was the bronze Sidonia, a grotesque figure in her evening frock, stockinged feet tucked up on the seat, a sable wrap beside her. She was busily adjusting her make-up.

"Good morning," he said.

She gave him a glance.

"Hullo! Just fixing my glamor. I look as though I'd been dragged backwards through a jungle by a tiger who preferred ash blondes."

"I saw your shoes on the step."

"Sure. Been washing the blood off. They're out there

to dry. What a night! The gay nineties all over again, I guess."

He went in and sat down facing her.

"Cigarette? I still have a few left."

"No, thanks. I crave coffee." She plastered lipstick. "This place is full of ants and earwigs."

"Sure to be. Do you feel any the worse for your rather horrible experience?"

"I feel out of this world! Why, I almost fell over him in the dark! Then, right outside the Powder Room, I saw my own tracks—all blood! Boy, was I sick!"

"You have my sympathy."

"A cup of coffee would make a bigger hit. I'd maybe used a few over the deadline last night, and I have a delicate stomach. What with that and the blood, I was never so sick in my life since I crossed the Atlantic in a hurricane. I just sat on some steps and gave all I had."

The bronze Sidonia, it seemed, was far from inarticulate, once she got going.

"And what happened next?"

She screwed on the top of her lipstick and took out a comb.

"I fainted—if you can believe it. I remember falling down the steps, and that's a blackout. Next shot I remember is Miss Elephant's Toe pouring a two-gallon pitcher o' water over me. Aw, hell!"

She began to comb her hair, making the queerest grimaces into a little hand mirror as she did so, and wincing once or twice.

"Head aching?"

"Somewhat. I fell on it."

As Storm Kennedy approached the house, making his way through a heavily armored battalion of thistles which invaded the gravel path, he saw Mrs. Muller coming toward him, a mink-enveloped figure more appropriate at a West End first night than in this rustic early morning setting. She was hurrying, but hesitated for a moment, glancing back over one furry shoulder, and then advanced as if to sanctuary. When they met, "I wonder if you would do me a favor," she said, "Mr. . . ."

"Storm Kennedy."

"Of course. Forgive me. But, really, I barely know my own name! There's no sign yet of the promised refreshments, and I haven't the least idea what the Scotland Yard men are up to. But I simply must get a breath of fresh air!"

"We all deserve that, at least."

"And I *must* escape, if only for five minutes, from my cavalier!"

"Lovelace?"

"Yes. Here he comes! Do you think, Mr. Kennedy—it would be so kind of you . . ."

"Leave him to me," said Kennedy, staring up the path to where Mr. Lovelace weaved an astigmatic course in and out among thistles. "I'll take care of him."

"A thousand thanks!"

Mrs. Muller gave him the accolade of a grateful smile and went on, battling in her high-heeled shoes and gossamer stockings through platoons of thistles.

When Mr. Lovelace, his eyes distorted by the thick lenses of his spectacles, drew near enough, Kennedy clapped a hand on his shoulder. Lovelace started so violently that Kennedy wondered, for a moment, and then, "The very man I'm looking for," he declared. "You and I must have a chat."

"Really! Er—that is, certainly. By all means."

Storm Kennedy took Lovelace's arm and turned him about.

"We'll walk this way. You see, what I have in mind is

rather important. It must be quite clear to you, and to the police, that you have no alibi. Had you thought of that?"

Lovelace pulled up so suddenly, and so determinedly, that Kennedy was brought to a momentary halt, also. Pale blue eyes behind the lenses were widely opened.

"Look here! What do you mean?"

"Just what I say. Have you told the police where you were between the time that I left you in the big room and the time that you appeared behind me on the steps? Don't misunderstand me. I'm not suggesting that you committed the murder. But, as a matter of interest, where did you go?"

Lovelace fumbled with his tie.

"I—er—went to the gent's toilet."

"Gent's toilet?" Storm Kennedy gave him a sharp glance. "And where might that be?"

The term had confirmed an earlier impression—an impression that Mr. Lovelace was not all his exterior suggested.

"In—er—a corner of the lobby."

"Indeed."

Kennedy thought rapidly. This was quite possible. After he had met Amelia Elphinstowe in the lobby, he remembered that they had gone straight through to the Powder Room to look for Hilary.

"Of course, I can't prove it, if that's what you're driving at. I never met a soul."

"No. That does make it awkward. I suppose you didn't notice the Egyptian gentleman about anywhere?"

"I didn't. Perhaps—er—you feel the same as I do? That he's the likeliest of the lot?"

They were walking on again. But Kennedy sensed the fact that Lovelace was keenly on guard, the fact (which, dimly, he had suspected already) that the man was hiding something.

"Why should he be?"

"Well—the dagger . . ."

"Oriental weapon? But he'd hardly be likely to leave it behind, do you think? You don't happen to know who or what he is, I suppose?"

"His name's Mohammed—something. I didn't quite catch it. He was telling fortunes."

"Oh, I see. One of the people supplied by the caterer?"

"No, oh, no! Nothing to do with Jarretts. The firm—I mean Jarretts—were responsible for the cold buffet and the dance band. Mohammed was one of the guests."

"Really? How queer! Who supplied the drinks, then?"

"Mrs. Faraway. Jarretts couldn't undertake that, you know, not nowadays. All—er—black market stuff."

Kennedy had a strong impulse to push the inquiry further, but prudence prompted that he reserve this for another time. As he and Lovelace passed along the northern end of the terrace, which was not barricaded, he could hear Peter Faraway's voice in the study, for the window was open. . . .

"Quite sure, Mr. Faraway," McGraw was saying, "you never saw the dead man before?"

"Positive. Complete stranger."

Peter sat in an armchair, wearing his tail coat, and a silk muffler in lieu of a collar and tie. McGraw leaned back against the desk, and Sample sat behind it.

"Want a complete list of guests invited last night. Got one?"

"Good Lord, no! It was Joan's party."

"Understand that printed invitations went out. Who sent them?"

Peter combed his hair with his fingers.

"Let me see. I must think. . . . Oh, yes! Cramp."

"Cramp?"

"Our butler."

"Then Cramp had a list of guests?"

"I suppose so."

"Like to have your London phone number. We'll call him."

"Oh, rather! It's Mayfair One—but wait a minute. Let me think—what day is it?"

"Wednesday, the twenty-third," came, in Sample's expressionless voice.

"Then he's not there!"

"Who's not where?" McGraw inquired.

"Cramp. He left on Monday."

"Is that so? Mrs. Faraway be home?"

"I shouldn't think she is. I hear she took the Fergusons with her. And the Fergusons live in Brighton."

"Too bad." McGraw chewed awhile in silence, then: "Not clear from your signed statement," he said, "where you were at the time the crime was committed. Where were you?"

"Let me see. Where was I? I remember I had a drink with what's-her-name-Sidonia. We were told the bar was closing, everybody buzzing off. Then—let me think—yes, by Jove! We wandered away in the fog, and, I believe—I can't be sure—I got rather serious with her."

"That's bad, too."

"I quite agree!" He grinned at Sample. "Don't you agree, Sergeant?"

"Yes, sir."

"Where did this occur?" McGraw drawled.

"I couldn't swear to it, but I think it was a potting shed!"

"Most appropriate. After that?"

"Let me see. . . . I began to feel sleepy, and rather cross. I sort of broke up the conference, and wandered back . . ."

"Leaving the lady in the potting shed?"

"I'm not sure, but I think she went out first."

McGraw's drooping eyelids flickered.

"On that point, Mr. Faraway, must have a clear statement. Did the lady leave you, or did you leave the lady?"

"Yes, I see your point, Inspector. You can see his point, can't you, Sergeant?"

"Yes, sir."

"Did I . . . ? Let me think. Ah, got it! *She* went out first. I remember she made some remark. When I followed on, she had pushed off. I thought she might get lost in the fog, and so I let out several yells and waved a flash-lamp I had with me. Just as I got to the steps . . ."

"Have you evidence on that point? May want you back, later."

Peter made for the door like a schoolboy released from classroom. McGraw didn't move. Sample stared after the departing witness.

"He's not over-bright for his years, sir."

"A man's only as old as his experience. There are Peter Pans with whiskers. Completed your list of cars?"

Sergeant Sample stood up.

"Here on the desk. There's a hired car in a lane by a back entrance, from a garage in Hanover Square. But the local police can get no reply from the office. I've put a cross against another. Note the owner of the Bentley."

McGraw walked around and sat in the chair. He glanced down and then whistled softly.

"Marquess of Glengale! Now—who came in *that* one?"

11

Storm Kennedy carried the old canvas deck-chair back to that spiderous shed in which he had found it. Here, with luck, he might hope to remain undisturbed for ten minutes. He was becoming bewildered; recognized the necessity of setting down known facts and trying to balance them.

He had a fairly clear idea of the nature of the "experiment" to which McGraw had referred. McGraw hoped to find out who had switched off the floor lamp in Larkhall Pike's study.

Seating himself in the chair, his back to the door, he took out a notebook and pencil, and began to write. First, he wrote:

> Witnesses who might, or who did mention this incident in evidence given to Superintendent Croker:
>
> 1—Mohammed Ibn Lahûn
> 2—Myself
> 3—Larkhall Pike

Chief Detective Inspector McGraw was a competent officer. He would have come to the conclusion that the murderer had run back to the house, retreated through the study window, which was open, and switched off the light.

Kennedy studied his notes, and then added:

> Persons present who might (in McGraw's view) have done this:
>
> 1—Myself
> 2—Mohammed Ibn Lahûn
> 3—Almost anybody else on the premises; excepting Peter. (His alibi resting solely on my evidence.)

He considered these notes awhile, and then wrote:

> Persons present who could be proved to have any motive in the killing:
> *Hilary* (assuming the dead man to be her persecutor)

He wrote on rapidly:

> Exact whereabouts of others present at the time that the crime was committed:
> *Unknown!*

He continued:

> Apart from motive (sure to come to light) Hilary's presence in the dark study immediately after the murder, is known to:
> 1—Elfie
> 2—Myself

Storm Kennedy lay back in the canvas chair, opened his cigarette case, and found that it was empty. He lolled, closing his eyes for a moment. He opened them again, and wrote:

> Why was Mohammed invited? (Question Peter)

To this he added:

> Who is Lovelace? (Get his background, when he isn't so scared.)

He lay inert for a long time, and then, turning to a new page, wrote:

> Could the dagger used have come from the collection in Larkhall Pike's study? (Check)
> Is there any explanation of Hilary's handkerchief lying beside the dead man other than that she was with him at the time of his death?

He considered these notes, and finally jotted down:

> What other evidence, unknown to me, have the police discovered?
> (Inspector Hawley—very capable—spent the night searching the grounds.)

He dropped back again, closing his eyes.

Hilary was lovely. He wished, with all the enthusiasm of a fancy-free bachelor, that he had never met her. In the first place, a woman could be no more than an intrusion in the life of a private investigator. The crowned king of them all, Sherlock Holmes, had been immune to sex allure. In the second place, assuming, for the moment, that a woman could be admitted to his career, Hilary was unattainable.

That she had (evidently) lived something of an undercover life, been in up to her neck with a modern Casanova, didn't disturb him in the least. He was willing to concede wild oats to a woman, having sown a few himself. The plain facts remained that she was adorable, that she had the courage of any man he had ever known, that she would be a wonderful mate. Elfie's fidelity, alone, bore witness to this. Fine woman, Elfie.

But, apart from the circumstance that she didn't seem to care a lot about him, Hilary was one of the few really wealthy girls mentioned in Debrett. And he was William Storm Kennedy, ex-officer with a decent record but no source of revenue (apart from a small gratuity) other than his earnings!

"*Nahârak saîd!*"

Kennedy opened his eyes, looked around, and saw Mohammed standing in the doorway.

"Hullo."

"Your spirit is troubled."

"Yes, it is, rather."

"You are surrounded, sir, by disturbing vibrations. It is as though one of the black efreets stood at your elbow. You speak Arabic?"

"I learned a little when I was in Egypt. Do you mind coming in? I shall have a stiff neck if I go on talking over my shoulder."

Mohammed bowed his head, and came into the hut, where he stood watching Kennedy with those brilliant, unfathomable eyes.

"I am of Egypt. My family owns much property in the Fayyum."

"Indeed? What are you doing in England?"

"I follow my star, *Khawâga*. I am a seer."

"You mean a fortune-teller?"

A slight frown disturbed the serenity of Mohammed's brow.

"I am the Sherîf Mohammed Ibn Lahûn. Ten times I have kissed the Kaaba. For many generations one of my family has escorted the Mahmal to Mecca. On our estates have been reared many of those milk-white camels which bear the Holy Carpet."

Storm Kennedy's sense of bewilderment began to increase. Was this man a lunatic or just an impostor? In either event, what was he doing here? He sat up.

"Sorry if I said the wrong thing. I had no intention of being offensive."

Mohammed bowed gravely.

"Where no offense is designed, let none be taken. This is a house of evil. And an evil man was slain here last night. Even in death, an aura of wickedness surrounds him."

Storm Kennedy was watching Mohammed now, closely.

"You appear to be uncommonly gifted."

"I am descended from the Prophet, may Allah be good to him; and the spirit of prophecy was born in me. It was written that this man should die as he did."

"Does the spirit of prophecy move you to point out the murderer?"

"It was not murder. It was the justice of God. *La il aha il'a Allah!*"

Kennedy hesitated. He found the mild, but fixed regard of those deer-like eyes almost hypnotic. At last, "I suppose you are a friend of Peter Faraway's, Mr. Ibn Lahûn?" he suggested.

"I have the honor to be a friend of Mrs. Faraway. I am her guest. Your spirit is troubled. You are concerned in the welfare of a lady who is here. I have looked into the minds of many of those present, as now, I look into yours. Compel her confidence, sir, or worse may befall. Evil passions, long pent up, have been released in this house. I heard the sound of their wings in the night. . . . I can do no more to help you."

He crossed his hands on his breast and bowed.

"*Alallâh!*"

He moved to the doorway.

"Thanks," said Storm Kennedy.

"Effendi forgets his Arabic!"

Mohammed Ibn Lahûn walked out.

12

The heavy draperies had been drawn in Larkhall Pike's study. A green-shaded lamp on the desk gave all there was of illumination, and the room lay cloaked in shadow. A thin shaft from a crack in the lampshade shone, like a stage spot, onto the brightly painted funerary mask of some Egyptian lady of long ago.

McGraw sat behind the desk. Sample stood near the door.

"This one no good for the lights," drawled McGraw. "But she's a possible for the necklace. That's why I sent for her."

"That necklace," Sample announced, "is the biggest puzzle of the lot, to me. You know where Inspector Hawley found it—fifty yards down the garden. Well, anybody might have dropped it, except . . ."

"Except that the dead man's fingerprints are on it! So *he* must have dropped it. As men don't wear Egyptian necklaces, have to find out who it belongs to."

"Case was stone-cold when we got here," Sample declared, his tone suggesting that he wouldn't have cared if it had been frozen.

"They generally are."

Came a rap on the door, and a police sergeant announced, "Mrs. Muller, sir."

Mrs. Muller came in, as the sergeant retired and closed the door. She had abandoned her mink.

"Ah, Mrs. Muller"—McGraw smiled, and his smile was surprisingly unfamiliar—"find it dark in here?"

"It is, rather, coming in from sunshine."

"Perhaps I could trouble you to switch on the floor lamp as you come by?"

Mrs. Muller, crossing to the desk, stepped aside and tried to find a knob or chain attached to the lamp. She shrugged and glanced at McGraw.

"There doesn't seem to *be* a switch, Inspector! But the present light is quite flattering."

"Suits me. Please sit down."

McGraw noted that her frock was wine-colored, offering the shapely contours of ivory arms and shoulders. A pair of thin gloves, dyed to match the frock, were tucked into a broad, barbaric gold bangle, so that they hung from her wrist like a scarf.

She sat in an armchair facing the desk. She was smoking a cigarette.

"Do you mind my smoking?"

"Smoke away. Now"—McGraw held up a typed page —"anything you want to add to the evidence you gave to Superintendent Croker?"

"I don't think so, Inspector."

McGraw nodded and dropped the page.

"See that you came alone in a hired car. This the car from Hanover Square?"

"Oh, dear! I'm dropping ash!" Mrs. Muller looked down at the worn carpet. Sample put a tray on the arm of her chair. "No. Mine was from Auto-Hire."

"Then where is it?"

"Well, my driver asked, shortly after I arrived, if he

could take some people back somewhere. He said he would be no more than half an hour. I can only suppose he was fogbound, like everyone else."

"Probably turn up. You're an old friend of Mrs. Faraway's?"

"Not really. I met her when we crossed together from New York years ago. But I hadn't seen much of her since her marriage, and had never met her husband."

"See her last night?"

"Unfortunately, no. She had already gone."

"Odd behavior for a hostess."

"Very! But Joan *is* odd."

McGraw flashed a comprehensive glance over her from under drooping lids.

"Now, Mrs. Muller, only one more point. Have you missed any jewelry?"

She looked almost startled, then shook her head.

"No. What I wore when I came I have now."

"Is that so? Tell me, then, did you see anyone last night who wore an Egyptian enamel necklace—sort of rising sun, crescent-shaped? Think. It's important."

Mrs. Muller stared unseeingly at the opposite wall, as if hypnotized by the death-mask, which seemed to be smiling at her. The curtained room was stuffy, its air heavy with that smell of ancient corruption which belongs to museums. Outside, the breeze which had blown the fog away had freshened. Faded velvet draping the windows billowed slightly. From somewhere at the head of the dark stairway came a soft, whispering sound.

This sound penetrated Mrs. Muller's abstraction. She turned sharply, glancing up at the shadowy arch.

"Think you heard something?" McGraw asked.

"Yes. But, of course, it was only the breeze." She recovered herself at once. "No, Inspector. I can recall no one wearing the kind of necklace you describe."

"Thanks."

Mrs. Muller stood up. McGraw decided that she had beauty, of an exotic kind, an alluringly husky voice and marked strength of character.

"Do you think I might be able to leave soon, Inspector, if my missing driver comes for me?"

"Hope so. But please wait, for the present."

Sample opened the door for her.

"I believe sandwiches and coffee are available," he said, his tone suggesting that he hoped they were not.

"Oh, thank you."

As she went out, Sample reclosed the door and turned to stare at the half-lighted figure of the Chief Inspector.

"Attractive woman," McGraw muttered. "Get the singing girl."

And a few moments later, with another rap on the door, the sergeant announced:

"Miss Sidney, sir."

Sidonia came in, walking like a mannequin and trailing her sables negligently on the carpet. She looked around through narrowed lids.

"Say, do I go blind, or does a fuse blow?"

"Sorry. Perhaps you'd just switch on the floor lamp as you pass."

"Me?"

"If you'd be so good."

Sidonia, scowling darkly, groped about under the wide lampshade, and then, "The darned thing's a prop," she said. "It don't light."

"Then leave it. Sit down, Miss Sidney. Find it darker than last time you were here?"

Sidonia paused on her way across to the armchair and, looking straight at the Inspector, said:

"Last time? There wasn't a last time. I've never been in this morgue before."

"Is that so?" Sidonia sat down, watching McGraw. "Well, as you're in it now, perhaps you can help me. Did you come alone last night?"

"I came with Sammy," she said, in a bored voice.

"Who's Sammy?"

"Sammy Sams. His band played here last night. Didn't you know?"

"Accept your word for it. Why didn't you go back with him?"

"Because I was nuts. Peter promised to drive me home."

"I see. Did you lose any jewelry?"

"Jewelry? I lost nothing, except my reputation."

"Here almost from the start of the party?"

"Right along."

"Then no doubt you can tell me this: Who was wearing an ancient Egyptian necklace, gold and enamel—very unusual?"

Sidonia raised a hand to her head, wearily.

"How much is in the jackpot for this quiz? Gold-enamel necklace? That's an easy one. Nobody."

"Sure? Lot of people here at one time."

"Maybe. But nobody wearing a thing like that." Her eyes turned fascinatedly to the funerary mask. "Looks like *she* might have worn it."

"Can't help me?"

"I guess not."

McGraw's shadowed regard remained fixed upon Sidonia's face.

"Why did you run out on Mr. Faraway?"

"For exceeding the speed limit."

"No other reason?"

"Reason enough."

"I see." McGraw held up a typed page. "Anything to add to what you told the Superintendent?"

Sidona shook her head.

When she had retired, trailing her sables behind her, "That's a tough baby," Sample said.

McGraw nodded.

"Inclined to think she's not the only one."

He stood up, walked around the desk, and began to pace the carpet, chewing steadily. Sample, who knew McGraw didn't use gum, had often wondered what he chewed.

"Worried, Chief Inspector?"

McGraw nodded again.

"I'm accepting the evidence that nobody drove out after Storm Kennedy arrived. But there's no evidence to show that somebody didn't *walk* out."

"You think our man's slipped through our fingers?"

"Nothing against it, except that there's an undercurrent here. Somebody hiding something. Conspiracy. Don't want to touch off the fuse until I know what I'm blowing up."

"Do you believe Kennedy came as a guest?"

"Came as a guest right enough. But he's got something up his sleeve. It's because *he's* here that I'm going easy. We can't afford another Mallory case!"

"If you're right, he's playing a dangerous game."

"Yes," McGraw mused. "That's why I'm considering accepting his offer. . . ."

And no one was more acutely conscious of the danger of the game he was playing than Storm Kennedy himself.

His singular conversation with Mohammed Ibn Lahûn had proved more than disturbing. He had rejected his first conclusion, that the man was an impostor, in view of the fact that Mohammed's position laid him open to expert inquiry. The possibility that he might be mad held good.

But, even in this event, one fact remained: He had some sort of uncanny knowledge of the truth—how acquired was another matter. According to his own account, by looking into the minds of those concerned.

Mohammed Ibn Lahûn must be watched.

How much did he really know?

Lovelace presented another problem. He was not, by long odds, out of the top drawer. At times, his accent betrayed him, apart from his choice of words. He was frightened. Why? What was he doing here?

Thus, two of Kennedy's written queries had been no more than partially answered.

Did the police suspect that footprints surrounding the body had been defaced *deliberately?*

Had anyone seen Hilary's handkerchief before he had removed it?

Peter, he could dismiss. What about Lovelace?

Sidonia remained an incalculable factor.

He was disposed to believe in Major Larkhall Pike (the man was a gentleman), with one reservation: he might be insane.

But that curious incident which had marked the night—an attempt by someone to reach the room in which the body lay—had been witnessed by Pike and frankly mentioned. Pike's impressions on this point were sane enough.

Would he pass on the new evidence to McGraw?

Storm Kennedy didn't think he would.

One problem—it took the form of a slender, bright-haired vision—occupied the forefront of his meditations.

What was the truth about Hilary?

He dreaded, now, the possibility that McGraw would accept his offer and enlist his services. Everything seemed to be against it. But McGraw was a dangerously clever man. He had had all the evidence needed to send Jim Mallory up for a long stretch, in the Mallory jewel case, when Kennedy—using the persuasion of a painful judo hold—had forced the young degenerate to disgorge. McGraw arrived with a warrant five minutes after Kennedy had left, taking the loot with him. . . .

These reflections had been whipped up by a vigorous walk around the eighteen acres surrounding Hangover House. Kennedy discovered a path, briar infested and thick with nettles, which followed the boundary of the property from the gate lodge to a point just short of a large pond adjoining a back entrance.

He saw a constable there, mounting guard over an empty car.

When he attempted to walk out, the man raised his hand.

"No one allowed out, sir."

Kennedy nodded.

He turned back and began to mount a steep slope, once a four-acre lawn but now become a miniature prairie. From this point, with his back to a mass of blanket weed masking the water of the pond, he had a good view of Hangover House.

It was a long, low building, and he could see that the northern wing in which were the study and Pike's bedroom, was probably Tudor, or earlier. The paneled hall had been added later, or else enlarged, and the upper floors bore evidence of Victorian "improvements."

A man and a woman strolled on the terrace—Lovelace and Mrs. Muller. A new idea flashed to his mind. Were these two secretly associated?

He paused, watching them.

Morning sunshine grew quite warm, but there was a freshening breeze. A sense of utter fantasy claimed him. That woman, in the distance, in her backless frock; Lovelace in his white shirt and tail coat, carrying her mink wrap! It was absurd, but gruesome.

For in that room which overhung the northern end of the terrace, an unidentified corpse lay—and Hilary Bruton could identify it!

He watched the pair on the terrace for a minute or more.

Mrs. Muller had the alluring carriage of an Oriental. Her burgundy-colored frock, molded to her hips, and then billowing out in fashionable abundance, accentuated voluptuous movements.

Flapping wings made him raise his eyes. A heron, in clumsy flight, passed right overhead and disappeared beyond clustering firs which flanked the pond on the west.

"Good fishing, heron!" he murmured.

He went on up the slope, and a considerable distance below the terrace, found a patch of grass which had recently been scythed and marked off with four stakes and a line knotted from stake to stake.

Here, he paused again, puzzled.

What new evidence had been found at this spot?

He made a rapid estimate, and decided that he stood about fifty yards from the house.

It was a damnable situation. Hilary remained a closed book, and he considered it highly improbable that McGraw would give him his confidence. He stared with unseeing eyes at the patch of grass, until, "Doing a little private investigation, sir?" came a melancholy voice.

Kennedy spun around and found Inspector Hawley standing only a few paces away. He must have been watching from the summer house in which Kennedy had talked to Sidonia.

"Not much to work upon," Kennedy smiled. "What clue did you find here?"

Hawley shook his head depressingly.

"I'm not at liberty to tell you, sir. Chief Inspector McGraw has methods of his own. . . ."

And it happened that, almost as the words were spoken, Chief Inspector McGraw was employing those methods.

Mohammed Ibn Lahûn sat facing him placidly in the museum-study.

"You state here"—McGraw glanced at a typed page—"that at the time when the murder took place you were in the courtyard, looking for Mr. Faraway."

"The statement is true, sir."

"Why were you looking for him?"

"To bid him good night."

"Already said good night to Mrs. Faraway?"

"Nearly an hour before."

"Why did she leave?"

"She was angry."

"What about?"

"Her husband."

"Why?"

"He was seeking to induce the lady called Sidonia to accept his embraces."

McGraw chewed thoughtfully.

"Is that so? And Mrs. Faraway objected?"

"Even the long-suffering do not suffer forever; and it is possible to overload a camel."

"I see. Known Mrs. Faraway a long time?"

"Since, with her father, she visited Egypt before war came to spread its poison. We had the honor to entertain them in our house. She was very young."

McGraw glanced again at the typed page. Mohammed Ibn Lahûn he decided to be one of the most difficult characters he had ever attempted to interrogate.

"As a matter of fact—no implications—there's nothing to prove your whereabouts, apart from your own statements, up to the time that you opened the door of this room and looked in. The room was dark?"

"Quite dark."

"You didn't see Mr. Kennedy until he lighted his torch?"

"I saw him quite well."

McGraw's eyes flicked open, and then the lids drooped again.

"How?"

"In outline against the open window."

"H'm. Is that so? Never saw the dead man before?"

"Never, sir. But in death, as in life, he was evil. It is well that he died."

Sample, in a dim background, cleared his throat.

"Think so?" McGraw drawled. "Judge of character?"

"I look into the souls of men and into the hearts of women."

"Why not into the souls of women?"

"Few women have souls."

There was a silent interval. Mohammed's large, limpid eyes remained fixed placidly upon McGraw. The thin shaft of light illuminated that Mona Lisa face reproduced by the death-mask. A vague whispering sound came from the head of the stair whenever velvet draperies swayed. And, grotesquely, sometimes as they moved, sunshine peeped into the shrouded room.

"Going to ask you," said McGraw, "to look at something. Gold and enamel necklace, ancient Egyptian, I believe. Sort of rising-sun design."

"Such a pectoral, sir, is not uncommon."

"Is that so? Recall which lady wore one last night?"

"No lady present wore such an ornament."

McGraw took a key from the desk drawer and held it out to Sample.

"Go get the necklace."

Sample nodded and went upstairs. Came the faint scrape of a key, and then, "Chief Inspector!" Sample called.

"Yes?"

"The door isn't locked!"

"What!" McGraw slowly raised his long, lean body from the chair. "But you locked it?"

"Yes, sir. The last time we came out."

"Don't go," said McGraw to Mohammed.

He went upstars, with long, springy strides, and joined Sample who stood holding the heavy door ajar. Reflected sunlight made the cell of a room bright in contrast to that below.

McGraw pushed the door wide.

"Window open! Accounts for that breeze under the door."

"But I remember closing it, sir. You opened it. I closed it when we came out."

The Chief Inspector stood stock still. His drooping lids were fully raised, and his eyes moved right and left, up and down in concentrated stares. He pushed Sample aside and walked in.

"Nothing seems to have been disturbed," said Sample.

His tone suggested that it would have been a matter of profound indifference to him if the place had been in flames.

McGraw crossed to the bed, gently moved the sheet. He replaced it. He turned to the table beside the bed. His teeth came together with an audible snap.

"Sergeant Sample."

"Sir."

"Said this case was cold?"

"I thought so."

"Use your eyes. What they're intended for. Look!"

On this small table had been set out the articles found in the dead man's possession. These were: a wrist watch; silver cigarette case; lighter; a leather wallet; a bunch of keys; a gold object resembling a fountain pen.

And the gold object was missing!

13

Not more than five minutes had elapsed when McGraw and Sample came down again. McGraw carefully carried the necklace spread out on a sheet of white paper.

Mohammed was standng before one of the wall cases, examining its contents with apparent interest. He turned as the Inspector set the sheet down on the desk, and his dark face remained quite expressionless.

"Please glance over this," McGraw drawled. "Don't touch it."

Mohammed crossed to the desk, his gait slow and graceful, and bent over the exhibit.

There was a momentary silence, and then: "I should judge, sir, this pectoral collar to be Seventeenth Dynasty Theban. But I am not an expert. If I may make a suggestion, the student who formed the collection in this room would be able to give you a better opinion."

McGraw chewed awhile. "Bear it in mind."

Mohammed stood upright.

"I cannot tell what theory you have formed, sir, nor even if you have formed any. But I can advise you upon one point: The owner of this gold collar did not kill the man who lies upstairs." He bowed. "Have I your permission to depart?"

Sample exchanged glances with McGraw.

"In one moment," said the Chief Inspector. "Little formality, first. Everybody going through the same, but you happen to be here. Be good enough to turn out contents of all pockets."

Mohammed's gentle eyes seemed to emit sparks. Then, they grew gentle again. Quietly, he removed his double-breasted black coat and tossed it onto the back of the armchair in which he had been seated. He wore no waistcoat.

"Turn them out yourself, sir."

Sample accepted the invitation, stolidly. Mohammed emptied his trouser pockets and exposed the linings. He stood there, a slim, straight figure, and raised his hands to the green turban.

"Don't bother," drawled McGraw. "Those things hard to tie."

He ran his fingers lightly over the silken folds. Sample replaced the various articles he had found in the tuxedo and returned those which Mohammed had carried in his trousers' pockets.

"Is that all, sir?"

McGraw nodded.

"Obliged for your co-operation."

When Mohammed had gone, "That's a dark horse," Sample remarked.

"Maybe. Only one of several. Get Inspector Hawley," McGraw directed. "All present to come in, and remain inside the house, closed doors. Send a car for female searcher from Lychgate, and someone to look for fingerprints on the window up there."

"Very good, sir." Sample paused on his way out. "Of course you saw there's wistaria with branches as thick as my wrist growing right up to that window?"

"Saw it. Just possible the wanted party escaped that way. But if you're sure you locked the door, someone must have unlocked it—and then come back here and replaced the key. May be fingerprints on that, too—as well as yours. Bring Mr. Pike in when you come back. Look him over, first."

"Yes, sir." But still Sample lingered. "I've been trying to remember when both of us were out of this room at the same time. . . ."

"Remembered?"

"Yes. When you sent me to find Mr. Faraway. I came back and you weren't here."

"Correct. That's it. Went to the men's room for a brush-up. In that five or six minutes somebody waiting for a chance slipped in. Likeliest place for the key—this drawer. Found it. Nipped upstairs and took the gold case. Hurried down. No time to relock door. But returned the key and slipped out again."

"That's my view, sir. But what a cool hand!"

When Sergeant Sample returned, he ushered in Larkhall Pike.

The Major remained attired in pajamas and dressing gown, and carried a newspaper under his arm. His parchment face was dusky with fury. He strode straight to the desk at which McGraw sat. His stoop had vanished; his stride was that of an angry soldier.

"Sir! There are limits, well-defined limits, to every man's powers of endurance!"

McGraw nodded.

"As someone just pointed out to me, possible to overload a camel."

"The simile is inapt. It might even be construed as insulting. But what I have to say I am going to say. That man"—a quivering forefinger accused Sample—"had the impudence, the blasted impudence, to search *me!*"

"Normal procedure."

"I believe you are a senior officer of the Criminal Investigation Department. I wish you to know, sir, that if this is the normal procedure of Scotland Yard, I regret that I am an Englishman!"

"Routine, sir. Sorry. But everybody here will have to submit to it. You see, important evidence is missing."

"And what, may I inquire"—Pike bent menacingly over the Chief Inspector—"have *I* to do with your damned evidence? I am harried from place to place, until even in the servants' quarters I can find no peace. . . ."

But McGraw had taken the measure of his man. He stood up, smiled.

"Sir! Tried to apologize. Can do no more. Sergeant Sample just carrying out routine orders. Better if I had explained the position, first. Have a duty to perform. Only ask you to help me. Won't you please sit down?"

Larkhall Pike sat down, and dashed his paper onto the floor beside him.

"Pshaw!"

McGraw closed his eyes, waiting for a moment, and then, "Believe you have lived here for some years?" he said.

"I have *existed* here."

"Why, sir?"

Larkhall Pike swallowed audibly, and it seemed with difficulty.

"My brother Benedict permits me to occupy the house during his lifetime. He has a perverted sense of humor. Some people have! He knew I couldn't afford to keep it up. He knew I couldn't sell it. And he insisted that the property must not be leased to anybody."

"Is that so?"

McGraw's drawl was sympathetic.

"I have one man, a semi-imbecile, who cultivates the vegetable garden, and looks after me. Sleeps out. I live on eggs. Produce 'em. This dodge of letting the place for parties was suggested by Jarretts, the London caterers. Damned undignified, but socialism doesn't recognize dignity. Have to eat. Fools come down to get drunk. Rich fools. Black market. Fiddling while Rome's burning. No closing time."

McGraw nodded.

"House mostly unfurnished?"

"Yes. We are at present seated in my living quarters."

"And you sleep upstairs there?"

"Unless there's a corpse in the bed, I do. The room described by the organizers as a Powder Room I normally use as a dressing and bathroom."

McGraw's sleepy eyes moved about.

"Valuable things here. Insured against loss?"

"I am, sir—by Jarretts. Furthermore, they undertake to put a responsible representative in charge. I have never met such a person."

McGraw lay back.

"And, during the time this tragedy was taking place, you were asleep?"

"I was aroused by the phone bell. I came down to find an ex-Sapper sergeant from King's Riding masquerading in another uniform, seated at my desk! I refer to Superintendent Croker. I was cross-examined in a manner for which there can be no excuse whatever. Compelled to view some fellow's body, and to have my fingerprints taken!"

"Very difficult for you, sir, I agree. Only one point—this piece of jewelry." McGraw indicated the Egyptian pectoral lying before him. "Formalities being over, I speak as a man in need of advice. You are an expert. May I ask your opinion of this exhibit? Please don't touch it."

Larkhall Pike, who had begun to adjust his pince-nez, dropped the glasses on their black ribbon.

"Don't *touch* it, sir? How the blazes am I to examine the thing without touching it?"

"Sorry. Thought a sight of it would be enough."

"Pshaw!" Pike fixed his glasses and glanced down. "Late

eighteenth Theban. Cloisonné good—if real. Gold work, first-class. If spurious, a clever copy. Identical piece in the Cairo Museum—found by Flinders Petrie." He removed his pince-nez. "Have I the permission of Scotland Yard to retire again to the kitchen?"

When he had gone, "Awkward old party," said Sample. "You kept your patience better than I could, sir."

"Only way." McGraw chewed thoughtfully. "Thumbscrews wouldn't force that man to talk. Even now, he hasn't told us half he knows."

"Another dark horse, in my opinion."

But McGraw's partly closed eyes were turning this way and that. He was surveying the bookshelves. And suddenly, "What's the family name of the Marquess of Glengale?" he drawled.

Sample was startled by the abrupt query. "Marquess of Glengale? You've beaten me. . . . Oh, I see! You're thinking about the Bentley outside?"

McGraw nodded.

"See if there's a *Debrett* here. Generally find a *Debrett* in a ruin like this."

Sample explored several rows of volumes, then pulled one out, banged the cover to dust it, and sneezed.

"H'm! My mistake. This looks like *Who's Who*."

McGraw stood up slowly.

"Put it back. *I'll* look. Never know who's who until you know what's what." He swooped and pulled out a stout volume. "*Debrett.*"

Resuming his seat, he began to turn the pages.

"Ah! here it is. Phew! Thought I was right!" He whistled softly. "Ronald Charringford Copley Bruton, 8th Marquess of Glengale . . ."

"Bruton?"

"Bruton! Let's see—h'm—ha—and so forth—h'm . . . *Ah!* 'Married, Agatha Mary Elphinstowe . . .'"

114

"Elphinstowe!" Sample echoed.

" 'No male issue. One daughter. Hilary Felice Mary.' "

"Well, I'll be . . ."

"Deserve to be." McGraw passed the volume to Sample. "Replace—and memorize appearance. Why I've left her out, so far. Daughter of the Marquess of Glengale a tricky job to touch. We're handling dynamite. . . ."

14

"You see, Hilary," said Storm Kennedy, "how hopelessly I am tied. McGraw's never likely to know that I found your handkerchief lying beside the dead man. But that is where I found it. Suppose this horrible thing should go to court, and I am put on oath as a witness? Must I commit perjury? Wouldn't it be wiser, my dear, to explain the mystery to a friend rather than to the police?"

Hilary sat, hands clasped between her knees, looking down at the littered floor of the summer house. Through a hole in its crazy roof a ray of sunshine drenched her bowed head with magic. Kennedy watched her.

"Yes"—a whisper—"it would."

But she said no more.

"What is Elfie's advice? Doesn't she agree with me?"

Hilary nodded, biting her lip.

"I could see she was glad when I hauled you away. Do, Hilary, I beg of you, give me something to work upon. I'm madly anxious to advise you, and I can't, unless you co-operate. The mere fact that McGraw has left you alone so far is significant. He may know who you are, already. That one blunder—giving a wrong name—will focus the inquiry on *you*."

Hilary sat upright and slowly turned to him. She was pale, but her eyes expressed neither fear nor defiance. They were hopelessly sad.

"I'll try to tell you."

Storm Kennedy's pulse accelerated madly. Hilary, evasive, Hilary scornful, was still utterly desirable; but Hilary submissive was just a lonely, adorable little girl he longed to take in his arms and comfort.

"My dear! I'm so glad."

The ardor in his voice brought a slow flush to her cheeks, which passed, leaving her more pale than before. She turned aside, fumbling with her gray-and-white handbag which lay on the broken-down seat beside her.

"Shall we smoke? I smoke very little, and so I still have a few left."

"Yes," he said quietly. "Mine are all gone."

She took out and opened an enamel case. There were cigarettes in it. Kennedy lighted Hilary's and then his own. She flashed him one swift glance over the flame, but read so much in the steady blue eyes that her courage faltered.

They smoked awhile in silence. In her deceptively simple dove-gray dress, Hilary did not provoke a sense of the incongruous, as was the case with Mrs. Muller and Sidonia. She seemed to be part of the morning, except that Kennedy had a dim impression that it was some morning of long ago. He watched her, and waited, until:

"Finding my handkerchief," she said, in a low, even voice, "where you found it, gave you the idea that I must have known the man. It's true. I did know him."

Kennedy didn't speak. He waited. Hilary's fingers holding the cigarette were quite steady.

"Only a few people—very few—were aware of this. If it were found out, if I admitted it, just the thing I was trying to hide would be dragged into the limelight. I thought, stupidly, that silence would save me from that. I had no right to think so. It forced Elfie to lie—to cover my lie. For Elfie knew him, too."

She lowered her head again, and again that ray of sunshine made a halo of her bright hair.

Kennedy was thinking hard. He had a glimpse of the pattern on the loom and visualized shapes yet to come.

"I don't want to interrupt, Hilary," he said. "But I believe it might be wiser if you don't tell me his name—yet. I have stated, truthfully, that I never saw the man before; but McGraw might spring the question in another form."

"All right. I'll do whatever you tell me. I came here to meet him last night—for nothing else but just that. Elfie knew all about it, and came with me. . . . Good heavens! What's this?"

A voice was heard shouting: "Miss Bruton wanted! Miss Bruton!"

Hilary sprang up, nervously, upsetting the handbag which lay open beside her. Its contents spilled out on the dirty floor.

"Damn!" said Kennedy. "Quick! We may not have another chance. Where had you come from when you ran into Elfie and me outside that study door?"

"I had just left him. . . ."

"Miss Bruton!"

Kennedy stooped and began to gather up feminine trifles. Hilary forced a smile.

"Thank you. I think that's everything."

A police sergeant appeared at the door.

"This way, if you please, Miss. You're wanted too, sir. Chief Inspector's orders."

"All right, Sergeant. I'm coming."

Hilary walked out composedly and went ahead with the sergeant. Storm Kennedy was about to follow when a faint gleam of metal attracted his attention. He dropped to one knee, peering under the seat. Something out of Hilary's bag had been overlooked.

He retrieved it—a heavy gold case, resembling a fountain pen, the top attached by a thin metal chain. Probably lipstick, he surmised.

Kennedy turned and went outside. But Hilary and the sergeant were already mounting ruinous stone steps which led up to part of the terrace. He slipped the gold case into his pocket. . . .

"Look at it this way," said Chief Inspector McGraw: "Whoever took the risk of stealing that thing must have had a big stake in the game. Clear?"

"Quite clear, sir."

Sergeant Sample sat at the desk. McGraw paced about the shadowed room, chewing.

"Right. In taking that chance, he or she must have known loss would be found out. Therefore he (let's call it *he*) must have guessed the theft would prove something we didn't know. What would it prove, Sergeant Sample?"

"It would prove," Sample replied, carefully choosing his words, "that the case wasn't as cold as we thought."

McGraw paused, stared across at him.

"Congratulations. That's so. Only person deep enough to stick his neck out so far would be the murderer. Clear?"

"I agree, sir."

"Therefore (the thing we didn't know) murderer is still in the house!"

"Or was, at that time."

McGraw pulled up again.

"A wise one, Sergeant! Inspector Hawley is responsible for covering all means of exit. But we can't be sure. Next point: In what way did this object nobody could open incriminate the killer? Why take such chances to get it?"

"I give that one up."

"Is that so? You're failing me, Sample. Because I'd given it up, too! When—if ever—we get fingerprint equipment from Lychgate, may learn something. But I doubt it. Let's believe in Inspector Hawley and accept as fact that nobody unauthorized left these premises since we arrived. What does that leave us with?"

"With what we had before. Except that one of 'em must have done it."

"Correct. Let's try to put a finger on that one." McGraw stood still, for he had closed his eyes. "Until dead man is identified, we can pin no motive on anybody. Clear?"

"I agree."

"We have following choice: Mr. Larkhall Pike, who is, Hawley tells me, a retired Indian Army officer. Any comments?"

"Bit of a dark horse. This room is uncanny. Gives me the willies. And he's got no alibi."

"Right. Mohammed Ibn Lahûn, a friend of Mrs. Faraway's, who claims he's staying at the Berkley Hotel, London. Checked it?"

"Yes, sir. He has a suite there."

"Any comments?"

"Fishy character. He seems to me to know a lot. But the puzzling thing is, he says so!"

"That, I agree, *is* the puzzling thing; but it may be a pose. Next, Mr. Allen Lovelace. Looked him over, didn't you?"

"I did, sir. Looked 'em all over, except Mr. Kennedy, as instructed."

"Anything from Lovelace?"

"On the desk here, Chief Inspector."

McGraw's closed lids opened. His eyes flashed on Sample. He crossed in three long strides.

"Show me."

McGraw took up a small, black-bound book, glanced

at the name, in gilt, on the binding, and then opened it at first page. He dropped the book on the desk, and nodded.

"Deal with him, later! We come to the Honorable Peter Faraway."

"He knows nothing."

"Didn't expect him to. Museum piece. English playboy with enough money (his wife's) to keep on playing with Comrade Cripps on his tail. . . . Storm Kennedy!"

McGraw resumed his promenade.

"We know all about *him*, sir!"

"Not all, Sample. First place, he's damn clever. Second place, he's one of these hand-picked, anvil-wrought characters they used to drop behind the German lines. He doesn't give a damn for anybody. And that means me. If—and I suspect it is so—he's here on a job, he'll stick at *nothing!*"

"We know that, sir."

"We do! Had some! Calling Mr. Storm Kennedy in for a chat, presently. Let's consider the women now. Mrs. Muller, wife of an oil engineer, on vacation in England. Staying at Hyde Park Hotel. Checked?"

"Report not come through yet."

"Attractive woman." The Chief Inspector smiled reminiscently. "Friend of Mrs. Faraway's. Delayed by an accident due to fog. Anything occur to you?"

"No, sir."

"Miss Sidney, known as Sidonia. Vocalist with Sammy Sams' band. Any impressions?"

"Very nice figure."

"So Mr. Faraway seems to think. Brings us to Miss Amelia Elphinstowe. That woman doesn't fit into the picture at all. But she's hard-boiled as they come."

"You haven't talked to her yet."

"Told you why. She's an aunt of Lady Hilary Bruton—who gave a wrong name."

"If I remember rightly, Mary *is* one of her names."

"Maybe. But she was trying to hide behind it."

"I think I can understand that."

"Can you?"

"A girl of that sort doesn't care to be mixed up in police business. I expect it was just an impulse."

"Impulse, eh? Only be one reason for it . . . Didn't want somebody to know she had been at the party."

Came a rap on the door, and Inspector Hawley looked in.

"Women have been searched. Missing evidence not found. Will it be all right for Wilson to go up and test for fingerprints?"

"Send him along."

Sergeant Sample sat tapping a pencil on his notebook and the Chief Inspector was still walking about when a sandy-haired young constable came in, carrying an attaché case. He peered around the darkened room in evident surprise.

"Wilson?" McGraw drawled.

"Yes, sir."

"Sergeant Sample, show him the window frame. Might try the table, too. You have the key?" Sample nodded and held up a white envelope. "Then go and ask Mr. Kennedy to step in for a chat."

When, a few minutes later, Storm Kennedy came in, followed by Sample who had gone to fetch him, he, too, betrayed surprise to find the study draped in shadows. McGraw had resumed his seat behind the desk.

"Please sit down, Mr. Kennedy."

"Why the spiritualist séance effect, Chief Inspector?"

"Trying to refresh people's memories. So forgetful." Kennedy sat in the armchair. "Perhaps you can help me. You told Superintendent Croker that you arrived late last night and could find nobody you knew. While you were looking around, you glanced into this room through the window. Was it lighted as you see it now?"

"No. Only the floor lamp was alight."

"And after the body was discovered?"

"I found it switched off."

"Is that so?" McGraw turned to Sample, who had made his way to the back of the Chief Inspector's chair. "Read out the statement signed last night by Miss Elphinstowe."

Sample cleared his throat.

"Very good, sir."

He began to read in the expressionless style peculiar to police officers called upon to give court evidence; and Storm Kennedy formed a vague impression of a piece of deliberate evasion in every way creditable to Elfie. For his brain was working too rapidly to allow him to pay much attention.

Here came the opening of the battle!

Sample's dreary recitation being concluded:

"Now, Mr. Kennedy"—McGraw lay back with closed eyes—"accept that as a true and exact account?"

"I suppose so."

"You suppose so. Don't feel Miss Elphinstowe was withholding any essential fact—such as someone's *real* name?"

"I am quite well aware that she was doing that," Kennedy replied quietly. "But I respect her loyalty. Lady Hilary gave her name as Mary Bruton—which *is* her name, by the way—on an impulse which I think you will understand, and I hope condone."

Sergeant Sample blew his nose.

"Thank you, Mr. Kennedy. Knew already, though." McGraw slightly raised the drooping lids. "And you don't feel Miss Elphinstowe was suppressing *another* name?"

"No name known to *me*."

"Sure of that, Mr. Kennedy?"

"Quite sure."

"There's no reference to Lady Hilary Bruton in your own statement."

"I had no reason to refer to her."

"But you had seen her."

"Certainly. Miss Elphinstowe, whom I saw first, said that she and Lady Hilary were ready to leave, and I volunteered to act as a fog pilot. It was while the ladies were preparing for the drive, in the Powder Room, that I heard Mr. Faraway coming up the garden."

"So you said. Known Lady Hilary a long time?"

"By the calendar, yes. But I had met her only once or twice before."

"Knew she was here, I suppose?"

"Certainly. Peter told me as I came in."

McGraw's drawled inquiries came like snipers' bullets, Kennedy thought. One never knew from which point the next one would be fired. Intense mental alertness was called for. It must be masked by a façade of nonchalance.

McGraw seemed to be thinking. He was silent for a long time. Sample was reading notes.

"Several questions I might ask," McGraw drawled at last. "But they can wait. Might ask, for instance, if you're prepared to lay your cards down. But I should hate you to say No. So, we'll leave it. Everybody else here been searched. A necessary formality. Important evidence stolen."

"What?" Kennedy rapped out.

"What I said. Any objection to turning out contents of pockets?"

Storm Kennedy stood up.

"None whatever." He grinned cheerfully. "Wish you luck!"

He plunged his hand, first, into the inside pocket of his coat, and found the envelope which contained Hilary's stained handkerchief. During that period of close concentration demanded by McGraw's questioning, he had temporarily forgotten that this damning piece of cambric was there.

But he laid the envelope calmly on the desk. It was ignored.

Next, he tumbled out his wallet; then an empty cigarette case, lighter, small tubular flashlamp—and his fingers closed around that gold object redeemed from the spillings of Hilary's bag. He placed it beside the other things which he had already laid down. . . .

McGraw rose slowly from his chair. His eyes flicked wide open. Sample bent over his Chief's shoulder.

"Mr. Kennedy!"

Storm Kennedy, who had begun to empty his trouser pockets, looked up, and met the fixed regard of two pairs of eyes.

"Yes?"

"Suppose you can explain how this piece of evidence"—McGraw pointed to the gold case—"stolen from my custody, comes to be in your possession?"

15

The heavy draperies swayed, billowing, as gusts blew in at partly opened windows behind them. Shafts of sunshine darted through the crevices, sometimes striking a group of books in bleached bindings, sometimes hitting a god of the Nile; a somber Thoth, a menacing Sekhmet, and, once, a graceful Isis, pure of outline as an Egyptian new moon, pale-green, mystic.

Silence lay heavy on the room as that silence which heralds Khamsîn, the desert wind.

Storm Kennedy, in one inspired flash, saw everything that had happened since he had come to Hangover House. It was a lightning panorama. His meeting with Peter Faraway and Sidonia as he entered, lived again before him. Peter very drunk, the bronze Sidonia more than slightly. A résumé of the incredible night passed in review. The mad reel seemed to pause, hesitate, at the point where Hilary had burst out of this room in which he stood now—Hilary, pale, agitated.

It went on again. He saw Peter's lamp moving erratically through fog wreaths, saw him pull up; joined him and bent over the murdered man lying on the steps. . . . The footprints in blood; Hilary's handkerchief. Sharp as etchings, picture after picture swept by. Each clear as a new record, he heard the voice of Lovelace, the musical tones of Mohammed, the gruff bonhomie peculiar to Amelia Elphinstowe.

And through them all he saw Hilary. Over every other voice he heard her voice.

But, first to last, he neither heard nor saw anything to prove her innocence!

This final shock had stunned him. Temporarily, he was at a dead loss how to proceed.

Had he committed himself to the defense of a murderess —whom he loved?

If the victim was indeed the man named by Lord Glengale, then Hilary had confessed that she came here to meet him. She had confessed to having just left him when she ran, panic-stricken, out of this room.

Now, some vital evidence—by appearance, either a gold fountain pen or lipstick container—had been stolen from the police.

And it had fallen from Hilary's handbag!

Storm Kennedy exercised yogi discipline. Perspiration must *not* show on his forehead.

He seemed to see his own handwriting, the letters moving in a *danse macabre*—notes made that morning:

> "Is there any explanation of Hilary's handkerchief lying beside the dead man other than that she was with him at the time of his death?"

His brain was functioning at phenomenal speed; and now he posed the question: Is there any explanation of my finding this stolen evidence in the summer house other than that it fell from Hilary's handbag?

In the interests of sanity, he must find one, and find it quickly. He focused on the summer house. It stood, concrete, before him. . . .

Yes—there was *one* explanation!

Hilary, before walking up to the terrace with the police sergeant, had said that whatever had fallen from her bag he had recovered. In short, she had missed nothing. This gold case he had found, later, under the seat.

And, not so long before, Sidonia had been in there adjusting her make-up, a large handbag open beside her.

She, and not Hilary, might have dropped the gold case!

It was a desperate situation. Useless, now, to fence with McGraw concerning where he had found the thing—and he had no intention of lying. But he could prevaricate. All was not lost. . . .

His reflections—so wonderful an instrument is the human brain—had, in fact, occupied less than thirty seconds. McGraw and Sample watched him steadily.

And Storm Kennedy smiled.

"The implication in your words, Chief Inspector, amounts to a charge of accessory after the fact. Shouldn't I be warned?"

"Depends on what you say."

"I'm afraid you'll be disappointed. I picked the thing up in the garden five minutes ago."

"Where?"

"In the summer house."

"What were you doing there?"

"Smoking."

"Alone?"

"At the time that I saw what I took to be a woman's lipstick lying on the floor—yes."

"But before that?"

"I had been talking to Lady Hilary. The case lay under the seat, and I didn't notice it until she had gone. As a matter of fact," Kennedy proceeded smoothly, "the summer house has been very popular. I saw Sidonia there this morning, too."

"Talk to her?"

"Yes. She was adjusting her make-up while waiting for her shoes to dry. Been washing off the bloodstains."

Sergeant Sample, busily writing, paused, looked up. "Did you say adjusting her make-up?"

"Yes."

Sample glanced at McGraw—and Kennedy knew that his red herring, for a moment at any rate, had put the pack off the scent. Sample had instantly jumped to the conclusion (as Kennedy had hoped) that the bronze, fumbling in her bag, might have dropped the gold case, unnoticed. He didn't believe that Sidonia had anything to do with the matter. If, by some freak of fate, she had, well, it was no part of his business to protect Sidonia.

McGraw had closed his eyes. Now, he partly opened them.

"Ask Constable Wilson to come down."

Sample nodded and went to the foot of the stair.

"Wilson, you're wanted."

The sandy-haired young policeman appeared promptly.

"Look over this pencil-case," McGraw directed. "Do it upstairs. More light."

"Very good, sir."

Wilson picked up the mysterious object with a pair of tweezers, gingerly, as though he handled some poisonous reptile.

"Any results from window frame?"

"Yes, sir. Two sets of fingerprints—quite clear. Men's."

"Is that so? Got your charts of persons present?"

"Yes, sir. From Inspector Hawley. But none of the prints taken correspond."

McGraw stood up, slowly. Then he sat down again, and smiled a wry smile. He glanced over his shoulder at Sample.

"Yours and mine! I opened the window. You closed it! Go up and check in a minute. Nothing else, Constable?"

"Nothing clear, sir. Just some smudges."

"*Over* the other prints?"

"In one case, yes."

"No lines discernible?"

"Not a thing, sir. Just smudges."

"Key?"

"One clear thumbprint."

"Mine," intoned Sample, as though the word had been a response in a church service.

McGraw chewed silently.

"Get on with that pencil-case."

This interlude had given Storm Kennedy time for further reflection. If, in addition to his own, Hilary's fingerprints were found on the gold case, only one conclusion remained possible. . . .

Inspector Hawley rapped on the study door and came in.

"I have to report," he said, "that Dr. Smithy isn't available. He's been called to a consultation in London."

"Is that so?" came McGraw's tired voice. "Doesn't help a lot. Better send for the wagon, and get a hospital opinion on real cause of death."

"I'll see to it immediately. Another point. This line is in service again, if you want to use it. I've spoken to the exchange."

"Good."

"The people outside are getting restive, Chief Inspector. So long as they don't attempt to leave, is there any objection to letting them out to wander about for a while in the garden?"

"None on my part. Found what I was looking for."

"I'll give them your permission, then."

When Inspector Hawley had gone, McGraw stood up, walked around the desk and leaned back against it, watching Storm Kennedy through half-closed eyes.

"Not compelled to answer any question I ask, Mr. Kennedy. But it might be better if you did. Are you covering someone?"

"Yes."

"Thought so. Want me to ask you who it is?"

"No."

"I won't—now. But I can guess. Is your story about picking up that thing absolutely true?"

"Absolutely true."

"Weren't *looking* for it?"

"I didn't know of its existence. I don't know, now, what it is or why it has any bearing on the case. I was going to show it to the women, as I supposed one of them had dropped it."

"Take your word for that. *I* don't know what it is, or why it bears on the case. But it was found on the dead man. Lay upstairs beside his body. Someone got into that room this morning and removed it. Clear?"

It was so clear that it was startling. For it explained the mystery of the woman who crept about in the night; the woman of whom he, himself, had caught a glimpse; whom Larkhall Pike had detected trying to steal upstairs to the room where the dead man lay. . . . She had been after this mysterious object.

"What does it contain?"

McGraw's sleepy eyes never flickered.

"Couldn't say."

"Why not open it?"

"Have *you* tried?"

"Never occurred to me to do so. I simply assumed it to be an unusually large lipstick."

"Is that so? Well, quite briefly, nobody has been able to open it. Some sort of trick fastener." McGraw was silent for a moment. "Entitled to carry on your own inquiry, Mr. Kennedy, provided it doesn't interfere with mine. Anything you think you ought to tell me?"

Kennedy's glance played over the envelope which lay on the desk behind McGraw, the envelope which contained a bloodstained handkerchief; then, "Yes," he said quietly. "There is. Whoever got into this room this morning attempted to do so, earlier—during the night. Now that I know the facts, I realize the importance of something that happened."

"Glad to have particulars."

Briefly, Kennedy related how he had been awakened by a creaking door, and had seen a figure stealing out of the study. He was fully alive to McGraw's tactics. By offering certain fragments of information, himself, he hoped to gain more than he gave. Of Pike's evidence, however, which identified the prowler as female, Kennedy said nothing. But Sample put the question: "Was it a man or a woman you saw, sir?"

He asked in a tone which suggested that he couldn't have cared less if it had been a purple elephant.

"Impossible to say," Kennedy replied. "Could have been either. I thought no more about it, at the time, as the explanation might well be a perfectly simple one."

"Sure," McGraw asked, "that whoever it was came out of Mr. Pike's study—this room?"

"Quite sure."

"Better have another chat with Mr. Pike. Obliged for your co-operation."

Constable Wilson came downstairs.

"The gold case is all over fingerprints, sir," he reported. "Mostly illegible. There's just a single thumb mark—recent —which I've identified with one of the charts. The name on the chart is W. Storm Kennedy."

McGraw glanced at Kennedy.

"Seems to confirm your story!" he said drily. "Nothing else, Constable Wilson?"

"Well, sir"—Wilson's sandy eyebrows registered puzzlement—"there is one peculiar thing, if you wouldn't mind examining the fingerprints through a lens."

"Can do." McGraw considered Storm Kennedy under drooping lids. "Go and have a talk with Larkhall Pike. May be able to handle him better than I can. . . ."

When Kennedy found himself out in the long corridor, and Sample had closed the door behind him, he stood still for a moment, weighing up gains and losses.

In recovering his property from the desk, he had resisted a strong temptation to snatch the envelope containing Hilary's handkerchief, and had left it lying there until the last moment, as if all but forgotten. His heart was still ticking above normal from the ordeal.

McGraw's purpose in asking him to talk to Larkhall Pike was plain enough. McGraw hoped to find out, in the event of Pike's evidence pointing in a certain direction, if he would try to obscure it.

How much did McGraw know?

Whatever he knew, he clearly suspected that somebody in the house had suppressed knowledge of the dead man's identity. It was reasonable also to assume that the person he suspected was the person in whom Kennedy was interested; a safe bet that he guessed this person to be Hilary.

And, damn it, the man was right!

McGraw was playing a waiting game, because a mistake in dealing with Lord Glengale's daughter might have serious consequences.

What was there in her statement to Superintendent Croker which had betrayed her? Or did McGraw's doubts concerning Hilary rest on no foundation other than her having given a misleading name?

His first job must be to find Pike (whom McGraw undoubtedly would interview later) and induce him to be silent concerning their early morning conversation in the kitchen. McGraw must not learn that he (Kennedy) had known all along the midnight powder to be a woman.

And Hilary?

At the thought of Hilary his heart sank.

Could it possibly be that the woman who crept into the study during the night and tried to slip upstairs was Hilary? Conceivable that she had taken the suicidal risk of repeating her attempt?

That she had the courage to carry out such a thing he must accept as a fact. But the incident seemed to mark this mysterious crime as one not of swift passion, but one coldly planned and coolly executed.

Why had the criminal (even now, he rejected violently thinking in terms of Hilary) wanted to recover that gold case? Possibly, it had had fingerprints upon it. And what was the "peculiar thing" which Wilson had asked McGraw to examine through a lens?

He made his way out to God's free air.

The effect, coming from the draped study, was similar to that of leaving a movie theater in daylight. Sunshine drenched the garden. Storm Kennedy looked down the slope.

Two figures moved slowly in the distance, away beyond the pond. He identified Miss Elphinstowe and Hilary. Three sides of the property were bounded by highways, that facing north by a narrow, unpaved and weed-grown lane which joined a secondary road near the back gate, where a constable mounted guard.

A car was being driven along this lane, cautiously, as the bad surface demanded. Kennedy could hear but could not see it.

There was no one in the paneled hall.

He went into the courtyard. Several cars were visible beyond locked iron entrance gates, and he saw a pair of constables on duty outside. Mohammed stood there, placidly regarding a group of men who argued hotly with the police.

"What's going on, Mr. Ibn Lahûn?"

The calm, dark eyes were turned in his direction.

"Reporters, sir, I believe. Chief Inspector McGraw has given orders that none are to be admitted. But reporters, like locusts, are hard to deny. I have been photographed several times through the bars, already."

And, even as he spoke, cameras were raised, and Storm Kennedy knew that his picture, also, would be in the evening papers.

He moved on, turning left, beyond range of the cameras, and following a path which he thought would lead him to those rambling domestic quarters in which he hoped to find Larkhall Pike.

Luck was with him, for just as he was about to enter that walled enclosure which embraced the kitchens, Larkhall Pike came out. He wore a raincoat over his pajamas, and a plaid cap of remarkable design. He was carrying a wicker basket.

"Hullo, sir!"

Pike paused, glared, and then the lined face relaxed.

"I am going to look for eggs. I hope to obtain permission from Scotland Yard to boil two for my breakfast."

Storm Kennedy fell into step beside the Major.

"In the way if I come along?"

"Not at all. If you can tolerate boiled eggs, you might care to breakfast with me."

"That's really kind of you, sir. But I doubt if the police will give me time."

"Badgering *you*, now, are they?"

"They are! McGraw has been asking questions about some woman who was prowling about in the night. I didn't repeat what you had told me, although I had some vague impression of the kind, myself. But I suspect that he may call upon you to say if anything disturbed you. If he does, no need, I think, to mention our earlier conversation?"

"I shall not mention it, Mr. Kennedy. Quite proper to respect information imparted in confidence. But this damned policeman might misconstrue your motives."

And Storm Kennedy experienced a pang of conscience. He was beginning to feel something oddly akin to friendship for this impoverished, bitter old soldier, and he hated being forced to play the hypocrite.

"He misconstrues them already!" he said hastily. "In fact, he asked me to see you and to try to find out if you could confirm the report in any way."

"Inform him that I declined to be cross-examined."

Kennedy laughed. It was not a really mirthful laugh.

"That will save a lot of trouble, sir!"

They walked on.

"Just look at my morning attire!" Pike exploded suddenly. "Disgraceful! Every stitch I possess hangs in my bedroom cupboard—and the room has been put out of bounds!"

"Oh, but wait a minute! I'll speak to McGraw . . ."

Larkhall Pike pulled up, turned and glared.

"You will do nothing of the kind, Mr. Kennedy! Please understand me. I forbid it. I accept favors from no man."

His tone was harsh, peremptory.

"As you wish." Storm Kennedy smiled. "I think I know how you feel."

They had come to a point where a road, striated with ancient cart-ruts, led from a boarded-up gateway westward across the grounds. Directly ahead rose a steep hill densely wooded, and, away to the left, Kennedy saw a number of chicken coops. A man carrying a bucket moved about among them. He could hear the clank of the handle whenever the man put the bucket down.

Kennedy turned, looked back, and then, "Hangover House must be very old?" he said, meditatively.

Larkhall Pike pointed.

"D'Angauverre Abbey stood on that hillside—a mile or so from the Pilgrims Way to Canterbury. It was abolished, and then demolished, in Tudor times. This place was the abbot's guest house. It later became the property of an ancestor, Sir Peregrine Pike, who rebuilt it as a manor house."

"Your roots are here, sir."

"True, Mr. Kennedy. But the tree withers. The present name, a vulgarized form of d'Angauverre, first appears in local records in 1742. Yes, Hangover House is very old, very sad and decrepit. It is appropriate that I shall probably be the last of my race to inhabit it. . . ."

16

Sidonia came out of the Powder Room and walked down the steps that led to the lily pond, carrying her sable wrap over one shoulder. On the last step she paused for a moment, seemed about to turn back, but then strolled ahead.

She had seen Mrs. Muller and the blond Lovelace together on a stone seat which overlooked the pond—and they had seen her.

"Hullo," she hailed, tonelessly.

"It is wonderful to be let out of jail again," said Mrs. Muller. "Don't you think so?"

"Everything's wonderful. I could cry like a child. Must go walk it off."

"Have you tried the promised refreshments?"

"Sure. I had a rubber sandwich and a cup of warm mud—and me with a lunch date at the Savoy grill!"

Mr. Lovelace stood up, stared, but said nothing. Mrs. Muller smiled.

"I'm afraid it's terribly inconvenient for all of us."

"I'll say so. We lead the gay life. And that sweet little number who searched us? Why, she even found my birthmark!"

And Sidonia went swaying away down a sloping, weed-choked path until she became lost to view amid overgrown shrubbery. Mrs. Muller watched her, half-smiling. Mr. Lovelace watched Mrs. Muller.

"Seems to be in a great hurry," she murmured. "I wonder if Peter Faraway is waiting for her."

"I don't—er—believe so. I think there's a certain—er—incompatability, this morning. But I was thinking that *we* get on very well together."

Mrs. Muller turned to him.

"Yes, we do—famously."

"Yes—er—I thought so, too. I have never met anyone who appealed to me so keenly."

"That's very sweet of you."

"Er—you are most appealing. You sort of reach—er—the poet in me."

"That is rank flattery!"

"No, not at all. It's a fact. I think I told you my name is Allen. Do you mind telling me yours?"

"Delilah."

Mr. Lovelace stared dumbly for a moment.

"Really?"

"Of course. Don't you like it?"

"It's—er—simply beautiful. Like music. But I never met anyone with that name before. I wonder—er—Delilah—if I should bore you terribly if I told you something about myself? Something very secret."

Mrs. Muller looked to right, to left, and all around, but with little hope of rescue. She had been civil to Sidonia, whom she disliked, with the sole purpose of detaining her long enough to effect her own escape.

"Suppose," she suggested, and electrified Lovelace with one of her glittering smiles, "you try first to find me another cup of coffee—bad as it is. I will wait here. May I trouble you?"

"Oh, rather! Er—certainly. It's no trouble. . . ."

And at about the time that Mr. Lovelace went stumbling up the steps upon his errand, Sidonia had discovered a path, bramble-haunted and dark, that path explored earlier by Storm Kennedy, which ran close to an ancient wall guarding the northern boundary.

Sidonia, behind a façade of bored tolerance, concealed a burning hatred of Hangover House and everyone in it. Moreover, she had urgent, vitally urgent, reasons for leaving without delay. It was a case of now or never; and Sidonia was not lacking in audacity.

She knew that there was a policeman posted at the back gate, for she had seen him. She knew, also, that the narrow lane outside the wall led to a road on which this gate opened. But it came out some distance away to the north.

The perils of the path no longer concerned Sidonia. Her shoes, her stockings, her frock, all were ruined. Her hair had never recovered from the cold-water treatment. How she loathed that arrogant old fool, Elphinstowe!

More narrow and yet darker the path became. No sunlight could ever penetrate through dense foliage which roofed it in. Nettles were abundant.

Then Sidonia stopped. She stood quite still.

"Sidonia!"

It was a chilling whisper.

Here, a little more light broke the darkness of the way. Close to her feet she saw mossy blocks, and, looking to the right, and beyond, could make out a gap in the wall, high up near its crest. Something seemed to stir, shadowly.

"Sidonia!"

She stared upward, intent, posed.

A face peered down at her from the jagged opening. . . .

In that room like a monk's cell which contained, in addition to Larkhall Pike's wardrobe, the body of a murdered man, Sergeant Sample laid down on the window ledge a strong lens through which he had been peering.

"An old hand, at a pinch, will sometimes use a rag or handkerchief," he remarked, "so as to leave no prints. That's what this looks like."

"Think so?" drawled McGraw. "What's your view, Constable Wilson?"

"Well, sir"—the young policeman flushed to the roots of his sandy hair—"I haven't had your experience. I'm fairly new to this business. It looks to me as though what the sergeant says may be right. The smudges on the window frame, as well as the marks on the pencil-case, seem to have been made by someone using some sort of covering. Could easily be, as he suggests, a piece of linen."

McGraw exchanged glances with Sample.

"Remarked, didn't you, it was a cool hand did this job? Begin to agree. Should like a little more background to some of these people."

He walked out, and went downstairs into the curtained study. When Sample joined him, "Wilson can go now," McGraw said. "Tell him to leave the charts upstairs. May want 'em. But I'm inclined to think we shan't solve this puzzle along that line."

When Wilson had left, McGraw began to walk about the room.

"Nobody in this house with an alibi that couldn't be broken," he declared. "But while we don't know the dead man's name, can't begin to look for a motive. There are three queries. . . . First, there's the unexplained incident of the lamp. That floor lamp is controlled from a point beside the window. Everybody, so far, has looked for a stud or chain. If we could find a witness who knew where to switch it on, said witness would be the party who had switched it off. Call this Query A. Clear?"

"Quite clear, sir."

"Should have told 'em all, 'Go home,' and had suspects shadowed, except for Query A and two other queries. Know what they are?"

"Yes," said Sample. "First: the business with the gold case. Query: Is the party still on the premises? Second: Storm Kennedy. Query: What's he up to?"

The Chief Inspector stood still; chewing became suspended. Then, feet and jaws resumed work.

"Going to recommend you for a step," he drawled. "Powers of deduction developing fast. You're right. Who employed Kennedy to come down here last night? And what was he employed to *do?* Looks as though somebody expected things to happen."

"Bodyguard?" Sample suggested.

"Could be."

McGraw stood still again. His eyes flicked wide open.

"Thought of something, Chief Inspector?"

McGraw stared at Sample.

"Yes." He spoke even more slowly than usual. "I have. Thought of the duties of a bodyguard. Job I've done, myself, before now. . . . When I was covering the Emîr of Bokhara I nearly had to murder a man who tried to knife him in Paris!"

A silence fell in which the faint swishing of velvet draperies sounded like a violent disturbance.

Then Sample blew his nose.

"Done Commando stuff, Mr. Kennedy, hasn't he?"

"He has. Might get rough in defense of a client."

"I suppose he came to protect Lady Hilary Bruton?"

"She's the likeliest."

"I wonder what she had to be afraid of?"

"To judge by happenings here last night—plenty!"

"What's the next move?"

"Next move," McGraw pronounced, "is to eliminate every other possibility. Want to be foolproof before we tackle the Bruton girl. Go and find that song bird. She *might* have dropped the thing."

But Sergeant Sample lingered. His weathered face, particularly in obstinate mood, sometimes reminded McGraw of an old ship's figurehead.

"I've got a new idea, Chief Inspector."

It sounded like a new idea for a funeral, but McGraw checked his promenade. He continued to chew.

"Unfold."

"Some of these mike queens have wealthy men friends. You'll have noted the sables? It's just possible . . ."

"See your point. Mean Kennedy might have been briefed by a diamond daddy to keep an eye on Sidonia?"

"Why not? But there's this against it: If *he* had slipped upstairs and pinched the gold case, he wouldn't have had it in his pocket."

"Didn't know he was going to be searched."

"That's right, too. But he mentioned Sidonia, and he laid it down as if not caring."

"Could be Commando stuff, Sergeant Sample! He'd have had to bluff it out, then."

Sample nodded solemnly and went to find Sidonia.

Ten minutes later the storm broke.

Sidonia could not be found!

17

STORM KENNEDY, having left Larkhall Pike among his chickens, returned along a rough path, made nearly impenetrable by rank undergrowth, which probably led to some point below the terrace.

It did. He found himself right down at the back of the summer house, and pulled up sharply. . . .

Even now, Hilary's fingerprints might have been found on the gold case! Even now, a police sergeant could be on his way to call her back for interrogation!

He saw her from where he stood.

There was a teak bench placed under a laburnum on the far side of the pond. Hilary and Elfie sat there.

Kennedy clenched his teeth—then stepped out onto the slope and began to walk down toward them.

He had gone no more than ten paces, when, "Hi! Bill!" came a hail from behind.

Kennedy stopped, turned. Peter Faraway was approaching at speed, a strange figure in his tail coat, a muffler around his neck.

"What's up, Peter?"

Peter, rather breathless, haggard and unshaven, joined him.

"I say—have you seen Sidonia?"

Storm Kennedy fixed Peter with a stare from angry blue eyes.

"Peter, your blasted Sidonia is a sick headache! God knows what you see in her. Joan's prettier, younger, and worth a platoon of Sidonias. 'Have you seen Sidonia' begins to fray me. I have *not* seen Sidonia—not for some time."

Peter looked surprised.

"Yes, but I quite agree, Bill. She was just a—let me think—just a tactical bloomer. Repeat that. A tactical bloomer . . . It's the *police* who want her!"

"The police?"

"Yes. The coppers. That cove Hawley got hold of me and asked where she was. I said I didn't know. Been huntint all over the place."

Kennedy glanced, once, toward the distant pond and then resigned himself. His only consolation lay in recognition of the fact that his red herring had proved so effective.

"She can't have found any more steps to fall down, Peter! Who saw her last?"

"Mrs. Muller and that queer bird Lovelace. After we'd been searched—don't know why—and the copper said we could go out, she told them she was taking a stroll in the garden."

"And did she?"

"They say, yes. They also say her manner was queer."

"Well"—Kennedy inhaled deeply—"Hilary and Miss Elphinstowe are down there by the pond. I might ask them if they have seen her." A sudden idea flashed through his mind. "By the way, Peter, you remember I dragged you off from Superintendent Croker last night and warned you not to mention Hilary's name?"

"Certainly I remember, dear old Bill."

"And you didn't?"

"Not to a soul, Bill."

It was a small point; but he might now assume that nothing in Peter's evidence had cast suspicion upon Hilary.

"All right. Let's go and ask them. Hullo! The coppers are ahead of us!"

Both stared in the direction of the pond. Inspector Hawley had appeared there. He was evidently talking to the two women, but, as he talked, his glance swept the prospect.

"They can't find her, Bill! I must think . . ."

But Storm Kennedy was thinking, too, and thinking hard.

The mere facts that Hilary had known the murdered man, had come secretly to Hangover House to meet him, had left him a few minutes prior to his death, might explain her behavior both before and after his body was discovered.

Sidonia's account of the incidents of the night could very well be a fabric of lies, her drunkenness feigned. She was tough as the Lord makes them, and by no means unclever. So far as he knew (and upon this point he would ask McGraw to show him any additional evidence the police might have) there was nothing to prove that Sidonia had not committed the murder!

If, as appeared to be the case, she had made a getaway, her reason for doing so was obvious.

The evidence stolen from beside the dead man had been in her handbag and not in Hilary's. Sidonia had only just learned that it was missing!

It was a theory to make him drunk with hope.

Had his red herring accidentally led the pack to the real fox?

"I'm further than ever, Elfie, from knowing what to do." Hilary's soft voice held a note of sheer despair.

She and Elfie sat on the teak bench by the weed-covered pond, watching a dragon fly like an emerald tie-pin darting over nearly invisible water. Miss Elphinstowe raised her head and stared up the slope. Peter and Storm Kennedy, with Inspector Hawley, walked back toward the house.

"Bill Kennedy wanted to talk to you. He didn't get a chance."

"I know." Hilary nodded unhappily. "I wanted to talk to *him*."

Elfie glanced aside.

"Have you made up your mind yet to tell him?"

Hilary grasped her hand. Hilary's palm was dry and hot.

"Oh, Elfie! It's the most frightful thing I have ever tried to do! I told you I got as far as admitting that we—knew one another; that I had lied about it. Even to tell him that much nearly killed me. Those steady blue eyes look as though nothing would hurt them so much as hypocrisy. Then I said (he asked me) that I had just left the man I came to meet when you both saw me running out of that room."

"But you mentioned nobody's name?"

"No. He said he would rather not know the name. You see why? He didn't want to have to lie about it. I know there's something—something urgent—he's anxious to tell me, or to ask me."

"He probably knows that the sleepy Scotland Yard lad who's very wide awake has found out who you are."

"He's sure to have found out, Elfie. Peter would have given it away, quite innocently. What terrifies me is that we haven't been questioned yet. As far as I can make out, everybody else has had an interview. Oh, Elfie dear! It's an awful situation!"

"It is," Elfie agreed gruffly. "Bloody awful. Our little deception might have worked if this gimlet-eyed C.I.D. lad hadn't come on the scene. It will never work with *him*.

The pair of us will be given a free ride in a Black Maria to Brixton Prison."

"Elfie, don't!"

"I believe they feed 'em better nowadays. And I'm starving for a square meal, however plain."

"You're a wonderful pal, Elfie. I could kick myself for dragging you into this thing."

"We couldn't foresee how it was going to end, dear. Yet, that Egyptian lunatic certainly warned me, earlier on. He advised me, most earnestly, to go home. His actual words were, 'Fly from this evil house.'"

"Whatever did you say?"

"I offered him ten shillings. He returned it with a pound note of his own, and requested me very sweetly to send both to the Red Cross."

Hilary clasped her hands between her knees, a characteristic pose, and stared down at rank grass growing around the bench.

"I am afraid of that man," she said in a low voice. "I feel he knows the truth about everything that happened last night."

"Certainly a bit of a mystery," Elfie agreed. "I suppose he's one of Joan Faraway's discoveries. But as Joan pushed off without as much as a sailor's farewell, I hadn't a chance to ask her."

"She was mad about Peter and that singing woman."

"H'm. It now appears that the singing woman has taken French leave. Though how the hell she got out beats me."

They were silent for a long time, Hilary staring down abstractedly, and Elfie watching a swift activity break upon this formerly drowsy scene. The early morning breeze had almost died away and the day promised to be warm. Police were moving all about the grounds, exploring bypaths and peering into thickets. Sudden racket of a motorcycle marked the progress of a dispatch rider along that narrow lane which came out near the back gate.

But Hilary never looked up.

"Elfie," she said, at last, "when the time comes, I suppose I shall have to make a clean breast of it?"

Elfie put her arm around the bowed shoulders.

"We shall have no choice, my dear. This is where we face the music. . . ."

"Elfie! I feel so ashamed, I hate my cowardly soul for bringing this—humiliating thing upon *you!* I don't believe you ever told a lie in your life, until you got mixed up in my rotten affairs! Elfie, darling, I can never forgive myself!"

"Shut up, or you'll get a bang on the head!"

"It seems to be my fate to do things to make the people I love most—despise me. I had to hide from Father when he called last night. I just couldn't meet him. Only because I know how dead straight he is. Sometimes—ever so many times—I have been ashamed to look you in the face. And now . . ."

"And now there's another angel joined the shining ranks—Bill Kennedy. Tell me you're ashamed to look Bill in the face and I'll really lose my wool! Listen, Larry (I only call you Larry when I'm angry. It's what *he* used to call you), you have been a heaven-inspired little idiot, and your own enemy. You have done the maddest things. You're as passionately wayward as a young mule, and now you have run into a stone wall."

Hilary raised tearless gray eyes to the older woman. "Elfie, what shall I do?"

"No need to ask *me*. And don't talk rot about your cowardly soul. You fell in love with Bill Kennedy the first day you met him, and he's in love with you. I know you, my dear. So, I know what you'll do. You will tell him the truth. You wouldn't have an hour's peace of mind until he knew it. You'd rather lose him."

Hilary's chin was firm as she looked up the sloping wilderness toward Hangover House.

"Do you think," she asked quietly, "I shall be arrested?"

"It's not impossible. I shall ask for an adjoining cell. . . ."

"Stay here in this room." McGraw's droopy gaze rested for a moment on Sample's rugged head. "Door doesn't lock. Going to make a tour of inspection."

He went out.

Hawley was in the long corridor with Storm Kennedy.

"All surrounding stations notified," said Hawley, sadly. "I don't think a woman wearing full evening dress and a sable cape has much chance to get through."

"Don't you?" McGraw drawled. He turned to Kennedy. "Looks as though you had something here. If Sidonia is in on this thing she has a hundred per cent more savvy than I gave her credit for."

Storm Kennedy smiled.

"Has she left her autograph on the gold case?"

"She has not. Been handled by someone experienced enough to use a handkerchief, or something of the sort. And we know nothing of this vocalist's background. Do you?"

"Less than nothing." Kennedy relaxed. Hilary's fingerprints were *not* there! "Have you opened the case?"

McGraw chewed reflectively.

"Going to ask *you* to try, presently. Meanwhile, sent to King's Riding for an alleged expert. If all fail, must smash it. Where's Mr. Pike?"

They had been walking toward the paneled hall. As they entered it, Larkhall Pike confronted them. A police sergeant stood beside him. The Major's parchment features were contorted with anger.

"It seems, Chief Inspector," he snarled, "that even at my Spartan meals I must be interrupted. I have never used influence to further my fortunes. If I had, I might be better off. But I have some slight acquaintance with the present Commissioner of Metropolitan Police, and, by God, sir, he shall hear of this!"

Even the imperturbable McGraw found himself temporarily silenced. Through the scarecrow outfit of pajamas and rusty dressing-gown, the Major's ferocious truculence shone, a searing flame. But Storm Kennedy saw an opening for soothing treatment—and for a hint to McGraw.

"I didn't know we had a mutual ally in Sir John." He smiled at Pike. It was a smile hard to resist. "The Commissioner is an old friend of my father's."

"Indeed, Mr. Kennedy?" Larkhall Pike swallowed as though he had a sore throat. "We were formerly brother officers. He went up, and I went down. Eggs are scarce in this merrie England today, but perhaps I may venture to defy the Food Ministry and boil two more." He glared at McGraw. "What do you want, sir?"

The Chief Inspector glanced aside at Storm Kennedy. He had not missed the implication which lay in that word "ally."

"Want you to be good enough to tell me how an important witness has disappeared, although all exits guarded. Some other way out?"

"There are walls. Men, as well as monkeys, have been known to climb them. Foxes penetrate occasionally at other points, through gaps in the netting. But if you say you have constables posted at both ends of Hangover Lane, I assume your missing witness would have been challenged."

McGraw nodded.

"What about the south side?"

"On the south the ground adjoins the property of Sir Nicholas Porter. It was formerly part of the Hangover estate. The boundary is a barbed-wire entanglement in a deep ditch. Sir Nicholas and I are not on speaking terms. The man is a vulgar city upstart."

"I've had that side thoroughly examined, Chief Inspector," said Hawley. "It's as Mr. Pike says—impassable."

"Take the north side," McGraw pronounced. "Obliged for your co-operation, Mr. Pike."

The party of three (Storm Kennedy had attached himself, uninvited) went out across the courtyard to the entrance gates. McGraw signaled for the gates to be unlocked and as this was done, the trio became surrounded by waiting reporters. Cars choked the lane. Cameras clicked. Notebooks appeared . . .

"Nothing for you, boys," drawled the Chief Inspector. "So don't bother me. When I'm ready to talk I'll say so." He set out with long springy strides, stopped, turned. "And don't follow me about."

Several enthusiasts who had started to do so, fell back.

"There's one point," said Hawley gloomily, "to which I'd like to draw your attention. Where the wall's partly broken away."

"How far down?" Storm Kennedy asked.

"About halfway between the lodge and the back gate."

As they walked along the lane—and it was necessary to walk fast in order to keep up with the long-legged McGraw—Kennedy was thinking, intensively. He had recognized the fact that they were proceeding parallel with that tangled path on the other side of the wall which he had explored earlier. He even remembered the gap to which Hawley referred. The wall was built of some kind of soft local stone, and ivy had dislodged several blocks, so that a number had fallen from place. They lay, already overgrown with weeds, in the thicket which bordered the path.

A few minutes walking (as McGraw walked) brought them to the spot.

"You see"—Hawley pointed—"the ground is soft, and there are clear tire marks. It looks to me as though a car had stood here, close up to the wall, and not so long ago."

"I think I can give you the time, approximately," Kennedy volunteered.

McGraw, standing on tiptoes, both hands clutching the stones, was trying to see over the edge of the gap. As Kennedy spoke, he dropped back and gave him a swift glance.

"How's that?"

"You will remember asking me to go and talk to Mr. Pike? Well, as I was on my way to look for him, I heard a car being driven, very cautiously, along this lane. I thought nothing of it then, but I see, now, that it may have been important."

McGraw's eyes were lowered as he consulted his wrist watch.

"Give me a buck up," he said to Hawley, and indicated the gap.

Hawley and Storm Kennedy shared the lift, until the Chief Inspector knelt in the jagged opening, his head moving right and left. A few moments only he remained there, then rose upright, turned and jumped down.

"Fallen blocks on the other side. Someone strong enough could have hauled her up, all right."

"Probably stood on the roof of his car," Kennedy suggested.

McGraw stared at tire marks in the lush grass, then looked at Kennedy.

"Which way was the car going?"

Storm Kennedy hesitated.

"Hard to say. My impression was—this way."

He pointed west.

McGraw's half-opened eyes were turned toward Hawley. "Same man on duty at back gate?"

"Yes." Hawley nodded. "Been on since seven this morning."

"Better talk to him."

They proceeded. And a few minutes later came in sight of the back gate, where a constable whom Kennedy recognized as the man who had spoken to him earlier stood beside an Austin seven. He saluted Inspector Hawley. But it was McGraw who spoke.

"Car came down Hangover Lane at about eleven-ten this morning. Passed you. What were your orders?"

The constable, a good-looking young Irishman, glanced once at Hawley and then answered nervously:

"Inspector's orders were, sir, to challenge anyone trying to leave the grounds or coming down the lane."

"Remember the car I mean?"

"Yes, sir. An old Buick."

"Who was driving?"

"A newspaperman, sir. He showed me his press pass. He said he couldn't get into Hangover House and was trying to find the nearest call-box to report to his paper."

"Name?"

The constable produced a small notebook.

"James Findlater, of the *Evening Herald*."

"Anybody with him?"

The constable frowned, thoughtfully.

"Well, nobody on the front seat, sir, and nobody in the back, except . . ."

"Except what?"

"I remember there was a dark topcoat, or that's what it looked like, lying piled up on the floor. I'll admit I didn't give it any particular attention."

"Not your fault."

McGraw turned and walked in at the gate. As Storm Kennedy followed, his glance sought the bench below the laburnum. But it was deserted.

"A getaway, Chief Inspector," he said. "Better check on Mr. Findlater. Sidonia, muffled in sables, may have been under that dark topcoat . . ."

18

A HAWTHORN tree stood in a secluded corner of the garden not far from an apple orchard. Its aged majesty was surrounded by a rustic seat. In spring, no doubt, it made a picture to delight a painter's eye, a trysting place for lovers. To this spot Mrs. Muller had retired, hoping to remain unobserved.

In repose, there was something tragic in her dark beauty. Or a haggardness which marked small, piquant features may have been due to a nervous ordeal which few women could have suffered unmoved. Often she glanced, furtively, toward an opening in a high, ragged yew hedge which concealed this restful hideaway from the lawns or from anyone standing on the distant terrace.

She had just two cigarettes left in her case, and now she decided to light one of them. In the act of doing so, she paused. The tiny flame of her lighter flickered, and went out.

"Hullo!" It was a voice she had learned to dread. "Er—I've been searching for you everywhere—Delilah."

Mrs. Muller snapped the lighter into action again, lighted her cigarette, and looked up.

Mr. Lovelace stood in the opening, balancing a cup and saucer.

"Have you?" she spoke coolly. "Well, here I am. I found it oppressive up there. This is a shady spot."

"It's—er—delightful. I don't suppose I should ever have found it, if—er—I hadn't been looking for *you*." He came across and placed cup and saucer on the seat. "I'm afraid this coffee is quite cold."

"Thank you, all the same."

She forced a smile. This unwanted cavalier was, perhaps, rather pathetic. She must try to be generous.

Lovelace sat down, and Mrs. Muller bravely sipped the gray and gruesome potion.

"Perhaps—er—you like cold coffee?"

"Iced—yes. Don't you?"

"Er—I don't think I ever tasted it iced. Please tell me if it's going to bore you terribly if I go on from—er—where I left off."

"It could not possibly bore me," she declared.

Indeed, Mr. Lovelace's conversation had reduced her to such a record low that further boredom was out of the question. He bent forward, earnestly. His spectacles glittered.

"Don't think I'm impertinent, Delilah, but you're French, aren't you?"

"No, I am not French. But does it matter?"

"I thought that might account for the fact that you're—er—so fascinating. I mean—your voice."

"I am glad you like my voice."

"Oh, I love it! I think it's the sympathy in your voice that—er—gives me the courage to talk to you about myself."

Mrs. Muller had draped her wrap behind her. She now reclined against it, one ivory arm extended along the back of the seat, her long, dark eyes half-closed in resignation. Lovelace's glance lingered for a moment on slim jeweled fingers and then returned to the provocative face.

"You see—er—you're so wonderful. You seem to be all

the beautiful women of poetry—er—in one, as it were. So I know you will understand if I tell you that *I* am two persons, as well."

It was not crystal clear, but Mrs. Muller said nothing.

"Poetry, and—er—music, don't pay awfully well, you know. A man has to—er—find some other job to keep him going."

"What a pity," she murmured, and flicked ash from her cigarette.

"Yes—it is a pity . . ."

Mr. Lovelace became suddenly silent. A change had crept over Mrs. Muller's face. She was staring past him, as if at once fascinated and repelled—and her gaze rested on the opening in the yew hedge. Lovelace turned, peering in the same direction.

Mohammed Ibn Lahûn stood there, placidly watching them. Finding himself to be observed, he bowed in his ceremonious manner, and was gone as silently as he had come.

"That man frightens me, for some reason." Mrs. Muller's husky voice was low pitched. "Don't leave me alone with him, Mr. . . ."

"Allen . . ."

"Allen . . . He spoke to me last night, just before—I had to go and look at the body. I felt as though I lay naked on a dissecting table."

"I'm—er—terribly sorry he upsets you. Rather a fishy character, in my opinion. . . ."

Voices became audible beyond the yew hedge. One, the softly musical voice of Mohammed, the other that flat monotone which characterized Sergeant Sample. A moment later, the sergeant stepped through the opening. He still wore his blue raincoat which he had neglected to remove since his arrival.

"I've been looking for *you*," he announced.

His remark was addressed to Mr. Lovelace, who sprang nervously to his feet.

"Oh, well, I'm here."

"Certain questions about a certain book . . ."

"Er—quite so. I quite agree. But not now, if you don't mind."

Sample nodded.

"Better come along. The Chief Inspector is waiting."

Mr. Lovelace focused a desperate glance upon Mrs. Muller.

"If—er—I have the chance—Delilah—may I see you again?"

"Of course," she smiled slightly. "In any case you can find me at the Hyde Park Hotel."

Mrs. Muller watched the two until they became swallowed up by the gap in the tall hedge. And they had disappeared for no more than a few seconds when Mohammed walked through. Mrs. Muller sat quite still. He crossed to her slowly, his gait graceful and leisurely.

"I have returned, Mrs. Muller," he said, the soft eyes gentle but compelling, "to speak to you in friendship. There are matters upon which I may be able to advise you. . . ."

The phone in Larkhall Pike's study had become a busy line.

James Findlater, it seemed, was really attached to the *Evening Herald*. News-hungry reporters outside the locked gates all knew him, knew his old Buick. Two of them had seen him slip away and drive along the nearly impracticable lane. He was said to be brilliant, but crazy. He had once served a prison sentence of fourteen days—rather than pay a fine. Serious drinker. Suspected Communist.

An alert was flashed to all points north, south, east and west of Hangover House.

Sidonia, according to the entertainment department of Jarretts, had recently been employed by Sammy Sams' Rhythm Seven as a vocalist. They believed her to be American. Mr. Sams, who might know more about her, couldn't be located. His band, with Sidonia, was programmed by the B.B.C. to broadcast at 2.30 that afternoon. . . .

Storm Kennedy wondered what had become of Hilary. He couldn't see her from the terrace and had failed to find her anywhere in the house. He was on his way out to the courtyard when he met Mrs. Muller coming in. She glanced down at her mink wrap, extended her hands and shrugged resignedly.

"Neither the occasion nor the temperature for furs, Mr. Kennedy!"

"I agree," he said, with a smile.

"But I went out there to speak to my driver, who has been waiting, I am told, for hours—and I didn't want to be photographed in décolleté in broad daylight!"

"He had been fogbound, I suppose?"

"Yes. The poor man spent the night in his car," she sighed. "Isn't it too provoking to be kept locked up like this? I cannot even call the Hyde Park, where I am staying, to let them know I haven't run away without paying the bill!"

Kennedy laughed outright. Mrs. Muller's dark eyes betrayed an admirable sense of humor. That husky note in her voice lent strange music to her words.

"Perhaps," he suggested, "the Chief Inspector might be induced to let you go. Shall I ask him?"

"Oh, Mr. Kennedy, that would be a truly Christian act! The Chief Inspector appalls me. I feel, when he speaks to me, as if I were back in the days of the Spanish Inquisition. My faithful cavalier, Mr. Lovelace, was summoned to an interview and I haven't seen him since. Do you think he has been arrested?"

"Your guess as good as mine, Mrs. Muller. But I can try to find out. Do you know him well?"

"Good heavens, no!" She laughed. "I had never seen him in my life until last night, since when I have seen him wherever I turn! He was interrupted in some revelation concerning his mysterious past when the sergeant came for him. And that appeared to upset him terribly."

"You mean he seemed worried?"

"Yes—very. I can't think what is bothering him—I mean, more than the rest of us are bothered."

Storm Kennedy was disposed to believe her. He dismissed a former, vague theory that Mrs. Muller and Lovelace might be secretly associated. In the first place, Mrs. Muller was cultured, although her nationality puzzled him. Mr. Lovelace was not.

"You have heard, of course, Mrs. Muller, that our songbird has deserted us?"

"Of course! Isn't it exciting? Do the police really think . . . ?"

"She has left them little choice. Why run away?"

"But she will be caught?"

"No doubt of it. A desperate try."

"Then, do *you* believe she did it?"

Kennedy hesitated.

"Considered coldly, her alibi is no better than mine, or yours, or anybody's. But, although she may be a poor singer, if she's guilty she is certainly an extraordinarily good actress."

"I quite agree with you. She told me, just before her disappearance, that she was going for a walk."

"Did you actually see her start?"

"Certainly. She went down those steps outside the Powder Room—the steps she had fallen down last night. And she seemed to be in a hurry."

This supported the evidence pointing to Sidonia's escape

over the wall; for the steps were one of the routes to that brambly path which skirted the grounds on the north.

"Was she wearing her sables?" Kennedy asked lightly.

Mrs. Muller flashed him an amused smile.

"She was carrying them!"

Storm Kennedy nodded.

"I am now growing really curious," he declared, "concerning the fate of your Mr. Lovelace. . . ."

And Kennedy's assumed concern even if real would not have been misplaced. At about this time the fate of Mr. Lovelace hung in the balance.

He sat, uncomfortably, on the extreme edge of a chair set before the desk in Larkhall Pike's study. McGraw watched him across the desk. Sergeant Sample watched him over McGraw's shoulder.

There had been some conversation, and now an uneasy silence had fallen. Presently, "Satisfied you didn't turn the light out," McGraw drawled. "Query A remains unanswered, Sergeant. But, before you go, one or two points to clear up. Described yourself to Superintendent Croker as a lyric writer and composer. Correct?"

"Quite correct. Er—certainly."

"Professional?"

"Well—er—I've been published."

"Any titles you could mention?" Sample intoned.

"Titles? Yes. Mrs. Muller was playing a published song of mine, last night—after the band had gone: 'Summer Is Winter When You're Not Around.'"

"Good title," McGraw pronounced. His eyes were closed. "Very good. But first point I should like to clear up is why you didn't give your real name to the Superintendent."

"Perhaps," Sample interjected, "you know the penalty for obstructing a police officer in the execution of his duty?"

Mr. Lovelace was mauling the relics of a white tie. His

pale face looked damp; so did his spectacles. His winged collar had given the whole thing up as useless.

"Er—if I may say something—I came in to—er—try to explain what happened. I intended to make my own position clear. But—er—you took me up on other things." He delved in a pocket of his tailcoat and produced a sheet of music. "I am known—er—professionally, as Allen Lovelace. I always think of myself as Allen Lovelace."

He offered the item to Chief Inspector McGraw. But Chief Inspector McGraw's eyes remained closed. The offering was ignored.

"Is that so?" McGraw murmured. "But according to your charge sheet, or inventory of fittings and refreshments provided, or whatever it's called, Jarretts think of you as Percy Bailey. Correct?"

Sergeant Sample passed a black-bound book across the desk to Mr. Lovelace.

"Your property. We've done with it."

Mr. Lovelace accepted the book and put it in his pocket.

"Clear to me what happened," McGraw continued, without troubling to open his eyes. "Fell hard for Mrs. Muller. Not blaming you. Attractive woman. Didn't want to blow prospects sky high by telling her you were the man from Jarretts. Said your name was Lovelace. Had to stick to it. Not unsympathetic, are we, Sergeant Sample?"

"*You're* not, sir."

McGraw's eyes became momentarily visible.

"Obliged for correction . . . Idiotic behavior, Mr. Bailey. If I took a different view of it, might prove serious. Employed by Jarretts to manage these out-of-town parties?"

"Yes, Inspector."

"Supposed to mix, unobtrusively, with guests; see that wheels run smoothly?"

"Just so, Inspector. Just so."

"Not supposed to make passes at ladies who happen to be present?"

"Allen Lovelace" pulled out a soiled handkerchief from his pocket and dried his forehead.

"Swear that the evidence you gave to Superintendent Croker and have given to me is the truth, the whole truth, and nothing but the truth? Think. You're in danger."

"I—I swear, solemnly!"

McGraw nodded.

"Checked up on you with your firm. Explained your absence not your own fault. Got a car outside, haven't you?"

"Yes—yes, I have."

McGraw opened his eyes and looked fixedly at Mr. Bailey. Then, he spoke again.

"Beat it!"

19

Storm Kennedy stood in the courtyard, wondering what had become of Mr. Lovelace's Morris, when the black wagon was driven in. Two men jumped down and dragged a stretcher from inside.

He turned and went in. The absence of Hilary and Elfie began to puzzle him. In the lobby he almost collided with Sergeant Sample, hurrying out.

"Just a moment, Mr. Kennedy. You're wanted."

Kennedy halted. Sample stopped the men with the stretcher.

"Stand by. Body to be moved later. Wait for the Chief Inspector's orders."

"What's happening, Sergeant?" Kennedy asked, as Sample rejoined him.

"Conference. We don't want to be interrupted. This way."

As always, the paneled hall, scene of last night's revelry, was deserted. Here, once, cavaliers and their lady loves had paced the stately minuet. Here, more recently, their descendants who still had the heart and the means to play among the ruins had danced to the hot rhythm of Sammy Sams. Beyond three opened windows, sunshine lent a wild beauty to a wilderness which had been a pleasure garden. There was no one in the long corridor.

Sample opened the study door and stood aside to allow Storm Kennedy to enter first.

On the threshold of the darkened room, Kennedy checked.

McGraw sat behind the desk; in a chair placed before it, Miss Elphinstowe; and in a third chair close to the draped French windows he saw Hilary. She was watching him from shadow. He couldn't read her expression.

"Be so good as to sit there, Mr. Kennedy."

McGraw indicated a worn leather settee near the door by which he had come in.

Kennedy sat down. Sample shut the door and crossed to his usual place at the Chief Inspector's elbow. That museum quality which pervaded the room seemed more marked than usual. Kennedy wished he had had something to smoke.

"May perhaps have wondered," McGraw went on, "what had become of these two ladies. Well, I held them incommunicado for awhile. Had one of the locked rooms opened for their accommodation."

"Why?"

"That's what I want to know!" Elfie growled.

"Simple," McGraw assured her. "Happen to be aware that Mr. Kennedy is interested in your affairs—yours and Lady Hilary's."

Kennedy darted a glance into the shadows. But Hilary sat motionless. Evidently she had already learned that her identity was known to the Chief Inspector.

"What of it?" Kennedy challenged.

"Didn't want any more conspiracy," McGraw stated bluntly. "Wanted you present when I interviewed these ladies, but didn't want a prepared case. I'm looking for facts." He glanced down at two sheets of paper which lay on the desk. "These statements made before Superintendent Croker are unsatisfactory—apart from a wrong name in one of them."

"That error of judgment I think you understand," Kennedy interrupted.

"Understand it quite well," McGraw replied drily. "Isn't the only error of judgment. For instance, Madame,"—he turned drowsy eyes in Elfie's direction—"you say here that at the time, approximate, of the murder, you came along the corridor outside, and—I quote your own words—'barged right into her'—meaning Lady Hilary. Does that mean she was running, or you were?"

"Well, I suppose she was speeding somewhat."

"Did she appear to be alarmed?"

"Chief Inspector," Kennedy broke in, "may I say a word?"

"In a minute. Want you to hear Miss Elphinstowe's evidence first . . . Did she appear to be alarmed?"

"More fed up than alarmed," Elfie answered gruffly. "I had taken a look outside to see how thick the fog was, and met Mr. Kennedy coming in. I went to tell Hilary that he'd gallantly offered to act as pilot and bumped into her, as I said."

McGraw chewed thoughtfully, then his glance explored the shadows which veiled Hilary. The breeze had died away. Velvet drapes no longer swayed to permit darts of sunshine to enter.

"Where were you coming from, Lady Hilary?" he asked.

"Well"—Hilary's quiet voice was perfectly composed—"it's rather difficult to remember, exactly. I had been on the terrace, outside the Powder Room. I suppose I had just come in, but I can't be sure."

"Better refresh your memory, Lady Hilary. Here's your statement." McGraw took up a typed page. "Pass it over, Sergeant Sample."

Sample took the sheet, and walked across to Hilary, to whom he handed it, and then returned.

"Switch on the light behind you," McGraw suggested. "See better."

Storm Kennedy was on his feet in a flash.

"Let *me* do it!"

But he was too late.

Hilary stood up, stepped to the right-hand side of the French windows and touched a switch set in the frame.

The floor lamp became lighted. . . .

Kennedy sat down, fists clenched. His pulse was racing. He couldn't control it. Sample coughed loudly. McGraw closed his eyes and leaned back in his chair.

"Might cross out Query A, Sergeant Sample," he drawled.

Hilary, who had resumed her seat, looked up. Her face was colorless, but her composure remained unruffled. Light from the standard lamp transformed her hair to liquid gold. She smiled at Storm Kennedy.

"Thank you, Bill," she said softly, and turned to McGraw. "If Query A, Inspector, concerns who switched off the light in this room last night, *I did*. . . . Is that what you wanted to know?"

McGraw's eyes opened widely. The expression on that gaunt, aquiline face, as he stared across at Hilary, was indefinable, except that it curiously resembled one of awe. But all he said was, "Obliged for your co-operation."

"May *I* speak, now, Chief Inspector?" Kennedy asked, urgently.

"Rather hear what else Lady Hilary has to tell us."

But, before Hilary or anyone present could speak, there was a ghostly interruption.

An agonized groan came from somewhere beyond the arched opening at the stairhead. Everyone seated in the study stood up. McGraw swung round on Sample.

"That bedroom door locked?"

"No, sir. Wilson left the key up there with other exhibits after testing for fingerprints. . . . But one of us has been in here ever since . . ."

A dull thud—sound as of shuffling movements shot an icy chill through Storm Kennedy's veins. His spine tingled.

"There can be no one in that room," he said, and wondered at the unfamiliar timbre of his own voice.

"No one *alive*," Sample agreed.

Shuffling continued. To it was added now, a wordless mutter. Storm Kennedy instinctively crossed to Hilary and put his arms about her, as she stood, back to him watching the stairs. He could feel her heart beating hammer-strokes.

Chief Inspector McGraw had got as far as the newel post when an apparition appeared on the stairhead.

It was that of the murdered man, partly enveloped in the sheet which had covered him! His face in color resembled dirty chalk, his eyes blazed feverishly. He began to stagger down.

"*La*"—he whispered, and stretched out one bare arm as if pointing—"*it was La . . .*"

He choked on the unfinished word.

"Geoff!" The name burst, a suppressed shriek, from Hilary's lips. "Oh! Merciful God! *Geoff!*"

The sheeted figure stumbled, fell. McGraw caught him, and eased an inert body to the floor. The Chief Inspector's glance flickered, momentarily, over Hilary, collapsed, now, in Storm Kennedy's arms.

Sergeant Sample ran forward.

"Leave him to me." McGraw's voice was hoarse. "Get a doctor. . . ."

20

A CAR which long ago had earned honorable retirement on the scrap heap, came noisily to rest outside The Effingham Arms, an inn itself a shadow of former splendor, four miles north of King's Riding. The driver scrambled down and stepped back to talk to his passenger.

"Shan't be two minutes, dear."

He turned to go, but a bronzed arm shot out from a sable cape and a grip not lightly discarded seized his loose tweed jacket.

"Take it slow, Jimmy! What goes on? Do you *want* the cops to grab me, or have you got a pain?"

"Neither, Sidonia. But I tell you I won't be two minutes."

Jimmy, a puffy young man whose face and figure were designed as a warning to Johnny Walker, stared angrily through black-rimmed glasses but couldn't shake off that tenacious grip.

"Then you're plain nuthouse! Do I have to tell you we're tailed—or are you aiming at a reward? London is where we're going, and if you figure I'm sitting out on the street . . ."

"Listen, dear. Nobody'll see you. Nobody ever stops here. Better still, come on in and have a drink while . . ."

"If I get out of this hearse it won't be to have a drink. It'll be to attend your funeral!"

Jimmy wrenched free.

"Put a cork in it," he advised, politely.

Turning, he ran up the steps which led to the saloon of The Effingham Arms, jerked the door open and went in.

A stout landlady presiding over an empty bar stood up as he appeared.

"Why! Mr. Findlater! Haven't seen you for a long time."

"Haven't been down this way, Mrs. Sprigg. Double Scotch. Could I use the phone in your back room?"

"With pleasure, Mr. Findlater. Go in. I'll bring you your drink."

"Much obliged."

And Mr. Findlater, who evidently knew the house, opened a door which faced the entrance and seated himself at a phone on a side table in a small, stuffy sitting room. Pulling a notebook from his pocket, he anxiously scanned its pages, his eyes contracted as he peered down in bad light. Then he began to dial a number.

Mrs. Sprigg entered and set a glass and a bottle of soda water beside him, and then retired as quietly as she had come in.

A sound of voices, raised in the adjoining bar, interrupted Mr. Findlater. He replaced the receiver and sat there listening. An expression of anxiety became one of outright terror as he gathered the nature of the conversation. Hurriedly replacing his notebook, and swallowing his Scotch, straight, he crossed the little room to another door, opened it, and looked out into a passage.

There was a staircase on the right, and on the left a private entrance from a side street. He went left, and began very cautiously to open the door. He saw no one in the street and, therefore, stepped out.

He was still holding the knob when a heavy hand fell on his shoulder.

A policeman had been standing against the wall.

"Your name Findlater?"

He twisted around and confronted a six-foot athlete whose face was principally composed of jaw.

"It is. What about it?"

"The Inspector will tell you what about it. Come along o' me."

He was led, gently but undeniably, around the corner to the front of The Effingham Arms. His veteran Buick no longer lingered alone. A police car stood just behind it, and another policeman stood beside the car.

"Here he is," Findlater's captor announced laconically. "Get the Inspector."

But before this second constable could obey, the side door of the inn was heard to bang noisily, and a plain-clothes officer came running around to join them.

"I've got him, sir!"

The Inspector pulled up. He, also, was a big man. (Superintendent Croker prided himself upon the physique of the King's Riding police.)

"Trying to slip away again, were you?" he said, unpleasantly. "That makes it worse. Don't waste time. Where is she?"

"Look here, Inspector . . ."

"And don't try bluster with *me*. Where is she?"

Findlater pointed, vaguely, to his car.

"Trying to be funny?" The Inspector came a step closer. "Where did you drop her?"

"I don't know what you're talking about. I didn't drop her. I left her out here!"

A fierce stare was the only reply, until, wrenching open a door of the police car, "Get in!" came an order like a bark. . . .

A few minutes later, news of the arrest of James Findlater, and of the unaccountable disappearance of Sidonia, came across the wire to Hangover House, interrupting a scene *à trois* among McGraw, Sample and Storm Kennedy. When he had listened to the report from Kings Riding, "Bring him back here at once," McGraw directed, and hung up.

The faded velvet drapes were opened wide. Sunlight mercilessly revealed the untidy dilapidation of Larkhall Pike's study. Shadow had lent its many relics a mystic quality. Seen now, they merely looked their age.

McGraw glanced aside at Sergeant Sample.

"Followed that?"

"Yes, sir—up to a point."

"Findlater admits he's an old acquaintance of this woman's, but holds out that he didn't know there was anything against her. Swears he can't account for her disappearance."

"Then why," Kennedy broke in, "did he help her to escape?"

"Admits she was mad to go. Planned to climb the wall and try to find somebody to interview. Found Sidonia. Known her a long time. Says he fell for it to pick up the story and pull off a scoop for the *Evening Herald*. Think he's lying?"

"Yes," said Sample, pronouncing the word as if it had been a reluctant sentence of death.

"I hope they find her." Kennedy spoke in a low voice.

"So do I," McGraw drawled, "for your sake."

"Why for *my* sake?"

McGraw uncoiled himself from his chair and walked around to lean back against the desk.

"Going to have trouble with present assignment, aren't you? Don't know what link, if any, there is between her and the missing woman, but your client is in this thing up to her neck. Speaking in everybody's interests, what about a straight showdown?"

Storm Kennedy sat still. He even contrived to smile.

"I admit that there are matters which call for explanation, Chief Inspector. For instance, a dead man coming to life."

"Thought you'd try that line," McGraw declared. "Charge of murder inadmissible?"

"Not what I was thinking about. That's a nice point for the lawyers. I had in mind Lady Hilary's pretending that she didn't know the man."

"Not what *I* was thinking about. Had in mind that Lady Hilary must have run into this room directly after attack took place, and switched the light off. Clear?"

"It certainly looks like that."

"Do you know it to be a fact?"

"I don't. But I suspect it to be. She has admitted switching off the light, but not when this occurred."

Storm Kennedy was putting in some hard, swift thinking —for he clearly foresaw the next question. Hilary, whose composure had crumbled when the "dead" man had staggered downstairs, remained in some room recently unlocked by McGraw's orders, in charge of Elfie. The Chief Inspector was prepared to wait.

But that stifled cry of "Geoff" had hopelessly betrayed her. She would be compelled, now, to reveal the man's name. Useless to prevaricate further.

"Any suspicions, Mr. Kennedy, about the victim's identity?"

It had come!

"Yes," Kennedy spoke quietly. "On a former occasion, when this point came up, I didn't know the man's name, and said so. But Lady Hilary's use of the word 'Geoff' has confirmed what was merely a surmise. The dead man (for the hospital report makes it clear, I believe, that he's really dead, now) was Geoffrey Arlington, the celebrated, or rather, notorious, traveler and explorer."

"Ever seen him before?"

"Never."

"Then how do you know?"

McGraw's drawl had become more pronounced. But his eyes were wide open.

"His name was mentioned when I accepted the assignment."

McGraw nodded, half-closed his eyes again.

"Glad you're not holding out on me. Had Lord Glengale on the line. Told me he'd employed you. Didn't tell me any more. On his way down, now. Get the name from his lordship?"

"Yes."

"In what connection was it mentioned?"

Storm Kennedy felt his forehead growing damp. He had an inclination to clench his teeth. He was being forced to blacken the case against Hilary. Vaguely, he became aware of the fact that Sergeant Sample was blowing his nose. But he had himself in hand again.

"Lady Hilary is a wealthy woman, Chief Inspector, and so has been surrounded by parasites, of both sexes. Lord Glengale believed that she had got herself involved in financial difficulties. He believed that her troubles were due to some of these undesirable acquaintances, and he named a number of those whom he suspected. Geoffrey Arlington was one of them."

"Think of any others, Mr. Kennedy?" Sample asked, looking up from his notebook.

The question sounded like a line from the burial service, but it was a very clever question, all the same. McGraw nearly smiled.

"Beside the point to try, Sergeant," Kennedy parried. "There was no other whose name was Geoff."

A brief silence came, and then, "Bit of a coincidence, though," McGraw remarked drily.

"Undoubtedly. But so is the disappearance of Sidonia."

"Any evidence that Sidonia knew this man?"

"None. But I consider her behavior to be more than suspicious."

"Is that so? What do you consider Lady Hilary Bruton's behavior to be?"

"Difficult to explain. But I believe she can explain it."

"Feel sure she can. What's more, she'll have to." McGraw turned to Sample. "Call headquarters for everything on Geoffrey Arlington."

Sample nodded and took up the phone. Storm Kennedy ignored a monotonous monologue which followed and concentrated on this maddening problem, growing tighter every minute.

But, try as he might, he couldn't get his ideas into focus. Was Sidonia really involved in the case? If so, Sidonia must be a consummate actress. He had decided already that Hilary's misstatements might be explained by her anxiety to conceal the connection (whatever this might be) between herself and Arlington. If, shortly after a secret meeting, some person at present not identified had attempted the man's murder, Hilary's anxiety would have grown greater.

Could this person be Sidonia?

Presently, he spoke in a low voice. (Sample was busy on the phone.)

"Sidonia's real name, I seem to recall, is Julia Sidney. Therefore, she can't be the person whom Arlington tried to indicate."

McGraw's sleepy regard was turned upon him.

"Thinking of the words, 'It was La——'?"

"I am, yes."

"So am I," McGraw drawled. "Not forgetting Sidonia

may have a pet name. Other La's are Larkhall Pike and Lahûn."

Sergeant Sample had just hung up.

"Two dark horses, sir," he intoned, like a parson giving out the name of a hymn to his congregation.

McGraw closed his eyes entirely, and then, "Ever hear of a tailor called Simon Artz, Mr. Kennedy?" he asked.

"I don't know if Simon Artz do tailoring," Kennedy confessed. "But they sell hand-me-downs of all sorts. Everything else as well. Why?"

"Arlington was wearing a jacket with that label."

Storm Kennedy's expression grew keenly alert.

"Then he had come from Port Said, in all probability."

"Is that so? Link with Egypt, again."

"What's the other link, Chief Inspector?"

McGraw paused for a moment before replying.

"Other link—" he seemed to be thinking of something else—"is an enamel, or cloisonné necklace which Mr. Pike has identified as late Eighteenth Theban, whatever that may mean. Found fifty yards from the terrace—with Arlington's fingerprints on it. Signs of a woman's high heels there, but when the grass was cut back, could make nothing of them . . ."

Storm Kennedy had not left the study more than two minutes when Inspector Hawley rapped on the door, opened, and announced, "Mr. Horace Merlin, from Kings Riding."

Mr. Merlin came in—a tall, thin man. He had the face, and the manners, of a comedian. He wore a chessboard jacket and flannel trousers, and on the threshold he paused, as if making a stage entrance, twirling a checked cap and grinning at McGraw and then at Sample.

"At your service, gentlemen. What can Merlin do for you?"

McGraw studied him under drooping lids.

"Come from Superintendent Croker, don't you, Mr. Merlin?"

Mr. Merlin bowed, humorously.

"Always at the Super's disposal, sir. He invariably engages me for the many charity affairs organized by the King's Riding police. Why be downhearted? Merlin's magic maketh merry."

"Thanks for the tip." McGraw yawned. "Told you can open anything that's shut, from a snuff-box to the door of a prison cell."

"Indubitably. That which is closed opens at my command. In the presence of His Majesty, the King . . ."

"Not here today, Mr. Merlin. Try your open sesame on this, in *my* presence."

From a desk drawer, McGraw took out the gold case and handed it to Merlin. The magician laid it in the palm of a large hand and regarded it. He closed his hand, opened it again—and the case had vanished.

"Sorry, gentlemen! But gold does slip through one's fingers." He apparently recovered it from an empty inkwell. "Now, let me see."

McGraw leaned back, lids wearily lowered. But Sergeant Sample watched the man of magic with naively wide eyes. Merlin was studying the exhibit closely. He pulled, twisted and shook. The case remained obstinately shut.

He took a pair of glasses from a pocket of his jacket, adjusted them and bent to peer at the puzzle. He moved it gently with long, sensitive fingers as it lay in his large palm. He finally inspected the flat end, then; suddenly, "Eureka!" he exclaimed, and held the thing aloft in theatrical triumph. "You are fortunate, gentlemen! Who but Merlin could have helped you? This is from the workshop of Silverston. Not more than six are in existence. The immortal Houdini possessed such a piece, and often wagered a hundred guineas that no one present but himself could open it. . . . Behold!"

Came a faint click . . .

The gold cap hung loose on its chain. The case had opened magically in Merlin's extended hand!

"Put it down here!"

McGraw was on his feet, drooping lids raised.

"Certainly. Shall I first reclose it—and challenge Scotland Yard?"

"No. Send the account to me. Good day, Mr. Merlin. Scotland Yard obliged for your co-operation."

And when Horace Merlin, grinning and bowing, had gone, McGraw and Sample bent over the desk.

The Chief Inspector with a steady hand tipped out a glass object onto the blotting pad. Then, using a long ivory bodkin which he had found among Larkhall Pike's desk equipment, he delicately explored the interior.

"Space down there for something else. But it's gone. Get Wilson with fingerprint outfit. See what this is?" He pointed, but didn't touch. "Recently used. Still wet."

"Yes, sir." Sample's voice sounded hushed. "But where does it get us?"

The object which had been concealed in the gold case was a hypodermic syringe. . . .

21

Storm Kennedy walked on, aimlessly. He had no particular goal in view, but just felt impelled to walk and think.

Foremost in his mind was the approaching interview with Lord Glengale. What account had he to give of his stewardship? He had accomplished exactly nothing. Even without the additional datum afforded by Hilary's blood-stained handkerchief, evidence to justify her arrest was piling up formidably.

She had confessed to entering the study at a time which could only have been shortly after the attack on Arlington. Her action in switching off the light was susceptible of one explanation alone. She had wanted to avoid being seen.

The dead man had held some mysterious threat over her; had used it as an instrument of blackmail. This, Glengale knew, and would be forced to admit.

But Kennedy obstinately refused to entertain the idea that Hilary had struck Arlington with a dagger. It simply didn't make sense. The defense, he knew, would rest upon a split hair—murder or manslaughter.

By what miracle a man certified as dead by a competent surgeon had returned to life, if only briefly, he simply couldn't conceive. He, himself, had seen not a few dead men, and McGraw was experienced in homicide. Both had accepted the fact that life was extinct. . . .

What little he knew about Geoffrey Arlington he had learned from Lord Glengale and from a brief telephone conversation with a fellow clubman who, he happened to remember, had once spoken of meeting him. This, just before setting out from London.

Arlington was a world wanderer and explorer. He had lectured extensively and had published a number of books of travel. Latterly, he had lain under a cloud. There had been some scandal, details of which Kennedy's friend couldn't recall. But he knew that Arlington had been asked to resign from the Travellers and other clubs. . . . "In my opinion, Bill," he had summed up, "the fellow's a bit of a Baron Munchausen. I think he was caught out on his account of discoveries around the headwaters of the Amazon. Has a rotten name with women, too. Not a bad looker, and cashes in on it. . . ."

And where, Kennedy asked himself, does Sidonia fit into the picture?

Assuming, as he must, that she was an accomplished actress, that her account of the night's happenings had been pure fabrication, what could have happened between her and Arlington to have provoked that murderous attack? Had he been her lover? Had jealousy—perhaps of Hilary —driven her to it?

If, as her flight strongly suggested, Sidonia was the culprit, then Sidonia must also be the woman who had risked so much to recover the gold case.

Kennedy wondered if the expert from King's Riding had turned up, if had succeeded in solving the puzzle of the fastener. But, now, another puzzle had intruded itself into the mystery. What was the significance of this ancient Egyptian necklace found on the lawn? Whose were those footmarks imprinted in the soft turf? An ornament so unusual in any case should prove to be a valuable link in the chain of evidence.

And at this point in his profitless meditations Storm Kennedy found himself near that gap in the wall by which Sidonia had made her escape.

He pulled up sharply.

Someone was climbing over from the lane!

Storm Kennedy had not consciously selected this path, in fact, aroused from his reflections, was surprised to find himself there. In its semi-darkness he stood, watching.

A pair of long, thin legs clad in corduroy trousers dangled down, one extended foot groping for the nearest block of fallen masonry. This found, the rest of the climber came into view—a man wearing an old Army tunic which had been dyed blue, a red handkerchief around his neck.

He descended with remarkable agility, turned—and stared.

It was Larkhall Pike!

"Hullo, sir!"

"Is that Mr. Kennedy?"

The Major's pince-nez dangled grotesquely on the black ribbon as he peered into shadows.

"It is."

"I feared it might be one of those damned policemen. They made me open the green bedroom, in which generations of my family have been born, in which Queen Elizabeth slept. Blasted insolence! And so I have taken the minor liberty of leaving my own property by an irregular route in order to borrow McAdam's razor. Had a shave, and exchanged my pajamas for his spare suit. His cottage lies just across the lane."

The Major's sense of propriety may have been gratified by the exchange, but McAdam's spare suit, apart from its originality, didn't fit him.

"I don't blame you, sir. This imprisonment is getting intolerable."

"It's a lot of poppycock, Mr. Kennedy—poppycock, sir! Anyone in Great Britain last night might have murdered the fellow—quite apart from the circumstance that nobody knows who the fellow is."

"His name has just come to light, as a matter of fact: Geoffrey Arlington."

"Geoffrey Arlington!"

Larkhall Pike lent to the words a quality of loathing quite peculiar.

"Yes. Did you know him?"

Pike had begun to walk back toward the house. Storm Kennedy had determinedly fallen into step beside him, as well as he could manage on that narrow, bramble-strewn path.

"I never spoke to him in my life. And I saw him only once—alive. It was when he had the brazen audacity to read a paper on secret passages in the Great Pyramid before the Royal Society. Mr. Kennedy,"—he pulled up, glared—"every word of his paper was fictional! No such passages have ever been discovered. Pshaw!"

"You think," Kennedy suggested, as they walked on again, "that Arlington was an impostor?"

"He was a rogue, sir! He merited his end. His exploration of the upper reaches of the Amazon was equally bogus. In my opinion, and in that of others better qualified to judge, the man never *saw* the upper reaches of the Amazon!"

"You failed to recognize him again?"

"Quite. My memories were vague, and his contorted face didn't help them."

"I suppose a man like that would have many enemies," Kennedy mused.

"Deservedly, sir! I was one of them. On my representation he was called upon to relinquish his fellowship of the Royal Geographical Society. . . ."

When Storm Kennedy parted from Larkhall Pike and watched him striding toward the kitchen quarters which were his only refuge, lean ankles protruding far below McAdam's corduroys, he turned along that overgrown path which led tortuously to the lower garden.

He had found more food for thought, and must try to digest it before facing whatever new ordeal might be in store for him.

Clouds gathered to mock the promise of a sunny day. When he plunged, desperately, into the wilderness of overgrown shrubbery, he grew aware of a darkening. Anxiety for Hilary became agonizing. Whatever her explanation, it could never amount to an alibi. If only he could see her, talk to her. If only he knew the *truth*.

One hope, and one hope only, remained: Discovery of the real culprit.

Those singular words of the dying man undoubtedly held a clue. What motive had inspired them? Storm Kennedy inclined to the belief that Arlington had known of Hilary's danger and—one decent act in an indecent life— had tried to pin the crime on the real assassin.

La.

If (which was all but inconceivable) he had meant Larkhall Pike, surely he would have tried to say *Pike?* If (a possibility) he had meant Mohammed Ibn Lahûn, then it seemed unlikely that he would have used the last name without its prefix.

In either case, a woman must be involved, for it was a woman who had stolen the mysterious object found on the dead man. . . .

Unless Larkhall Pike lied!

And whoever had taken the gold case from beside Arlington's body had used some hand covering to avoid leaving fingerprints.

His brain working with a queer, cold precision, Storm Kennedy, unknown to himself, stepped softly, in harmony with subtle thoughts. Silent as an Indian hunter, he moved along the tangled path—paused, awakened and looked. . . .

He was passing behind that rustic summer house in which he had found the gold case. Through crannies in its crazy wall, outlined against light from the entrance, he had seen something move. Trying, consciously now, to retain his silent tread, he crept nearer. He peered inside, checked his breathing.

For what he saw there was dramatic, revealing as a curtain rising on a scene wholly unexpected . . .

The green bedroom referred to by Larkhall Pike may, at some time, have been painted green or draped in green. At present it possessed no definable color scheme, unless faded silk curtains attached to a vast four-poster bed had begun life as green curtains.

Beyond all argument, this impressive bed dominated the room. It could, without crowding, have accommodated a small family. It stood so far above the floor that anyone but an acrobat trying to get into it must have required one of those stepladders which add so much to the discomfort of sleeping-cars. Its vast surface was covered by a quilted satin bedspread—of the same color as the curtains. No doubt this carved and twisted mass of oak was the very couch upon which the royal Tudor virgin had reclined.

Upon neutral walls, blotched in patches to a melancholy sepia, hung several large, melancholy pictures, mercifully faded too. A mighty fir tree grew so close to the house that the green bedroom must always have harbored shadows.

It smelled like a vault. A once fine French carpet had been elderly when Queen Victoria was young.

In one of the recessed windows a spinning wheel attracted the visitor's attention.

There were oak chests, a dust-coated dressing table with nothing on it, a pair of capacious tapestry-covered armchairs.

One of these was occupied by Miss Elphinstowe, the other by Hilary.

"Have a cigarette, dear," Elfie suggested, and held out a yellow packet. "I bought these from a policeman."

Hilary shook her head and smiled.

"What a grand pal you are, Elfie! Whatever should I have done without you?"

Elfie lighted a "gasper."

"You've always been able to play the fool, dear, without help from anybody. This little jamboree is your star turn, to date. If only you had counted ten instead of singing out 'Geoff!'"

"But, Elfie! It was—ghastly! How *can* a dead man come to life again? I thought it was his ghost."

"So did I. But I kept my mouth shut."

"Perhaps you were struck dumb?" Hilary suggested.

"I was! I'm only just recovering. It isn't that the truth wouldn't have had to come out, sooner or later. But you might have picked a better moment. What I mean is this: Instead of confiding the facts to the discretion of Bill Kennedy—who is more than sympathetic—you are going to be carpeted by that terrifying C.I.D. lad with the half-closed eyes."

"But Bill would have had to tell him."

"No doubt. But Bill could have suppressed non-essential details. In fact, I'm sure he would have done."

Hilary didn't speak at once. She was staring at, but perhaps not seeing, a brass clock on a side table. It was exhibited under an inverted glass bowl. It wasn't going. On the evidence afforded by its construction, there seemed to be no reason why it should have gone at any time.

She shuddered slightly.

"This is a gruesome room, Elfie. I feel as though hundreds of people had died in it."

"People die in all sorts of places, Hilary dear. We all have to peg out somewhere. But a scaffold is not my selection. And I'm told that Dartmoor prison is unhealthy for permanent guests. Do you, darling, or don't you, realize that the police have a case against you which no mutton-headed jury could turn down?"

Hilary clasped her hands between her knees, and stared at the worn carpet.

"I quite realize it, Elfie. And I don't care a bit. That's not what bothers me. All I'm worrying about is that I dragged *you* into this mess! Oh, Elfie darling!" Hilary moved so swiftly that she had crossed and was kneeling before the elder woman even as the words were spoken. "Say you forgive me! I'm so utterly miserable."

Bright head bowed, arms thrown about Elfie, Hilary knelt, pathetic in her penitence.

Elfie looked for somewhere to put her cigarette, but failed to find any place. She stabbed it out on the oaken arm of the chair and stroked Hilary's hair. When she spoke, her voice was peculiarly gruff.

"Be quiet, Hilary. I'm ashamed of myself for being so coarse—Dartmoor and all that nonsense. But we have to face facts, darling. That dreadful man (his death hasn't altered my opinion) was the cause of all your troubles. This fact is sure to come out. And that's what the police call a motive."

Hilary knelt in silence, her bowed head resting on Elfie's knees.

"Bill is our only hope." Elfie spoke grimly. "And I'm

afraid the McGraw has a downer on him. But I'm going to ring the bell—if there is one—and say, as a qualified nurse, that you are unfit for a police interview but would be ready to answer any questions put to you by Bill Kennedy, who is a friend."

Hilary pressed her face against Elfie's knees.

"That doesn't mean I shall have to tell him everything —yet?"

"Everything that happened last night."

"He is sure to ask about—Geoffrey."

"Say you were afraid of him. *Why* is nobody's business —except that you'll have to chance explaining it to any man you want to marry. Otherwise, tell Bill the whole story. Then, leave it to him to put the facts before Inspector McGraw. Shall I ring the bell?"

"Yes, darling." It was a small, smothered voice. "Ring the bell, if there is one . . ."

22

Mohammed Ibn Lahûn sat in the summer house. His dark eyes were turned, impassively, in the direction of approaching dark clouds. The opening was cloaked by creepers, but he could see the clouds through their tendrils.

Of all that mixed catch trapped in the police net cast over Hangover House, at this stage of investigations Mohammed made the best showing. His shadowy beard and mustache were more strongly marked, but, on that dusky face, were not inappropriate. His dress clothes appeared to be far less creased than Peter Faraway's, his green turban was correctly folded. In an atmosphere of apprehension, turmoil, he remained philosophically undisturbed.

Swift, approaching footsteps drew his gaze from distant thunderclouds to the more immediate aquiline features of Chief Inspector McGraw, now appearing in the opening.

"Ah, Mr. Ibn Lahûn. Came to look for you. Needed exercise."

"He who travels gleans wisdom on the way."

McGraw dropped onto a seat facing Mohammed.

"Seem to have heard so."

McGraw chewed industriously.

"A cigarette, sir? I rarely smoke, myself, and have a number."

Mohammed courteously extended a cigarette case.

"Thanks, no. When I think, I chew. When I get my man I light my pipe. May be able to help me. Ever hear of Geoffrey Arlington?"

Mohammed spread eloquent palms, one still supporting the cigarette case.

"Every cultured Egyptian has heard of Geoffrey Arlington. His book called *The Secret Places of Egypt* made him ridiculous from Alexandria to Aswân. Geoffrey Arlington is a liar."

"*Was*, no doubt."

Mohammed's deer-like gaze became fixed upon the half-closed eyes of McGraw.

"Has reformation claimed him?"

"No—death. Didn't know, I suppose?"

"The news is fresh to me, sir, but not unwelcome."

"Is that so? When did you see him last?"

"I never saw him. But his picture was on the wrapper of his book."

He replaced his cigarette case in a pocket of his dinner coat.

"And you didn't recognize him? I mean last night?"

Mohammed was silent for ten seconds, and then:

"You imply, sir, that the man who died here last night was Geoffrey Arlington?"

"That's so."

Mohammed slowly shook his head.

"He had changed, greatly."

McGraw nodded.

"They do, you know, when they've been murdered."

Mohammed Ibn Lahûn stared, raptly, into space. He looked toward the east.

"I understand why, even in death, an aura of evil surrounded him. He died as he lived—a liar, a hypocrite, a

190

wicked man. God is great, and Mohammed is his only prophet."

He touched his brow, his lips and his breast, and inclined his head. McGraw's eyes were closed.

"Checked up on you, Mr. Ibn Lahûn. Matter of routine. Any idea, as a prominent figure in the Moslem world, if Arlington might have made religious enemies?"

"He was unworthy of attention by the faithful, sir. His fate the Almighty had hung around his neck. His own deeds condemned him. By virtue of his own deeds he died."

McGraw chewed.

"Is that so? Can't help me, then?"

Mohammed did not reply immediately, but at last, "Only in this," he said gently. "Those whom you believe to be guilty are innocent. Kismet—the law of things as they are—ordained that he should die. . . ."

So that when McGraw returned to the study he was in a bad humor. Sergeant Sample looked up from shorthand notes as his chief opened the door.

"Got the report on Arlington yet?" McGraw inquired.

"May take some time, sir. I don't think he's ever been on the books. But two other reports have come in."

"What are they?"

"One's from headquarters. The Hanover Square garage. Their line's out of order. One of our men called, and they told him the car standing down here at the back gate was hired, self-driven, to Geoffrey Arlington last night. He phoned for one. The manager knows him."

"Where did he phone from?"

"They can't say. He came in a taxi and picked up the car."

"What time?"

"Ten-fifteen."

"Had a call posted for the taxi driver?"

"Yes, sir."

McGraw elbowed his way to the chair behind Pike's desk. Sample made way for him.

"Other report?"

"Detective-officer Brayle, our department, arrested Sidonia ten minutes ago. She was going into the block of flats in Jermyn Street, where she lives. He had been waiting there."

"Who was she with?"

"Sir Wilfred Willerton. Nothing known about him except that he's a Second Lieutenant in the Grenadier Guards. According to a statement made to Brayle, Willerton, on his way back from the coast, pulled up at The Effingham Arms for a drink. Sidonia jumped out of another car standing there and begged him to give her a lift to London. He's an admirer of hers. He agreed."

Sample had been reading, hesitantly, from his shorthand notes. The effect was that of a nervous schoolboy trying to recite Shakespeare.

McGraw pondered this information.

"Is that so?" he remarked. "Any more good news?"

"Yes, sir. James Findlater is outside, under escort."

McGraw chewed in silence for quite a long time, and then:

"Let him stay there," he drawled. "What explanation does the woman Sidonia offer?"

"Says she's on the air at 2.30. That a big engagement hangs on it."

"Pity. May ruin her career. Told them to hold her?"

"Yes, sir."

A rap on the door heralded the entrance of Inspector Hawley.

"I have a message from Lady Hilary Bruton, Chief Inspector," he announced. "Miss Elphinstowe states that

Lady Hilary is still unfit for interrogation. But, knowing the importance of time, she would try to answer any questions put to her by Mr. Kennedy. I understand that Mr. Kennedy is a personal friend."

Chief Inspector McGraw appeared to have fallen asleep, but presently he aroused himself.

"Get Mr. Kennedy," he instructed.

Inspector Hawley went out. McGraw glanced aside at Sample.

"Watching my step, Sergeant. Getting on dangerous ground."

"Yes, sir."

When, ten minutes later, Storm Kennedy was ushered in by Hawley, he appeared as one rejuvenated. In spite of an unshaven chin, disheveled dress clothes, he looked like a winner of the Irish Sweepstake. His blue eyes were dancing.

"Seem on top of the world," McGraw commented drily. "Got a clue?"

Kennedy sat down facing the Chief Inspector.

"I have learned never to jump to conclusions; and I know it's going to be hard to pin this thing onto the real culprit. . . . But I think I know who the real culprit is!"

"Is that so? Have a kind of notion I know, too."

Storm Kennedy challenged drowsy eyes.

"Have you? We can all make mistakes."

McGraw nodded.

"Recently pointed out to me that those whom you believe to be guilty are innocent. Kismet, the law of things as they are, plays a big part."

"Sounds like Mohammed."

"It was!"

McGraw laughed, and barriers were swept away. This simple, human quality established an affinity which had not been there before. Injured *amour propre* was forgotten in the birth of a new understanding. All this laughter can do.

"But he's a dark horse, sir!" Sample intoned.

Any further comments Sample may have had in mind were interrupted by the buzz of the phone. He took the call, listened, and scribbled busily. When he hung up, "Hospital?" McGraw suggested.

Sample nodded.

"They say, yes. There's the mark of a recent injection on his left arm."

"Actual cause of death settled yet?"

"No further report, sir. I believe they are waiting for a special opinion."

"Hope it isn't Dr. Smithy's. Ought to try to find a doctor who knows a dead man when he sees one."

"We were all agreed," Kennedy pointed out.

"Not all doctors. Listen, Mr. Kennedy. I know what you're doing here, and who employed you. Trying to shield Lady Hilary Bruton. . . . Don't interrupt. Your turn later. Had experience of your methods. Mallory jewel case. Grant you're good at the game. But it's one thing to grab the evidence of a robbery and stymie the C.I.D. It's another to try to cover up evidence of attempted homicide. A last word—I want you to go and talk to Lady Hilary."

The drooping eyes opened fully. Their glance clashed with Storm Kennedy's equally steady regard.

"I shall be glad to do so."

"Know you'll be glad. Been waiting for a chance. But here's a friendly tip. Expect you to report to me *exactly* what she tells you. If it clears her, good enough. If I think you're doing any editing, I'll have her here on the mat, whoever's daughter she is."

"That's agreed," Kennedy said quietly.

"Right. Get busy."

And the door had no more than closed behind Storm Kennedy when Hawley rapped on it again, stepped in, and announced:

"Lord Glengale, Chief Inspector."

Lord Glengale wore a neat checked suit and a soft-collared white shirt with a regimental tie, very tightly knotted. The whole agile figure, that nut-brown face, conveyed the same impression: tightly knotted. His uncompromising gray eyes were strangely like the eyes of Hilary when she was angry.

He stared across the room, as McGraw slowly stood up.

"Chief Inspector McGraw?"

"At Your Lordship's service. This is my assistant, Detective-Sergeant Sample. Will you please take a seat?"

Glengale sat down on the leather couch just inside the door.

"Where is my daughter?"

McGraw dropped back in his chair.

"At the moment, sir, in charge of Miss Elphinstowe, upstairs. All had a nasty shock a while ago."

The steely eyes of Lord Glengale never moved.

"Possibly you misunderstood me?"

"Understood you perfectly, sir. But Your Lordship knows the meaning of discipline as well as I do. At the first moment possible you shall see Lady Hilary. Acting under orders from Superintendent of Department. My duty to carry them out."

They were an odd couple, these two men. McGraw's clipped dialogue was not unlike that used by the old soldier, except in the matter of its delivery. The detective was every whit as tough as this survivor of a ruling class whose decline had been foreseen by Rudyard Kipling, whose requiem was chanted by Somerset Maugham.

"Explain these orders."

McGraw leaned back.

"Relate to details connected with the case which I must ask you to consider."

"Give me the details."

The Chief Inspector chewed reflectively.

"Man called Geoffrey Arlington was stabbed here last night. Highly mysterious circumstances. Lady Hilary first declared she didn't know him. Now, she's admitted she did. No one else present who'd ever met him."

Lord Glengale stood up and took a step forward.

"You are not daring to suggest to *me* that my daughter is the criminal?"

Sergeant Sample blew his nose.

"Suggesting nothing, sir. Merely answering your question. You see, there's evidence to show that Lady Hilary was probably the last person to see Arlington alive."

"What does *she* say?"

"So far said nothing. Mr. Storm Kennedy, with my permission, has gone to ask her for the real facts. While we're waiting, Your Lordship might be able to supply a few details about this man."

Lord Glengale returned to the couch and sat down again.

"Man was a blackguard. Bad as they come. Never met the fellow face to face. But knew him by sight. Discovered by accident that he'd induced my daughter to put up capital for a wild-cat oil well in Arabia. Damn oil well didn't exist! Absconded with the money. Could do nothing. Had his record looked up. Terrible! Fired from all his clubs. Rank outsider."

"Sounds like it," McGraw agreed. "How long ago was the oil deal?"

"Couple of years."

McGraw considered this, and then, "Anything to suggest association had been renewed?" he inquired.

"Nothing definite. But, lately, my daughter's been gallivanting about with her Aunt Elfie. . . ."

"Miss Elphinstowe?"

"Yes. Knew in my bones there was something going on. Why I employed Storm Kennedy. How he traced her to this ruin, God knows."

"His business." McGraw chewed awhile. "Any suspicion, Lord Glengale, that Arlington may have been trying to blackmail Lady Hilary?"

The Marquess stared fixedly at McGraw. But McGraw's eyes were closed.

"Quite capable of it."

"Knew he was in England?"

"Saw him! Nearly bumped into the fellow, in Knightsbridge, only yesterday."

"Knightsbridge," McGraw mused. "Was he alone?"

"Woman with him. Would be."

"See you?"

"He did not."

McGraw was silent for awhile, then, "What I'm anxious to know, sir," he went on, "is, had he, to your own knowledge, any hold over Lady Hilary?"

Lord Glengale stood up again. He crossed to the desk, rested his brown, nervous hands on it, and focused angry gray eyes upon McGraw.

"You mean, anxious to know if she had any motive for murdering him?"

"Merely anxious to learn the facts."

"Must say, Chief Inspector, your attitude is one of insufferable stupidity. Must decline to answer any further questions."

"That's for you to decide, sir."

"Have decided. But allow me to tell you this: Fellows like Arlington could never get what you call a 'hold' upon Hilary. Members of my family do not submit to blackmail. If they make mistakes, they face consequences. That clear to you?"

"Quite clear, sir."

"Wait outside in the car. Perhaps you will be good enough to notify me when I have your permission to see my daughter."

Lord Glengale crossed to the door, jerked it open, and went out.

As it banged behind him, "Phew!" said McGraw. "Another case like this and I'm for chicken farming."

"Wouldn't suit your temperament," Sample assured him, and added, "While Lord Glengale was blowing off steam I got an idea."

McGraw glanced at him.

"So did I," he drawled. "But hadn't the pluck to carry it out. What's your idea?"

"Well, you've seen the marks Wilson found on that hypodermic syringe. Same as those on the case and the window frame. Kind of fine mesh. Now, it seems to me that nobody could use such a delicate thing as a syringe with a handkerchief wrapped round his fingers."

McGraw closed tired eyes.

"Conveying what?"

"I don't know, sir. But I've been thinking." His tone suggested that he might have been crying. "There seems to be a theory there, somewhere."

"Probably is. Let me know when you find it."

The terrace outside the open window lay in shadow. Over that wooded hill where once d'Angauverre Abbey had stood, a black cloud hung like a pall. Rain began to patter gently on the mossy pavement. . . .

23

Chief Inspector McGraw sat, silent, with closed eyes so long, that Sergeant Sample began to wonder if he had really fallen asleep. He glanced up from his perpetual notes, and was reassured. A faint chewing movement might be discerned.

"This case my last, if I'm not careful," McGraw began presently. "Mere fact of the Bruton girl stooping to lie to Croker tells its own story. In deep with Arlington. Something big in the background. Clear?"

"Quite clear."

"Once a girl with those traditions tells one lie, there's no limit."

"Same with drink, sir," Sample observed, in a tone which would have earned high commendation from the Salvation Army.

McGraw ignored the interruption.

"Lord Glengale knows she's in deep. Why he put Storm Kennedy on her tail. Kennedy got here too late. Mischief was done. What's the betting, Sergeant, on the suspects?"

Sample registered reflection, and then, "I'd lay evens Sidonia's in it," he concluded. "Side bet. Two-to-one on Mohammed. But, on pure form, I agree with you, Chief Inspector, the big money on Lady Hilary."

"Larkhall Pike?"

"Not in the running, now, in my view."

"If only Hilary began with La," McGraw murmured.

"That's a catch, I agree. But a man in his state might just have been raving."

"Doubt it. Rational enough . . . Think of the girl's nerve, Sergeant. Never turned a hair when she found out we knew her real name. Admitted switching the light off without hesitation. Had a good look at her chin?"

"Yes, sir. Like her father's—but prettier. Oh, she has the guts for the job. All my money's on Lady Hilary."

McGraw fell silent again. He was aroused by a knock on the door.

Inspector Hawley came in, depressingly.

"Thunderstorm brewing," he observed, *en passant*, and then, "Mrs. Muller would like a word with you, Chief Inspector, if convenient."

"Convenient," McGraw drawled. "Send her in."

Mrs. Muller entered presently, her wrap discarded, as if she were conscious of the appeal which belongs to a shapely figure and an ivory skin. For she came to ask a favor.

"Please sit down, Mrs. Muller."

She selected the chair set facing the big desk, and smiled. It was a rueful smile, almost that of a child begging candies, but like her voice, oddly fascinating.

"Please tell me, Inspector, if I am asking the impossible. But I suppose Mr. Lovelace has been allowed to go, and so I was wondering if there's any objection to my going, too? My driver has been waiting for hours, and really it *is* distressing to stay in evening dress all day!"

McGraw returned her smile with one which had a quaint, unfamiliar charm of its own.

"Don't believe there's anything against it, Mrs. Muller. Glad you reminded me. Though we'll be sorry to lose your company. Any objection, Sergeant Sample, to letting Mrs. Muller go home?"

"No, sir. None that I know."

McGraw turned again to Mrs. Muller.

"Staying at the Hyde Park Hotel, I remember. Don't live in England?"

"No, Inspector. My home is in Beirut. I expect to return in two weeks' time."

"Beirut? Things a bit disturbed in that area?"

Mrs. Muller's smile grew sad, and then faded.

"Unfortunately, yes. My husband, an engineer, is in oil—ghastly way of putting it! Makes him sound like a sardine!"

Then McGraw laughed. They all laughed. And the Chief Inspector stood up and extended a large, shapely hand.

"Good-bye, Mrs. Muller. Been a pleasure to meet you."

"That's very sweet. Thanks ever so much for your courtesy."

Mrs. Muller departed. McGraw sat down again. And Mrs. Muller rejoined Hawley, who was waiting in the long passage.

"It's all right, Inspector. I am allowed to leave."

"Glad to hear it, madame."

"I'm just going to get my handbag and wrap. I wonder if you would be kind enough to ask my driver to bring the car into the courtyard? I haven't the courage to face all those reporters outside the gate!"

"I'll see to it. See that you're not held up, too."

But Inspector Hawley had been standing beside the car for nearly ten minutes before Mrs. Muller, wrapped in her mink, appeared.

Her appearance aroused Lord Glengale from a savage reverie. Seated in the back of a Rolls town car, he had been cursing under his breath so that even Binns, his chauffeur, had flinched. The dainty figure of Mrs. Muller diverted his ideas into a new channel. The Marquess notoriously had a quick eye for a horse or a pretty woman. He studied the piquant profile, petulant lips, with approval.

In fact, he stared pointedly until Hawley opened the door for her; then, as the door was closed and the Inspector went ahead to clear a path through hungry news-hunters:

"Do we know that lady, Binns?" he demanded.

"No, milord. Not to the best of my knowledge, that is."

"Queer. Thought we did. Ought to."

Mrs. Muller's car was driven away along an avenue formed by disappointed reporters.

In the green bedroom Storm Kennedy smoked one of the "gaspers" bought by Elfie from a policeman. He stood in that recess which harbored the spinning wheel, looking at the bole of a giant fir reared like a mast just outside small leaded panes.

"Now that the crisis has come"—his tone was quietly conversational, but every word cost him nervous effort—"I want to make my own position clear. I want you both to know that my arrival here was not an accident. Since I left the Army I have been working as a confidential agent. . . ."

"Known in some parts," Elfie interpolated, "as a private eye."

"Quite so. I was called in by Lord Glengale to try to avert what happened here last night."

Then, Hilary's voice reached Kennedy. It was a cold voice.

"What, exactly, do you mean by 'what happened here last night'?"

"I mean your meeting with Geoffrey Arlington."

"You are not trying to persuade me to believe," Elfie inquired gruffly, "that Ronnie had sense enough for that?"

There was a cordiality half-hidden under the words which encouraged Kennedy to turn.

"I am."

His reply was addressed to Elfie, but his glance became arrested by challenging gray eyes in which he read something both of reproach, and of scorn. His skin tingled hotly. He could face other men, in debate or in physical battle, but his powers of self-control threatened to let him down under the scrutiny of those beautiful eyes—which yet, inexplicably, were so like Lord Glengale's.

"You mean"—Hilary's voice remained cold—"that all you have done, for which I have been so grateful, you did because . . ."

"Because I was paid to do it?"

"I wasn't going to say that."

"But you were thinking it. And it isn't true. I have not been paid. I shall not be paid. I consented to act for your father because he was a man in deep distress, and because, from the first moment I met you, I wanted nothing better, nothing more than to serve you. On those terms alone I consented to do my best. But my best has failed."

Hilary's long lashes flickered, then veiled her eyes. She stood up and crossed to Storm Kennedy, both hands extended.

"Forgive me, Bill—if you can." But, as his fingers closed over hers, she knew that he had. "I am far more caddish than any man, sometimes."

It was these sudden about-turns, Kennedy realized, the complete generosity of her apologies, which made Hilary so lovable.

"I don't believe it!" He smiled, drew her nearer for a

moment—then released her hands. "You are a bundle of bewildering but adorable impulses."

"So is a pet monkey," Elfie growled. "Also a blasted nuisance to everybody. Listen, Bill. We're two liars caught in our own net. Hilary is ready to give you all the facts about what happened last night. If they help you to get us out of it, you're a better man than Sherlock Holmes—or was it Gunga Din?"

Storm Kennedy turned and rested his hand for a moment on Miss Elphinstowe's shoulder.

"Elfie—you are a very wonderful woman. Before we start, let me explain something else. I am here by permission of Chief Inspector McGraw. And I have passed my word that I will tell him *everything* that Hilary tells *me*. The decision must rest with McGraw. So, do you mind, Hilary, if *I* ask the questions and *you* answer them?"

"I should prefer it."

Hilary spoke gravely, reseating herself in the great tapestry chair, where again, as once before, she stirred some memory buried in Kennedy's subconscious mind. Perhaps that of an illustration to a story read in childhood—the picture of a fairytale princess . . .

"Suppose I outline what I imagine to have happened, and you correct me where I go wrong?"

Hilary nodded, and clasped her hands on her knees. Elfie lighted a fresh cigarette.

"You came to Hangover House to meet Geoffrey Arlington." Storm Kennedy spoke slowly, mustering his ideas. "You must have arranged this with him. Because he, I presume, had not been invited?"

"No. I didn't even know he was in England until he phoned me last night. I had not seen him for over a year."

"You didn't want to see him. The meeting was forced upon you. Now, let me suggest (although I know, Hilary, it isn't the whole story) that he had used you in some way to float a shady transaction—used your money, too—and that he threatened to expose the facts to your father unless you did meet him. Is that true, as far as it goes?"

"Yes—as far as it goes."

"And so you put him off and thought the thing over. Or you may have been interrupted."

"I was interrupted," Hilary said. "My father called at Elfie's flat."

"You were planning to leave London? Did this journey concern the same matter?"

"It did," Elfie broke in. "We were going away to try to stymie his game."

"Then you had anticipated his turning up?"

"He had written to say he was on the way," Elfie replied again. "Hilary wouldn't read his letters. . . . But *I* read 'em!"

"You didn't want to be seen in this man's company," Kennedy went on. "And so you suggested a secret meeting here."

Hilary's hands moved restlessly.

"I thought there would be a crowd at Joan's party. I hadn't meant to come. But I was here once before—to a garden fête—and I remembered the summer house, and the back entrance. At ten o'clock last night I called him and made an appointment for 12.30. I thought I could slip out unnoticed."

"Now, something I don't know: What was your object?"

Hilary bit her lip, and hesitated for a moment.

"To prevent him forcing his way into Elfie's flat, which he had threatened, and to make it quite clear to him that, whatever he chose to do about it, I should never consent to see him again."

Kennedy nodded, thoughtfully, and then, "Arlington was delayed by fog," he continued, speaking as one who thinks aloud. "Nearly everyone had gone before he arrived. Were you waiting for him in the summer house?"

"No. I had given him up. He found his way to the house. I turned and saw him standing behind me."

"And what did you do?"

"I made him come out into the garden. I didn't want to be discovered with him."

"The fog was dense by that time. Where did you go?"

"Down the slope, toward the back gate."

"How far, Hilary?"

"Oh, forty or fifty yards."

"And what happened?"

Hilary hesitated again. But it was only to collect her thoughts.

"He—Geoffrey—refused to believe what I told him. You see, I had met him when I was very young—and he tried to appeal to my silly sentiment as he had done in those days. When he realized that it didn't work any more, he changed his tactics."

"You mean—he threatened you?"

Hilary's chin was firmly set. She was entirely composed.

"He tried to. That was where he made a mistake. I may be soft as putty. Elfie says I am. But no one, man or woman, can bully me. It brings the worst out. And the worst is pretty bad. I had in my bag the only present he had ever given me. It was an Egyptian necklace. . . ."

Storm Kennedy called on the powers of yogi. His expression remained unchanged.

"I had brought it, wrapped in a handkerchief. I wanted no link, no memory, to recall the misery he had meant to me. When I told him to go, I thrust the thing into his hand. This convinced him, I suppose, that I meant what I had said."

Hilary became silent. Her fingers were locked, now,

between her knees. She was stairing down at the faded French carpet.

"You must tell me"—Kennedy spoke gently—"what appeal he tried to make to your sentiment."

Hilary glanced swiftly aside at Elfie. And Elfie shook her head.

"The knife from Mecca," she prompted gruffly.

"He made all sorts of appeals," Hilary went on, her soft, musical voice quite under control. "But, in particular, he tried to convince me that his life was in danger."

"From whom?"

"He said, during the year he had been in the East, that he had lived for some time, in disguise, in Mecca. He showed me a knife, which he took from a sheath. He swore that it was one of the holy relics, that it had belonged to the Prophet's wife. I forget her name . . ."

"Possibly Ayesha?"

"Yes, it sounded like that. He declared that fanatics had followed him to England—had followed him here, to Hangover House. He claimed to be penniless."

"He wanted money?"

Hilary nodded, miserably.

"He said he must get away—hide. And he asked me to help him. . . ."

Her voice faded.

"What did you say?"

"I may have been wrong—unjust. I shall never know. But I said that I didn't believe him. I said that I didn't care in the least *what* became of him. It was then that he grew violent and—threatened me. I turned and ran. Somehow, I got back to the terrace. He was running after me. I heard him call out, '*Larry! Larry!*'"

On that word Hilary ceased, as though a hand had been clapped over her mouth. She and Elfie exchanged swift glances. Storm Kennedy's forehead grew moist. . . .

Vividly, a phantom appeared before his mind's eye. He saw again a ghastly figure on a shadowy stair, chalky face, extended arm. He heard that croaked, accusing whisper:

"*La . . . It was La . . .*"

24

"I know what you are thinking," Hilary said in a quiet voice. "And you may even be right. He—Geoffrey—always called me Larry. . . ."

"He had a tonic sol-fa mind," Elfie broke in. "He probably gave a pet name to every woman he knew, one beginning with Do, Ra, Me, Fa, So, La or Te."

The gruff interpolation was meant to help Kennedy; to enable him to conquer a momentary lapse of control. He rewarded Elfie with a grateful smile.

"You mean, Hilary, he may have meant to say, 'It was Larry'?"

"Quite possibly." Hilary spoke with composure. "He was a devil—a vindictive devil. I had dared him to do his worst. He may have been trying, even then, to do it."

Storm Kennedy, every minute, became more completely convinced that the association went deeper than any shady financial transaction. But he must forget it. Lady Hilary Bruton he must think of as a client, unprofitable but lovely. His business was to get her clear, and then—get out.

"I should like to make sure of the facts so far."

Hilary flashed him an appealing glance, bit her lip,

and looked away. The change of tone had registered, harshly.

"Please do. They are quite simple."

"You returned an Egyptian necklace (the police have found it) which you had wrapped in a handkerchief. I presume, so that it didn't get mixed up with the other odds and ends in your bag?"

"Of course."

"When you put it into his hand, it was still wrapped in the handkerchief?"

"Yes."

"He evidently dropped the necklace but retained the handkerchief. Now, if you can bear it, let's go on. The dagger which he claimed to have stolen from Mecca—was this the dagger found beside his body?"

"I think so. I never saw it very well, out there in the fog. But I think so."

"Did he actually hold it in his hand when you turned and ran back to the house?"

"Yes. He was waving it about—raving. He said his death was inevitable unless he could escape the fanatics who had followed him. His only hope was to slip out of England, secretly. He would have to bribe someone to smuggle him over to the French coast, as they would be watching the ports."

"Mr. Arlington might have succeeded as a sensational novelist where he failed as an explorer," Kennedy remarked bitterly. "What was your part to be?"

"He claimed that the custodians, or the Arab League, or someone—truly, I can't remember, exactly—would pay a big ransom if he could entrench himself and bargain with them. He spoke of twenty thousand pounds."

"Which he asked you to advance?"

Hilary nodded; her averted face was expressionless.

"At least suggested it."

"In what form! Such a cheque would not be met by my bank without inquiry."

"I have jewelry worth that amount."

Storm Kennedy's hands clenched convulsively. How, in heaven's name, could a girl like Hilary have become involved with such a cheap scoundrel?

"I see. You defied him, told him to do whatever he had threatened to do, and ran back to the house. By the way, McGraw is sure to ask, what *had* he threatened to do? May I suggest—don't answer if you don't want to—tell the whole story to your father."

Hilary's hands moved to clasp the arms of the tapestried chair. She stared down at the carpet again.

"Yes."

"All right. That's clear enough. Now, you say he followed you?"

"He did. That was when he called out. I dashed onto the terrace. I don't quite know how I found the steps. I ran along until I came to an open window. I didn't care what window it was. I had only one thing in mind: to get away from him. I rushed through—and found myself in a room I had never been in before."

"Yes, Hilary? Go on. This is important."

"Only one lamp was alight. There was nobody in the room. At random, and simply because it was right by my hand, I pressed a switch—and the lamp went out."

Storm Kennedy seemed to hear his own heart beating.

"And then?"

"Then I listened for just a moment. I thought I heard voices . . ."

"Where?"

"Outside. Don't ask me *whose* voices, because I was too upset to know. I stumbled across the room to where I had seen a door. I found it, opened it—you and Elfie were standing in the passage."

Elfie was watching Storm Kennedy with an expression hard to define, except that it was charged with some potent message, some message he failed to read. He turned to Hilary. She sat quite still, her lashes lowered.

"And that is all you know about what happened?"

"That's all I know."

"You left Arlington at the spot where the argument took place?"

"Yes."

"Had you any suspicion that someone else might have been near in the fog?"

"Yes. But there was nothing to confirm it. It may have been due simply to my fear that someone might overhear us."

"And you have no idea what happened afterwards?"

Hilary raised her gray eyes and looked steadily at Storm Kennedy.

"On my word of honor, none whatever."

A zig-zag of lightning split the darkness, followed by an angry roll of thunder drums over the hills. . . .

Chief Inspector McGraw stood at the partly opened window, his hands clasped behind him. He was watching torrents of rain turn terrace and steps into racing rivulets and tumbling cascades, watching that blackly frowning cloud low over a distant slope from which the once great abbey of d'Angauverre had ruled the valley. He spoke without turning.

"Lady Hilary's story sounds straightforward enough. Pity there was no witness."

"But there may have been."

As Storm Kennedy made this retort, McGraw turned. His expression, in semi-darkness, back, now, to the window, was indecipherable.

"Such as?"

"That remains to be proved. She mentioned a distinct impression that someone else was near, hidden in the fog."

"Is that so? Assuming she was right, any theory who this someone else might have been?"

"Anybody's guess. We know, now, where the necklace came from; but if (it's a hundred-to-one chance) Arlington's story of the Mecca dagger had any relation to fact, this story seems to be significant."

"Dagger might have been another present," McGraw suggested. "Appears to have had original ideas."

Storm Kennedy inhaled deeply.

"You mean, Chief Inspector, that you are rejecting Lady Hilary's evidence?"

"Not rejecting it. What a court of law would accept, *I'm* prepared to accept. Her evidence is unsupported. You're implying, I take it, that story of theft of Mecca relic suggests the work of a fanatic?"

"It's not impossible."

"Odds on Mohammed," Sample murmured.

McGraw stared at him. Sample sat behind the big desk. He had switched up the lamp, so that his face, in greenish light, resembled a kind of exhibit different from any in that room of strange memories. The Egyptian death-mask had come to life again. McGraw's glance was drawn to it, and he thought that it smiled, contemptuously.

"Suppose"—Storm Kennedy's voice was cold—"instead of wasting time, we settle once and for all the point whether Mohammed has or has not anything to do with the matter?"

McGraw beckoned to Sample.

"Get Mr. Ibn Lahûn." Then, as Sample went out: "Don't want to suggest antagonism, Mr. Kennedy," McGraw added. "Nobody happier than I shall be if Lady

Hilary is cleared of suspicion. Hard luck for me if I have to charge her. Lord Glengale is here—with his daughter, at the moment."

Kennedy said nothing.

"Difficult type," McGraw continued. "But in the C.I.D. have to face realities, however unpleasant. What we're paid for. You think you know the guilty party. I'm waiting for more facts on that. Present facts, as I see them, are these: Lady Hilary Bruton is the only person present who had both motive and opportunity. Clear?"

"I can't dispute it."

"You bank on her character. Not overlooking that. Does seem unlikely a girl with her background would stab a man—even in anger. But has admitted to you, herself, he held the weapon in his hand. Sudden impulse. Feasible?"

"Unfortunately, yes."

"Don't know the strength of this story about Mecca. Without offense, it might be (A) an invention of Lady Hilary's; (B) invention of Arlington's. Still clear?"

"Still clear."

"But agree it has to be checked up. Nothing's impossible."

Storm Kennedy began to walk about restlessly. Long strain was telling. He struggled to retain that cold detachment lacking when clear thinking becomes fogbound.

"When we are through with Mohammed, Chief Inspector, may I ask you one simple question?"

"Many simple questions as you like."

McGraw, a tall silhouette against the window, remained immovable. Lightning flashed viciously behind him, and then came that rolling of thunder drums.

The phone buzzed. McGraw took the call. After a few words, "Mrs. Peter Faraway," he drawled. "Knows nothing about what's happened. Like to talk to her?"

Storm Kennedy nodded and crossed to the desk.

"This is Bill Kennedy, Joan. Where are you?"

"Why, Bill!" came Joan's high-pitched excited voice, "so you *did* turn up? Bill, what a party it must have been!"

"It was, I assure you."

"I only got home from Brighton half hour ago. Do you tell me you're still celebrating?"

"Celebrations are over, Joan. Peter will give you a detailed report when he gets back to town."

"Hasn't he left?"

"Not yet. Starting shortly."

"Where is he?"

Storm Kennedy saw again, vividly, a scene he had witnessed during a final ramble around the ancient property—a reconnaissance from which he had been recalled by Sergeant Sample. He visualized a tumble-down lean-to, untidily stocked with gardening implements, broken hen coops, logs, flower pots; a heap of sacking.

"Well, when I saw him last he was asleep in the potting-shed."

"Alone?"

"In solitary splendor."

"All right, Bill. *Do* come back here and stay to dinner. Is my old friend, Mohammed, still there too?"

"He is."

"Then *do* bring him along, as well . . ."

As Kennedy hung up, Mohammed Ibn Lahûn entered, with Sergeant Sample. The sergeant's expression was one appropriate to a chief mourner.

"Ah, Mr. Ibn Lahûn"—McGraw indicated the couch by the door—"please sit down. Think you may be able to help."

"All life is service," the Egyptian stated, placidly seating himself. "But many serve evil causes."

McGraw made his way to the leather chair behind the

desk, and Sergeant Sample took up his usual post (on a hard wooden stool) near McGraw's left elbow, opening his notes. Storm Kennedy leaned against a bookcase. The Chief Inspector's angular jaws began to work automatically, and Kennedy wondered, as others had wondered, what McGraw chewed.

"Told me, not so long back, Arlington beneath any consideration by the Moslem world. Not so sure, now. Appears, on recent evidence, that the knife, or dagger, found beside his body, is a holy relic which Arlington stole from Mecca. Belonged to the Prophet's wife. Know that?"

Mohammed extended slender palms.

"I know that this is not true, sir. Certain possessions of the Prophet (may God be good to him) remain in the custody of those charged with their safekeeping, in Mecca, El Medineh, Damascus, and elsewhere. The dagger of which you speak is not one of these."

"Sure?"

"I am well acquainted with all the holy relics, sir. I would, also, beg to draw your attention to this fact: If recovery of the weapon had been the assassin's motive, he would not have left it there."

"Thought of that." McGraw glanced across at Kennedy. "Had you?"

"Certainly. But we must allow for some unexpected interference."

"Fate interfered, *Khawâga*," Mohammed assured him. "It was written when and how the man should die."

Only a sound of falling rain, an amplified hiss, broke the silence, until, "Might be a good idea," McGraw suggested, "if you enlarged, somewhat, on statement to Superintendent Croker. Not clear to me what one of your type is doing here."

"Certainly." Mohammed inclined his head, courteously. "I am in England, sir, to attend a conference of those responsible for preserving the faith of Islâm. Light is dying from the earth. The world grows dark. The revelations of the Prophet (secure in Paradise) no longer touch the hearts of men."

"How true," Sample intoned, looking up from his task of sharpening a pencil.

Mohammed smiled sadly.

"As an old friend of Mrs. Faraway's (we have corresponded ever since her visit to Egypt), I naturally called to pay my respects. She is, as you know, sir, very wealthy, but you may not know that she is also very unhappy."

"Not uncommon," McGraw drawled. He glanced again at Storm Kennedy. "Didn't think the Honorable Peter was a man of means."

"He isn't," Kennedy answered promptly. "But his wife is the daughter of Cornelius Corkoran, known in the United States as the Railroad King."

"Is that so? Accounts for a lot."

"Peter is her second husband."

"Inherit the title?"

"Yes, if he doesn't drink himself to death before his father."

"I see." McGraw looked at Mohammed. "Believe I interrupted you."

"Life is dotted with many punctuation marks, sir, but with only one full stop. Mrs. Faraway confided to me her belief that her husband was entangled again. She believed, knowing something of those small powers with which the All Knowing has endowed me, that if I attended the party here I might perhaps discern the object of the Honorable Peter's affections. She wished to learn if the matter had grown serious enough to justify divorce."

"Didn't know it was as bad as that," Kennedy muttered.

"Laughter is sometimes a mask for sorrow." (Sergeant Sample sighed like a bellows.) "I learned that the Honorable Peter was seeking to induce the singer called Sidonia to accept his embraces. He pressed his attentions upon her so hotly that Mrs. Faraway departed, in just anger. I remained, to endeavor to pursue this unfortunate affair to its termination."

McGraw had closed his eyes. Now, he partly opened them.

"And what was its termination?"

"Unfortunately, sir, I lost sight both of Mr. Faraway and of Sidonia. But I believe the damsel rejected his love. Possibly he failed to offer suitably rich gifts."

"Quite likely," McGraw agreed. "About these small powers to which you referred, Mr. Ibn Lahûn. Helped you to learn anything more definite than that those I believe guilty, are, in fact, innocent, and so on?"

"Many things, sir. The singing woman is without guilt in this matter."

"Think so, too."

"Lady Hilary Bruton can be cleared of suspicion by one person, alone. I have already advised this person to tell the truth."

"To what person do you refer?" Storm Kennedy asked rapidly.

"To Mrs. Muller, *Khawâga*."

"*Mrs. Muller!*"

Chief Inspector McGraw, hands on the desk, began to stand up, his eyes fixed in a stare almost of ferocity upon the Egyptian's face. Kennedy suppressed an exclamation, took a step forward.

"I don't know what has led Mr. Ibn Lahûn to this remarkable conclusion, Chief Inspector. But I have certain evidence to support it. May I suggest that we ask **Mrs.** Muller a few questions?"

McGraw sat down again.

"Mrs. Muller on her way to London. . . ."

25

Hangover House became a center of urgent activity. Some echo of this penetrated even to Larkhall Pike, locked in the kitchen with a copy of that day's *Times* belatedly delivered by McAdam. Only one occupant of the premises remained oblivious to what was going on. Peter Faraway, undisturbed by thunder, snored peacefully, but unmusically, in the potting-shed.

An emergency call had been sent out to intercept Mrs. Muller. Sergeant Sample sped north in the Yard car in an endeavor to overtake her.

And Chief Inspector McGraw was deeply dissatisfied with himself.

He stood staring from the window, his gaze following that angry cloud moving eastward and away to an accompaniment of drum rolls, diminuendo. Sunshine peeped, nervously, over its ominous shoulder. Rain continued to fall, but softly now. He spoke without turning.

"Stepped in on me in the Mallory case, Mr. Kennedy. Got me bad marks. Looks as though I have to be grateful you stepped in on this one."

Storm Kennedy laughed, shortly. There was no one else in the study.

"That may be true. But no credit to me. A pure accident led to my discovery of the clue. I wasn't looking for it."

"What Mohammed calls Kismet."

Then, at last, the Chief Inspector turned.

"The law of things as they are?" Kennedy suggested, and smiled.

"Just so. But Assistant Commissioner may never have heard of said law. Want to get the facts straight. Make sure I haven't been wearing smoked glasses. When you walked down the garden and came out behind the summer house, weren't heading that way *deliberately?*"

"Not at all. Just walking, and thinking."

"Is that so? Saw somebody moving in there, through a crack in the back wall, and took a good look. It was Mrs. Muller. Searching for something under the seat where you'd found the gold case."

"Exactly."

"At this moment she was disturbed by appearance of Mohammed. She gave up the search. You *think* before he caught her at it? They walked off together."

"Yes."

"You stepped in. Among a lot of dust and rubbish found these." McGraw pointed to two objects lying on a sheet of white paper. "Didn't make sense at the time. Couldn't get the connection. But that's where you'd found the gold case, and you assumed the gold case to be the thing Mrs. Muller was looking for."

"Naturally."

McGraw nodded. He had resumed chewing.

"Inference sound enough. Didn't come straight back. Went on walking. Still walking when Sergeant Sample came to look for you. Fond of walking—or trying to think up a way of holding out on me?"

Storm Kennedy flushed hotly.

"That's damned unfair, Chief Inspector!"

McGraw smiled, held out his hand.

"Know it is—now. Wanted to be sure."

Kennedy's blue eyes remained hard for only a moment longer. Then, he returned McGraw's smile and grasped the extended hand.

"I was trying to think of some way to confirm what was no more than a strong suspicion. You see, I didn't know what the gold case contained. What I found, this second time, under the seat, suggested no association. It might have had none. Nothing to go upon, really, except the fact that Mrs. Muller had been searching there. *She* didn't know—but she may have suspected—that the gold case had been found. I argued that she wanted to make sure. Inference—that she had hidden it there, herself."

McGraw nodded.

"Inference sound enough. Already said so. Now, what you found was a small, empty phial. Kind chemists use to put up a hypodermic shot. Also a moistened swab smelling of iodine. Conjurer from Kings Riding opened the gold case . . . There was a hypodermic syringe inside—and a place to hold the charge. Smelled of iodine, too."

Storm Kennedy became conscious of excitement so intense that it was hard to control.

"Which answers the simple question I told you I wanted to ask. The question was, what did the case contain?"

"Know now. Arlington got the shot, all right. Hospital reports evidence on left arm."

"*After* he was dead—or appeared to be?"

"After. Someone crept up to that room where he lay, opened the gold case and made an injection."

Kennedy could think of nothing to say. This incredible incident seemed to point to the intrusion of a lunatic, except for one circumstance: the concealed syringe had been in the dead man's possession.

"Same prints on phial," McGraw added, "as on syringe and window frame."

"What kind of prints? I thought that Wilson reported they were illegible."

"Most of them were. But one common factor. All show marks of some sort of fine-meshed material." McGraw paused, stared at Kennedy. "On the syringe and phial these are the *only marks*."

"Looks like a laboratory job."

"It is. Same with the drug used. But autopsy may trace that. Sit down."

McGraw went around and seated himself behind the desk. He left the lamp alight, although hesitant sunbeams began to venture into the gloomy room. Storm Kennedy took a chair opposite to McGraw.

"Have you any theory, Chief Inspector, to account for these marks?"

"Yes." McGraw leaned back, wearily closing his eyes. "Owe the idea to Sergeant Sample. Didn't germinate until Mrs. Muller was pushed into the limelight. Going to try a little experiment."

"Does your theory explain why someone should give a dead man an injection?"

McGraw's jaws began to work mechanically, and then, "No," he drawled. "Doesn't. Any suggestions?"

When Storm Kennedy had gone, with orders to stand by, Chief Inspector McGraw proceeded, methodically, to clear up certain details which he was anxious to dismiss. He gave instructions for the release of Sidonia. ("Should hate to disappoint the B.B.C."); and he gave Mr. James Findlater a dressing-down which lingered long in the memory of that alcoholic ornament of Fleet Street. Findlater's interview (in shorthand) with Sidonia, McGraw tore up.

"That story's killed," he drawled. "Had your news desk on the line. Nothing to be released without my authority."

Alone in the study, McGraw took a call from Scotland Yard which seemed to be of surprising importance. He made detailed notes before hanging up, then sat, eyes closed again, for fully five minutes, chewing meditatively.

Storm Kennedy learned from Inspector Hawley that Lord Glengale was still in the green bedroom, and he decided not to intrude upon this family conference. Disclosure of the new facts which had come to light would be premature in any case. These facts had to be measured and tested.

His accidental discovery, implicating Mrs. Muller, had brought sudden, lurid illumination to dark places. Her charming self-possession, which made her seem at ease under any circumstances, had blinded him as it had blinded McGraw. He had been prepared, reluctantly, to concede first-rate acting ability to the missing Sidonia. The true artist had remained, unsuspected, in their midst.

But, because she had gaiety, and a rare sense of humor, Storm Kennedy felt a pang of unhappiness when a police sergeant brought a message from the Chief Inspector.

Mrs. Muller was on her way back. . . .

He was in the relic-lined study, with its odor of ancient decay, a room which would haunt his dreams, when Inspector Hawley rapped on the door and announced:

"Mrs. Muller is here, Chief Inspector."

Storm Kennedy had been staring out of the window, which he had fully opened to enjoy the fragrance of Mother Nature fresh from a rain bath. He turned as Mrs. Muller came in. She wore her long mink wrap. Her face was pale. Sergeant Sample followed.

She ignored Kennedy, fixing a gaze of narrowed dark eyes upon McGraw. The desk lamp was still alight.

Kennedy noted that the usually courteous Chief Inspector did not stand up. He merely pointed to the chair set facing his own.

"Be good enough to take a seat, Mrs. Muller."

She stood still for a moment, watching him, and then, "May I ask why I have been brought back here?" she demanded.

"Be good enough to take a seat. Matters we have to discuss."

She crossed to the chair, her carriage slow and graceful, and sat down. Sample resumed his perch on the hard stool left of McGraw, and prepared to write. His expression would have suited the First Gravedigger in *Hamlet*.

"You haven't answered my question, Inspector."

Mrs. Muller's huskily vibrant voice broke a tense interval. McGraw was watching her, his lids half-lowered.

"Any need to?" he asked. "Nearly made a bad mistake. Saved by the law of things as they are. Ever hear of that law, Mrs. Muller?"

"I know why you mention it." Mrs. Muller had herself well in hand. "That man, Mohammed, has been talking about me. He talks in parables. You may have misunderstood him."

"Think *you* misunderstood him. Believe he offered you certain advice?"

Mrs. Muller shrugged.

"He is a fanatic. I'm afraid he is also a hypocrite. He made a strange, veiled suggestion to me—yes. It appears, as I did not adopt it, that he came to *you*."

"Didn't come. Was sent for. Obliged for his cooperation. Let's get to matters we have to discuss. Something here I want to show you."

Mrs. Muller threw off her mink wrap. Storm Kennedy automatically stepped forward and draped it over the back of her chair. He observed, as she lifted her arms, that she had put on the gloves which formed part of that wine-colored ensemble worn at the party.

She glanced up under black lashes.

"Thank you, Mr. Kennedy. Are *you* in this conspiracy?"

"I'm afraid I am, Mrs. Muller," he answered gravely.

McGraw, from a desk drawer, took out the gold case. Storm Kennedy noted that he held it delicately by one end. The Chief Inspector offered the case to Mrs. Muller, saying:

"Good enough to tell me if you recognize this?"

She accepted it calmly, turned it over between flexible fingers, and bent to peer at it—closed, as when it was found. Mrs. Muller's hands were quite steady.

"I don't, Inspector." She returned the case. "What is it—a pen?"

"No." McGraw took it gingerly by the tip. He turned to Sample. "Pass this back to Wilson, upstairs."

Sample accepted the exhibit by its other end and went up the short stair to disappear into that arched opening which led to Larkhall Pike's sleeping cell. McGraw closed his eyes and lay back in his chair as if deep in thought. But Storm Kennedy knew that he was waiting for Sample's return before continuing the cross-examination.

Outside, moisture dripped reluctantly from leaves refreshed. A smell of wet loam competed with tomblike odors of the room. Mrs. Muller broke an oppressive silence.

"I still fail to understand, Inspector McGraw, why my journey to London has been interrupted."

"Do you?" McGraw didn't open his eyes. "Sorry, but I can't believe it."

"What do you mean?"

"Mean what I say. Always do. Nothing more difficult in the work of a detective, Mrs. Muller, than to browbeat a woman. But you leave me no choice. Criminal Investigation Department composed of men, not of machines. Come into the open. Give me the facts I want. Pay you better in the end."

Storm Kennedy had changed his position, so that, now, he had a clear view of Mrs. Muller's fascinating profile. For the first time, as McGraw spoke, he detected a faint twitching of the full lips. Mrs. Muller was a clever woman. She was also a cool, daring gambler.

Her quick brain (he determined) calculated the odds against her. She couldn't know what cards the police held, but McGraw's attitude had warned her that he had a good hand.

For uncounted seconds the issue hung in the balance, and then, just as Sample returned quietly to his place, "I don't think I have any facts to give you," she said.

Sample cleared his throat, a fair imitation of recent thunder. Storm Kennedy wished he had had the power to instruct Mrs. Muller, hypnotically, to reply in a different way. McGraw didn't move, nor open his eyes, but presently, "Sorry you think that." He spoke in a low tone. "Wouldn't like to reconsider your answer?"

He was leaving the door open. And Mrs. Muller knew it. Perhaps she misconstrued his motive—for she shrugged her shoulders again.

"Why don't you say, outright, what it is you want to know?"

McGraw slowly raised the drooping lids, and looked at her.

"Very well. Can do so." He opened a desk drawer, taking out the swab and the phial on a sheet of white paper, which he placed on the blotting-pad. "Believe you mislaid these recently."

Mrs. Muller glanced hastily at them—and again Storm Kennedy observed a slight tremor of her lips. She shook her head.

"They are not mine. What led you to suppose they were?"

"May not be yours," McGraw admitted. "But you used them recently."

"Used them? What for?"

The Chief Inspector laid a second sheet of paper on the desk.

"To charge this hypodermic syringe."

Mrs. Muller sat quite motionless and silent. She was still seated so when a red-headed policeman appeared on the stair. He coughed discreetly. McGraw glanced up.

"The same, sir."

McGraw merely nodded; and as Constable Wilson went upstairs again, the Chief Inspector did an odd thing.

He ceased to chew. From his mouth he took out a small piece of whatever he had been masticating and tossed the fragment into a wastebasket. He glanced at Storm Kennedy.

"Putty rubber. One bit lasts me through the longest inquiry."

From a coat pocket he produced a huge briar pipe and a leather case on an equally outsize scale. When he had got the bowl filled to his satisfaction and the tobacco well alight, he lay back, puffing luxuriously.

Mrs. Muller watched him, in silence.

"Should hate to think," the Chief Inspector said, "prepared to keep quiet, Mrs. Muller, and see an innocent girl accused of a crime she didn't commit."

"Why do you make such a suggestion?"

"Facts explain themselves. *Someone* murdered Geoffrey Arlington. . . ."

"Geoffrey Arlington!"

"Name new to you? Or just surprised I know it?" But, as Mrs. Muller made no reply, McGraw continued, "As an old timer at this game, Mrs. Muller (real ambition, chicken farming) must say this: Never met a cooler hand. Viewed the body. Gave a convincing statement to Superintendent Croker. Walked out of this room without a stain on your character. Have declined to give *me* the facts. Shall now give the facts to *you*."

Mrs. Muller half-rose from her chair. Storm Kennedy saw a flash of white teeth as she bit on that full underlip. Then, came an interruption, excited voices outside the closed door.

"Please wait one moment . . ."

"Go to the devil!"

The door burst open and Lord Glengale came in, Inspector Hawley at his heels.

"Lord Glengale," Hawley began.

McGraw signaled with his pipe, and Hawley retired, closing the door. Lord Glengale looked neither right nor left. He crossed to the desk, stared down at the Chief Inspector. He didn't appear to have noticed either Storm Kennedy or Mrs. Muller.

"Perhaps a little unceremonious," he remarked. "Patience exhausted. Have applied to that officer just gone out—without result. Tired of tomfoolery, sir. My daughter has given me a full account of what happened. In short, knows nothing whatever about it—except misfortune to have been acquainted with dead blackguard. Have I your permission to leave, with my daughter and Miss Elphinstowe?"

McGraw replaced his pipe between his teeth, his eyes focused on the steely gray.

"Could answer Your Lordship in several ways. This **is** a criminal inquiry. I am in charge. Inspector Hawley quite correct in declining to disturb me. Directly other witnesses are free to leave, shall be glad to advise you."

Lord Glengale remained perfectly still, stiffly upright.

McGraw puffed at his pipe. Sergeant Sample blew his

nose. The Marquess took a deep breath and stared angrily at Storm Kennedy. He stared at Mrs. Muller—and then stared harder, until suddenly, "Got it!" he exploded. "Knew I'd seen you somewhere!"

Mrs. Muller, who had sunk back into her chair, looked up at him. Her expression was one impossible to define. McGraw fully opened his eyes which he had partly closed.

"Where did you meet Mrs. Muller?"

"Never met her. Spotted her driving off a while back. Vaguely familiar. Remember now where I had seen her before—in Knightsbridge yesterday evening with that fellow Arlington . . ."

26

Storm Kennedy stood again by the open window. He was listening to a diminishing drip of rain from foliage, to the sigh of earth drinking thirstily. Above these sounds he had detected the confident purr of an aristocrat engine. . . . It might be the Bentley. Or it might be the Rolls. One, certainly, had left.

For Lord Glengale had obtained McGraw's consent to take his departure (with Hilary and Elfie) shortly after his sensational identification of Mrs. Muller. Kennedy could see him, now, marching stiffly to the door, opening it, and then marching stiffly back to shoot out a brown, nervous hand to the Chief Inspector.

"Thanks."

And McGraw, smiling grimly, as he gripped the proffered hand, "Thanks for your co-operation. . . ."

Now, Lord Glengale was gone—perhaps Hilary, too. No further sounds reached Kennedy's ears from the paved courtyard. Behind him, in the room, a throbbing silence had fallen. He wished he could have willed that it should never be broken, that he be spared witnessing the torture of a woman who, whatever her faults and follies, had high courage and a sense of humor. The smell of McGraw's strong tobacco annoyed him.

It was Mrs. Muller who ended this suspense. And as she began to speak, Kennedy turned and watched her.

She was marble-pale under the slight make-up she used, but her voice remained softly modulated, even, and quite without tremor.

"You need not trouble to ask me any more questions, Inspector, unless to help. I will tell you everything. I know now how wrong I was not to tell you before. You meant to be kind."

"Might start at the beginning," McGraw suggested, eyes closed as if concentrating. "Useful information."

Mrs. Muller nodded, almost imperceptibly. She was watching that ancient Egyptian mask on the wall, before her and behind McGraw.

She told her story with a courageous frankness which carried conviction. It was not in her make-up to adopt half measures. . . .

Mrs. Muller had been born in Beirut. Her father, at that time, was Italian consul; her mother, still living, was Syrian.

"Speak perfect English," McGraw commented.

"I was educated in England. Joan Corkoran—Mrs. Peter Faraway—and I were at the same school. But I had no invitation to come here. Joan didn't even know I was in London. . . ."

She had lived with Geoffrey Arlington as his mistress for four years. Her husband, a German technician responsible for the maintenance of the pipelines which carry the Persian oil, had never divorced her. "He always said I should want to go back one day. Carl is a very sweet man. . . ."

It had not taken her long to find out that Geoffrey Arlington was an impostor. ("But it made no difference, even when I did find out. I still went on loving him.") While they were in Egypt, he had news of the death of his wife, said to have been an invalid for years. Upon receiving this news, he had suddenly decided to return to England. He was desperately hard up at the time.

"Wife's estate?" McGraw suggested.

"No. She had nothing to leave. I suspected another motive. Not long after I went away with him he started a secret affair with an English girl. She was very young, pretty—and wealthy. He never knew I had found out. At first, I thought her money was the attraction. Then I began to be afraid, it lasted so long, that he was really in love with her. . . ."

Storm Kennedy's mental reactions threatened to betray him. He tasted the bitter humiliation of one compelled to listen to statements concerning a woman who is not present to defend herself. The fact that no defense might be possible merely made the situation more poignant. He must just listen. He was, as Elfie had said, "a private eye."

The association came to a head during a stay in the south of France. . . .

"I must make it clear that we never met. She had no idea of my existence. Then—they both disappeared for over a fortnight! But he returned, penitent, and full of lies. We left together for Egypt. I never saw Hilary Bruton again until I saw her here last night. You see, I knew he was coming to meet her."

McGraw, laying his pipe in an ash tray, inquired, "Listening-in from adjoining room?"

Mrs. Muller temporarily lost her composure.

"Yes. But how can you know?"

"Report from headquarters. Geoffrey Arlington (checked in as 'Mr. Geoffreys') had the room adjoining yours at the Hyde Park Hotel. . . ."

They had flown to London from Paris. Lord Glengale must have passed by as they arrived. Geoffrey Arlington had had some mysterious business to transact in France before crossing on to England. Mrs. Muller had been unable to find out what it was. ("But I know it concerned Hilary Bruton.") On his bedside phone, Arlington had called a number; and Mrs. Muller, listening in a wardrobe closet of the room adjoining, had heard him talking to Hilary.

Hilary called him back at ten o'clock. He repeated the name, "Hangover House" and her directions how to get there. Then, he ordered a car from a firm he had often employed. He knocked on Mrs. Muller's door and said that he might be late.

"And *you* started," McGraw broke in, "at ten-fifteen in a car from Auto-Hire. Got here first."

"I thought, now that he was free, he had come to ask her to marry him—and I meant to stay while Hilary Bruton stayed. I rarely let her out of my sight all night. I was still in the big room, at the piano, after nearly everyone had gone. Mr. Lovelace had persuaded me to play some ridiculous song, and Miss Elphinstowe came and joined us. She was so whimsically amiable that it occurred to me she might really be mounting guard. I said I must get my wrap, and I hurried off to the Powder Room."

Storm Kennedy's nervous tension grew with every passing moment. He had witnessed the piano playing and now was listening to what had followed. . . .

Hilary was not in the Powder Room. But the glazed door was wide open. Mrs. Muller ran out onto the corner of the terrace, closing the door, then around to the front. She stood there, listening—and faintly heard Arlington's voice, and Hilary's. She made her way down the steps, and down the lawn, guided by their voices. They were quarreling furiously, somewhere quite near.

"Before I could get any closer, Hilary Bruton came running past. She didn't see me. I heard Geoffrey shouting, 'Larry! Larry!'"

Mrs. Muller ceased. Resting her elbows on the desk, she covered her face with gloved hands.

"Inspector McGraw!" It was an agonized appeal, a tremulous whisper. "As God is my judge, I meant him no harm. I—loved him. He burst suddenly out of the fog. He was in one of his mad rages. In his left hand he held something white. It may have been a handkerchief. In the other he had a short dagger." Mrs. Muller's tone grew more clear, except that, now, it held a note of restrained hysteria. "He saw me. I stood right in his path."

Again she fell silent, her head bowed in her hands. No one stirred until she went on:

"He used language so vile that—I must try to forget it. But I would not let him pass. . . . Until he threatened me with the knife. Then I ran back to the steps. There I turned and faced him again. He was breathing hoarsely. His eyes glared. He sprang on me. I caught his wrist, twisted it—and I felt the blade go into his body. He tripped and fell forward. And I ran around and in through the terrace door of the Powder Room."

The Chief Inspector knocked out and then carefully refilled his briar. Mrs. Muller lay back in her chair. Her pallor was alarming. Sergeant Sample cast sympathetic glances from time to time. McGraw, his pipe well going, dropped the match.

"Brings us to final point. Gold case you handled, Mrs. Muller, had been cleaned and lightly powdered. Your lace gloves have a small, but distinctive pattern. Paris?"

"Yes."

"Slipped up those stairs this morning"—he pointed—"while this room was empty, opened case and took out syringe. Same marks on all. Same on window frame. Did you charge the syringe and give an injection?"

"Yes." Mrs. Muller's voice, while steady again, was very

low. "I hadn't time to relock the door. As it was, you nearly trapped me when I came down to put the key back. I had, instinctively, looked for it in the desk drawer. . . . I had tried to get to him during the night. But Mr. Pike is a light sleeper. I opened the window because my first idea was to throw the case out into the shrubbery. Although I wore gloves, my hands were hot, and I was afraid fingerprints might be found if I left it there. Then, I decided the shrubbery wasn't safe."

She tried to escape from Lovelace (who met her in the passage), and hurried down the garden, but knew he was following. It was then that she had enlisted Kennedy's services, asking him to detain her follower. Mrs. Muller knew, of course, that when the case was missed, there would be a thorough investigation. As she passed the summer house, Sidonia called out to her. She had to go in and talk to her. Sidonia left when she had completed her make-up and Mrs. Muller was wondering where to hide the case when she heard someone calling her name. She was afraid everybody was going to be searched—and threw the case under the seat.

"Why hadn't you replaced the container and the swab?" McGraw wanted to know.

"I had no time to get them back. I had wetted a handkerchief to moisten the swab, and it had swelled. I threw those away as well."

"Went to look for them, later?"

"Twice. The first time Mohammed interrupted me. The second time was just before I left."

Storm Kennedy remained in purgatory. McGraw's insistence upon details irritated him to the uttermost edge of endurance. But the Chief Inspector went on smoking.

"How long had Geoffrey Arlington carried that case?"

"For three years. Ever since his first attack of catalepsy."

"Catalepsy!"

The echo burst, explosively, from Kennedy's lips. . . .

It was a strange story Mrs. Muller told, in an ever fading voice. Three years before, during a violent scene in a Casablanca café, Geoffrey Arlington had collapsed, apparently dead. He was certified to be dead, and would have been buried—except that a great Italian physician (a friend of Mrs. Muller's father) happened to be in Casablanca. He called to offer his sympathy. He examined Arlington's body. . . .

"And he became as one inspired! It was his subject—these obscure nervous diseases. He hurried back to his hotel, returned, and made an injection."

Mrs. Muller's strength was deserting her. As her voice failed, her accent became more marked. But she forced herself to go on.

"The dead man came to life. . . . God! That moment! Dr. Lombrosi made up a charge of this injection. It had to be renewed every three months. He gave it into my keeping. He knew I should never be far away from Geoffrey."

But it was Arlington who employed Silverston, an expert who invented illusions for stage magicians, to make the gold case. No one but he, or Mrs. Muller, could open it.

An interval immeasurable in terms of time was ended by McGraw.

"One more question. What is your first name?"

"Delilah."

"No other?"

"To Geoff I was always—Lala . . ."

It was Storm Kennedy who caught her as she toppled forward and slipped from her chair.

27

Kennedy awoke late on the following morning and tried to remember what had made him so miserable. The explanation came swiftly—a stab of pain.

Hilary had left Hangover House without a word of farewell. Lord Glengale had gone, too. But Glengale was angry with everybody, probably including his "private eye." Kennedy had delivered Peter Faraway at his own door, leaving him to explain to Joan that vital affairs necessitated his rushing away. He had rushed no farther than his own flat. And, after waiting for more than an hour, had called Miss Elphinstowe's number.

No reply. He had rung again, up to midnight, at half-hour intervals.

No reply.

He groaned, and wondered why he had a headache; then recalled how much whisky he had drunk before finally going to sleep. Clearly, he had offended her. It was just as well. There was some deep secret in that outwardly sparkling life. Hilary knew that he was aware of this—and had no intention of disclosing it to him.

Kennedy was sorry for Mrs. Muller. But, in McGraw's opinion, the Public Prosecutor would make no charge against her. Geoffrey Arlington had not died of the wound;

he had died as the result of an attack of angina pectoris, probably induced by violent anger. Catalepsy, to which obscure disease he was subject, had supervened. Dr. Lombrosi's injection had restored him, temporarily, but could not restore the damaged heart.

Mrs. Muller had acted in self-defense. Moreover, to take the case to Court meant calling Lady Hilary as a witness.

"Advising Assistant Commissioner to drop prosecution of Mrs. Muller," McGraw had told him. "Hope she finds Mr. Muller well . . ."

Sergeant Whittaker entered, in near-silence. He carried a tray.

"I didn't ring, Whittaker."

"No, sir. But I thought a cup of strong tea would be suitable. It is eleven-fifteen—and Lord Glengale is here."

"Lord Glengale!"

Storm Kennedy came fully to life, swung his legs out of bed and groped for his slippers.

"Yes, sir. He instructs me to tell you that the matter is urgent. I will fill the bathtub."

Ten minutes later, Storm Kennedy walked into his office.

"Good morning, sir."

Lord Glengale stood up. He had been sitting in an armchair, reading a copy of *The Daily Telegraph* which Whittaker had thoughtfully provided. He glanced at his wrist watch.

"Don't believe in early rising?"

His manner remained brusque as ever, but the steely eyes were not hard. Rather, their expression was speculative.

"I turned in rather late."

Lord Glengale stood watching him, analytically; then, "Done a good job," he announced. "Pleased with you. Hilary's bolting. Know who she's bolting from?"

Kennedy's heart was misbehaving, that is, as a heart passed fit for Commando work.

"I can't imagine."

"You!"

"From *me*, sir?"

"Said so, if you were listening. Hilary's an easy looker and full of mettle. But she needs a strong hand on the curb. Shall I go on?"

"By all means."

Lord Glengale took an envelope from his pocket.

"Seat on the Golden Arrow. Hard to get at short notice, but still have some influence. She and Elfie are on it. Something Hilary ought to tell you. Will, if you ask her. Told me. Never mind about money. Money not everything. Note enclosed to friend in Paris. Passport in order?"

"Yes."

Lord Glengale glanced again at his watch.

"Just time to make it. Binns outside with the Rolls. Wizard traffic driver."

Storm Kennedy wondered if he were yet really sober.

"But I haven't time to pack even a toothbrush and razor . . ."

"Been a soldier, haven't you? Buy 'em in Paris."

Sergeant Whittaker opened the door.

"Your suitcase is ready, sir."

"Good man, that," said Lord Glengale.

The Golden Arrow pulled out of Victoria just twelve seconds after Storm Kennedy stepped on board. . . .

They were in the forward coupé of the same car. Hilary wore a black-and-gray checked traveling coat, a beret to match. Elfie was attired in a blue suit with red facings, and a peaked cap, so that she looked like a postman.

When Storm Kennedy appeared in the doorway, Elfie stood up as suddenly as if a wasp had stung her.

"Thank God you made it, Bill!" She lurched toward him, grasped his hand. "Top marks to Ronnie. *I* tipped him. What's the number of your seat?"

"But, really, Elfie . . ."

"Shut up!" she whispered gruffly. "Engage the enemy more closely! Strike while the iron's hot." She glanced back. "Hilary, I'm leaving you two to fight it out. Drinks on me when I come back."

And then suddenly she was gone, closing the door softly behind her.

Hilary's chin was so firmly set as to be reminiscent of her father's. She was staring out of the window at those pathetic memories of the blitz which decorate the outskirts of Victoria Station. As Kennedy took a seat beside her, he saw her color fade.

"Hilary." He rested his arm lightly on her shoulders. She turned. And the gray eyes were swimming. "Are you very angry with me?"

She shook her head, almost desperately.

"I'm not angry with you at all."

"But you ran away without saying good-bye."

"I know I did."

Her eyes now were absorbing every detail, flitting from the dark hair to a rather grim jaw, to his tie, in that eternal, all-embracing glance seen only in a woman's eyes when she looks at the man she loves. Storm Kennedy was peculiarly modest, but he knew, at last. And something sang deep inside his spirit.

He tightened his clasp on Hilary's shoulders, drew her toward him.

"Hilary! I have no right, no right in the world—but I can't help myself. I simply adore you!"

It was a long kiss, for the first. He felt her tears on his cheek when he released her lips.

"I have no right, either, Bill"—a whisper—"until you

know the truth about me. But *I* can't help myself. . . . That's why I ran away."

"Perhaps I know quite a bit of the truth, Hilary, and can guess the rest."

Her eyes challenged him. But there was no longer any hint of anger in their gray depths.

"How can you possibly know?"

"Surely you can't have forgotten that you gave me an outline of the story only yesterday?"

"Oh, that," Hilary murmured, and turned away, staring out of the window. "It left out the most important part, altogether."

He drew her close to him again.

"I know it did, Hilary. Your father already knew about the Lebanon oil-well business. So that Arlington would have been wasting his time in exposing the facts to him. Quite apart from which, you were completely innocent in the matter."

Hilary nodded.

"It was finding out that I had put money into that dirty swindle which led Father to find out about—Geoffrey." Her hands were clasped between her knees in the familiar way, her lashes lowered. "You see, Bill, I was very young, very vain and very silly. Under Mother's rather foolish will, poor darling, it was easy for me to get hold of far too much money. I was only eighteen when I met him. I thought he was the most wonderful and romantic creature in the world."

Kennedy squeezed her shoulders, gently.

"And you fell madly in love with him. At least, you thought so."

"Yes, I did. He was a dangerous man. Even then, he tried to rush his fences, as Father would say. He didn't succeed. But all the same, I was badly in the toils. We used to write to one another regularly. I was always longing to see him again. Then came the oil-well affair—and Father discovered the whole story."

"I can imagine the scene."

"It ended with Father absolutely forbidding me to have anything whatever to do with Geoffrey in future. He talked in terms of horsewhips, if he ever caught us together. And you see, I know Father. He meant it."

"But you did meet him again?"

Hilary nodded, unhappily.

"In Cannes. Secretly. None of my friends knew. Thinking of it now, in cold blood, I can only suppose it was spring madness. But"—she paused, conquered a momentary weakness—"I went away with him, to a little Alpine village, where . . ."

Then she ceased altogether. Kennedy held her fast.

"Yes, dear?"

"Where we were married by the village curé."

And, now, it was Storm Kennedy who fell silent. He was dumbfounded. Hilary stole a quick glance at him, and went on hurriedly:

"Geoffrey was forced to leave Europe shortly afterwards—and I simply *had* to tell somebody. That was when I went to Elfie. . . . It was Elfie who discovered that he had a wife already, living in England . . ."

"Good God! But, when you found out . . ."

Hilary turned. Once again, her glance absorbed him.

"Unfortunately, Bill, by the time I found out, it was too late. Now, you know what he threatened to do. . . ."

Kennedy drew her head down to his shoulder and kissed the bright hair cascading from below her tilted beret. Smoky London was left behind. The Golden Arrow ran smoothly through outer suburbs. Presently, without moving her head, Hilary went on.

"Elfie took me to someone she knew in France—when the time came. They are sweet people. They don't know my real name, of course, and they have—looked after him, since—he was born. Somehow, that foul brute found out. He called on them. They sent Elfie a telegram at once."

She was silent for a moment.

"His proposal," she continued quietly, "was that we should go through another marriage ceremony, now that he was free. When I completely lost control and told him that I would rather be publicly executed than marry him, he began to rave. He said, as the child's father, he would bring him to England, and . . ."

Hilary's voice shook.

"How old is he?"

"Nearly four months. I am on my way to see him now."

"I'll come with you," Storm Kennedy whispered.